A FRESH SET OF EYES

BOOK TWO OF DAVID LLOYD INVESTIGATIONS

BY LIZ STRANGE

GORDIAN KNOT BOOKS

"Hello, my name is Sandra Klassen, and I am calling to arrange a meeting with David Lloyd. I'm hoping that you might be available to take on my son's case. His name is Nathan, um, Klassen. I am happy to give more details. Please call me back." She left a number, which David dutifully wrote down.

Now that's interesting, he thought. The name Klassen had immediately set off warning bells. Anyone who read or owned a television had to have at least heard the name, even if they didn't catch all the details. It had been a sensational case, fed by the ever-eager media and a population hungry for every twisted, degrading detail.

Nathan Klassen had been one of three teenage boys accused of and eventually convicted for the murder of two young brothers. At the time of his arrest he had been eighteen years old. His fellow convictees were John Dean, sixteen, and Alex Snider, eighteen. The investigation and trial had both been lengthy affairs, neither coming to a fully satisfying conclusion. Fingers had been pointed at several individuals, and in the end many were not content with the legal conclusions. Evidence had been circumstantial at best, the popular opinion being that the teenagers had been convicted because of their bad reputations, rather than for any actual responsibility in the deaths of the two young boys.

AUTHOR'S NOTE

This novel was inspired by the infamous "West Memphis Three" case, an investigation and trial I have long been fascinated with. Names, events, and details have been changed or, in this novel's case, created only from my imagination.

To all those wrongly accused, and to the men and women whose hard work and dedication has righted the darkest of wrongs.

MAY 5TH, 1991 2:37 A.M.

The man struggled with his bulky load, at one time stumbling down onto his knee, bringing about a surge of pain. He didn't have time for injuries. Plowing on despite the throbbing in his lower leg he finally made it to his intended destination. The air held a chill and a funereal silence enveloped the shadowy landscape.

He knew the risk of bringing the night's end result to such a public place, but even in his fury he understood it was a better place for the discovery to be made, an area accessed by the unmonitored public. The time of morning also meant he had next to zero chance of being interrupted. The neighbourhood lay in its typical middle-class slumber, bodies tucked into beds to recharge for the next day's work or school attendance.

As he struggled with the second bundle the twine caught on his belt, and in the near-complete darkness he didn't realize that his oversized buckle had been pulled loose. As he retreated back through the underbrush he also missed the piece of metal coming free and dropping to the ground. He didn't look back, and once he'd made it to his vehicle the blinding rage he'd felt earlier dissipated, making it impossible for him to even fathom how such a thing could have happened, how he could have lost control so completely. He drove home, leaving the terrible events behind.

Though he may have cleared his mind of any sense of remorse or shame, for one mother, five families, and the public consciousness, the world would never be the same.

CHAPTER 1

The house lay in complete disarray, though David couldn't remember a time when he'd felt more at peace. After a bumpy couple of months recuperating from the gunshot wound received during the tail end of his last case, and the endless open houses that finally attracted a buyer for Jamie's downtown condo, life had begun to take on a smooth, dependable pattern. February was nearing the end of its run, a great time to tackle the home renovations the couple were currently involved in.

David could hear Jamie singing along to the classic rock station he had playing as he finished up the final coat on what would be his new home office. When last he'd peeked in on him, Jamie had been sporting a light spray of tan paint on his forearms and his sandy hair had been tousled, neither occurrence able to dim his model-class good looks. After deciding to finally move in with his long-time partner, Jamie had been full steam ahead, orchestrating the lucrative sale of his own place and the upgrades to the home he'd share with David. The house had been owned by David for more than a decade, and though he was faithful in keeping it clean and in good repair, he hadn't done much by way of improvements. His idea of home décor consisted of matching sets, and buying everything in the same neutral beige-brown colour palette. Jamie had other ideas.

"Take me down to paradise city…" Jamie wailed, bringing a grin to David's face.

He wiped a trail of sweat from the side of his face with his shirt and allowed himself a few moments to survey the work accomplished so far. He felt a surge of pride at the job he'd done replacing the flooring in the bathroom. Jamie had picked out tiles with hints of sea life visible in them, a type of natural flooring David couldn't recall the name of on a dare, but appreciated for its understated beauty. With the new vanity and toilet in place the room would be thoroughly modernized.

A hand slid into the hair on the back of his head as he knelt on the floor. He turned, finding Jamie watching him. "Nice work," he said, letting his eyes drop to David's jean-clad behind. "And other things."

David stood, laughing. "I'm busy here. I don't have time to be ogled." In truth he still found it amazing that someone as handsome as Jamie had fallen for his rugged looks and burly physique.

"That right?" He stepped closer to his partner, a teasing glint dancing in his green eyes.

David wrapped a muscled arm around Jamie's waist, pressing his mouth to the warm skin on his throat. "Okay, maybe I can take a break."

A cough behind them broke the moment. They turned to find Sean, David's brother, standing in the hallway with a fine dusting of drywall coating his hair and shirt. He had three beers in his hand, which he offered once he had their attention. Then, totally ignoring what he had just interrupted, he stuck his head into the bathroom to check out David's progress.

"This place is going to look awesome when we get done," Sean said.

David took a swig of his beer, nodding. "Yep. How's the basement going?"

"Good. Everything is sanded down and ready for primer. I was hoping I could steal Jamie so we could get the whole thing done before I bail."

"Sure. Just give me a minute to clean up the office."

Jamie left the brothers alone. Sean leaned against the doorframe, taking a long swallow from his bottle. The movement drew David's gaze to his brother's hand, now sporting a wedding band. He and his girlfriend had taken a trip to Las Vegas over Christmas break and decided to get married while they were there.

"So how's married life, little brother?"

"Good. Not much has changed really. I mean we've been living together for a couple of years now."

"I guess."

"Same as you two, you know. We just have paperwork."

The comment came in an off-hand manner, but made David think. He and Jamie had taken a big leap moving in together, one that he had every intention of making stick.

"All set," Jamie said, making a re-appearance.

As his brother and partner made their way downstairs he let himself reflect on how good things were going. Many emotional hurdles had been cleared in recent months, leaving the future wide open. Once Jeremy Black was taken care of, life would be perfect.

The phone rang, followed by a brief one-sided conversation from the lower level. Footsteps sounded. "David, it's for you," Jamie called up to him.

He moved into the bedroom, where he had another extension. "Hello," he said, hearing Jamie click off on the other line.

"It's Jenny," a breathy female voice said.

"Well hello sunshine. How's it going?"

"Honestly, your grandmother is driving me crazy. There's only so much cookies and pep talks I can take!"

"So many," he corrected, chuckling.

"Whatever. Can you bring me over to your place for a while?"

"Sure. I'll come get you for dinner. I have some stuff to finish up first."

"Fine. I'll go take a nap till you get here." She hung up.

Jenny was a young former prostitute that David had crossed paths with some months before. She'd been beaten horribly, a murder attempt, but managed to pull through via her unparalleled tenacity. David felt for the girl, and not only because her attempts to help his case had put her in the line of fire. She'd finally been released from the hospital about a month earlier, to move in with David's grandmother. Rhea kept an eye on the girl, making sure she ate, rested and attended all her physical therapy. David had found the girl a counselor she was still seeing, and he took that as a good sign. The next step would be to get her enrolled in an administrative course, skills she would be able to parlay into a job as David's secretary. He intended to keep her off the streets once and for all.

A couple of hours later the tiling was done. He cleaned up the scraps and tools, knowing he was far from done; grouting, trim and installations still waited, but he felt satisfied and purposeful. As he washed his hands in the kitchen sink, he knew there was no way he had the energy to cook anything for dinner. Instead he placed an order for several pizzas. He'd grab another case of beer on the way to get Jenny.

With keys in hand he started down the stairs to let Jamie know where he was going. He caught sight of his partner sitting on an overturned milk crate, laughing at a terrible Mick Jagger impression Sean was in the middle of. He looked so relaxed and happy, something David had been afraid would be difficult given how recently Jamie had made such drastic changes to his life.

Jamie looked his way. "I'm heading out to get Jenny. Listen for the door 'cause I ordered some pizza."

The other two men said goodbye and David was on his way. Looking at the gritty, slush-covered streets he prayed for a quick turn into spring. Though he didn't mind the winter season, this particular one had been grim.

Jenny came out the door and down the driveway as fast as her mending legs would take her, aided by a stark metal cane. David's grandmother rushed out after her to plop a homemade toque on the young woman's head. David couldn't help but grin at Jenny's reaction. He waved to his grandmother as she returned to the house.

"What is with that woman!" Jenny said upon entering the car. She ripped the toque off her head and threw it into the backseat.

"There are worse things than being looked after," David answered.

"Yeah," she said, flicking her hand in his direction and turning away from his gaze.

He let the matter drop. Over the preceding months he'd

picked away at her suspicious and prickly demeanor, learning some alarming though not entirely surprising information about the girl. She'd been given a tough break in life. He'd never deny that. He could understand why she found it hard to believe in David's good intentions, and why it was hard to let go of her old life.

Jamie and Sean were at the kitchen table eating when he and Jenny arrived. David dropped the case of beer he'd picked up into the fridge then joined them. His mouth watered as he grabbed a slice with the works. Jenny took a piece from the pizza with bacon and green olives that he'd ordered especially for her, giving David a small smile of thanks.

For a few moments there was no conversation, yet the feeling was not in any sense uncomfortable. In an odd way they were family, not by blood, but by circumstance and mutual appreciation. The understanding was reassuring, and not to be taken lightly.

"So, you're looking good, Jenny. Can hardly tell anything happened to you," Sean said after wolfing down six slices of pizza in quick succession.

She did look much better than the first time David had laid eyes on her. Grandma Lloyd's cooking had put some meat on her bones, which she desperately needed. Hair that had been bleached to a shocking ivory had grown out to its natural golden-brown colour, a decent cut removing several inches of damage. The bruises had faded, and without the harsh makeup that had been her go-to she was quite a pretty girl.

"Once I'm rid of this thing, I'm golden," Jenny said, referring to the cane that rested between her and Sean.

"That'll be gone sooner than you think. Gran says you're doing really well with the rehab," David said, trying to sound positive instead of condescending.

"Yeah, Ron said I should be able to move on to regular exercise in another month. Maybe I can join the gym with you guys?" She looked to David then Jamie for acquiescence.

"Sounds good to me," Jamie said.

The rest of the night passed quietly. Sean headed home after dinner, leaving the other three to watch a couple of movies.

Jenny spent the night in the spare room, and though neither she nor David said as much, they were both happy for each other's company. Jenny had become the little sister David never had.

Sunday came and went in a flurry of painting and repairs. David fell into bed that night exhausted, without a hint of the turbulent events to come.

Monday morning filtered in with soft shades of grey. Jamie had hit the shower at six a.m., as per his usual custom, and was on the road by seven. David enjoyed the muted sounds of his puttering about, and the fact that Jamie never failed to leave a pot of coffee waiting for him. Thirty minutes after Jamie's car had pulled out of the driveway David set about getting ready for the day.

He found a spot to park only a block away from his building, not always an easy task in downtown Toronto. Once inside the office he started his opening day procedures; coffee, phone messages, and mail. The mail yielded nothing intriguing, though he was happy to find payment for a case he'd settled a few weeks back. At present he had a deadbeat dad to locate and a father who wanted his daughter, attending first-year university, to be checked out. The last time she'd come home her behaviour had been questionable, and the father suspected drugs.

The phone messages were much more interesting than the mail.

"Hello, my name is Sandra Klassen, and I am calling to arrange a meeting with David Lloyd. I'm hoping that you might be available to take on my son's case. His name is Nathan, um, Klassen. I am happy to give more details. Please call me back." She left a number, which David dutifully wrote down.

Now that's interesting, he thought. The name Klassen had immediately set off warning bells. Anyone who read or owned a television had to have at least heard the name, even if they didn't catch all the details. It had been a sensational case, fed by the ever-eager media and a population hungry for every twisted, degrading detail.

Nathan Klassen had been one of three teenage boys accused

of and eventually convicted for the murder of two young brothers. At the time of his arrest he had been eighteen years old. His fellow convictees were John Dean, sixteen, and Alex Snider, eighteen. The investigation and trial had both been lengthy affairs, neither coming to a fully satisfying conclusion. Fingers had been pointed at several individuals, and in the end many were not content with the legal conclusions. Evidence had been circumstantial at best, the popular opinion being that the teenagers had been convicted because of their bad reputations, rather than for any actual responsibility in the deaths of the two young boys.

The actual events had happened nearly a decade before, and David was a bit fuzzy on the details. He decided the best course of action would be to review the history of the crime and trial before getting in touch with Sandra Klassen. After retrieving a new cup of coffee he spent the better part of the next three hours poring over everything he could find on the internet. The accused had a staunch following of people certain of their innocence, who had been both vocal about their beliefs and financially supportive to the cause of having them released, though there had been many to speak of the boys' odd and criminal behaviour in the years preceding the murders.

With a twinge of sadness David found that one of the three had committed suicide just before Christmas. At that time David had been wrapped up in a case that ended with him being shot. Considering how emotionally involved he'd been in that case it was no wonder he'd missed the news.

The more he read, the more glaring the lack of concrete evidence and the questionable behaviour of many involved in the case became. None of it was sitting well with him, and he decided he needed an expert to bounce his concerns off of.

Despite the lingering cold, the sun sat high and bright in the grey-blue sky as David walked back to his car. He travelled toward the city centre, home of the Ministry of the Attorney General's offices. The price to park in the nearby city-owned lot caused him to suffer minor heart palpitations, but it was better than hoofing several blocks back to his destination.

As he stepped into the building's main foyer, walking past the sign boards listing the various government and private business offices the space held, he felt a twinge of unease. He'd only be there on one other occasion, nearly dinner time on a Friday when most of the offices had been deserted. This would be the first visit where he'd likely be seen by a number of Jamie's colleagues.

Oh well, first time for everything.

The elevator door opened up, revealing the office to be directly opposite. He hesitated, unconsciously touching his hearing aid. Once he realized what he was doing he dropped his arm and strode with purpose across the hallway. Inside, two young women sat behind an enormous desk, one typing madly away on her keyboard, the other reading from a file with a telephone pressed between her ear and shoulder. She smiled in his direction, giving a small nod to indicate she'd be right with him.

Less than a minute later she dropped the phone. "Can I help you?"

"Yes. Jamie Brennan's office."

"Is he expecting you?"

"Ah, no. Tell him David's here please."

She nodded and her fingers punched in the extension. After a brief conversation she turned back to David. "He'll be right out."

"Thanks." David looked around the open space, noting two large meeting rooms with the doors ajar and an area of cubicles where many serious-looking young people were hard at work. A crisscross of hallways obviously led to offices beyond his current view. A small waiting area had been decorated in soothing tones and blah artwork.

Jamie came around the corner looking crisp and conservative, a contrast to the well-worn jeans and sweater David wore under his winter coat. Jamie's brows were pulled together and David noted a flush creeping up from the edge of his starched collar.

"Hey, David. Something the matter?"

"No. Do you have a minute to spare? I have a question about an old case."

Jamie's eyes flicked in the direction of the reception desk before he answered. "Sure. Come on back."

He turned, and David followed him through a series of interconnected hallways until they arrived at the back of the suite, where the senior prosecutors had their offices. Jamie's gait was stiffer than usual, and upon seeing two older men standing in the doorway of the office next to his, his shoulders drew in. One of the men glanced in their direction, giving David a cursory look-over.

Jamie stopped. "Pete, Harry, this is David Lloyd. David, Pete and Harry are the Ministry's top prosecutors."

"Please, not with men like you making their way up the ranks. I'll be put out to pasture soon I suspect," Harry said. He was the older of the two, with a sharply receding hairline.

David shook hands with both men in turn. "Nice to meet you."

"Are you a lawyer, David?" Pete asked.

"No, no. A private investigator actually."

"I see."

Harry seemed to understand, and his expression softened. "This is your David, Jamie?"

Jamie nodded.

"Well now. Nice to finally meet you. I've heard some great things about you."

"You have?" David asked, surprised to hear such a statement.

"Yes. So are you here to drag this guy out for lunch? He works much too hard."

"I know he does, but this is a business visit actually. I need a legal opinion."

"Ah, well, I won't take up any more of your time."

Jamie opened the door to his office and stood aside to let David enter. Pete looked mildly perplexed, not having picked up on the conversational cues. The door closed and Jamie took his seat behind the desk buried in legal files. David lifted another set off the chair opposite him and sat down.

"You okay?" he asked.

Jamie smiled. "Yep."

"I should have called first, huh?"

"It's fine David. I have to get used to this. No more secrets."

David let the matter drop. "Do you remember the Gagnon case?"

Jamie appeared surprised at the question. "Of course. One of the first that I helped with as a junior prosecutor. Very gruesome. What's your interest?"

"Sandra Klassen left me a message. I figure she wants me to do a new investigation for her son. You know the boys have always maintained their innocence. I just figured I'd get your take on the whole thing before I call her back."

"It was a mess. Conflicting stories and recants. Bad behaviour on the part of suspects, parents, and the police. Shaky evidence. To be honest I was surprised they were able to make the case stick."

"Did you have doubts? I mean, did you think the boys could have been innocent?"

Jamie was quiet for a few moments, pulling at his lower lip. "I certainly considered it. There were no clear motives for any of those considered as suspects, but in the end the boys seemed the most likely. They knew the suspects, had histories of violence and criminal behaviour; in fact one had been institutionalized for a period of time after assaulting his own sister. And their only alibis had been each other."

"Wasn't there a fourth boy involved somehow?"

"Yes, Sam Miller. He was going to drive them to a party in a nearby borough, maybe Richmond Hill, I can't remember. Anyway, he got grounded so the other three ended up back at the Klassen boy's place, supposedly to smoke some pot. The mother worked the night shift at the hospital, so there was no one to verify if they'd been there or during what time period."

"And the boys were killed when?"

"I'd have to double-check, but I believe sometime between eleven p.m. and four a.m. They were last seen at a park close to their home around seven."

"There's no way the other kid could have joined them?"

"Nope. The house had a security system, which the father had engaged. If he'd tried to sneak out, the alarm would have gone off."

"Sometimes people lie, especially where their loved ones are concerned."

"Of course, but it didn't seem likely in this case. And the other three were adamant Sam wasn't with them. I can't understand why they'd let him off like that if he'd been there."

"Hard to say. People do strange things sometimes."

The men had both seen and experienced some of the odd, thoughtless, and downright cruel things that human beings were capable of. It was par for the course with both their occupations.

"Do you think there might ever be a retrial?"

"Could be. They certainly have some expertise and financial support for the effort. And forensic science is evolving every day."

"You know that one young man killed himself a few months back?" David asked.

"Yes, I read that."

"What if it turns out they're innocent? How in the world could anything make up for their treatment and for stealing ten years of their life?"

"The justice system isn't perfect, we both know that."

"That's not a real answer. That's lawyer talk."

Jamie nodded, a ghost of a smile playing on his lips. "It would be a travesty. Nothing could make up for such a transgression."

"Your gut feeling?"

Jamie sighed. "I never bought it. I just couldn't understand how this group of immature social misfits managed to kidnap two boys in broad daylight, subdue them, take them somewhere to torture them for several hours and then dump the dead bodies. There were too many things that didn't add up, the fact we never found the vehicle for one. They had to have had a car." He looked pained and flustered, the idea of innocent peopled wronged in such a way obviously not sitting well with his by-the-book sensibilities.

"I guess I'll be returning Ms. Klassen's call after all."

CHAPTER 2

Sandra Klassen arrived promptly at ten thirty the next morning. David had a fresh pot of coffee brewing and had remembered to put more effort into his outfit than he might have otherwise. As such he'd pulled on a long-sleeve button-down shirt and a dark pair of dress pants. He'd vetoed the tie Jamie had offered him, an accessory he rarely wore outside of weddings and funerals. He'd been putting off getting a haircut, a fact he now regretted, but simply brushed the shaggy mess from his face. His hand hovered over the ear that wore the small hearing aid, feeling a familiar rush of self-consciousness. At last he turned away knowing there was nothing he could do to reverse the handicap.

The weather had taken a downturn overnight, bringing on that bitter Ontario cold that made vehicle engines resist starting in the morning. Sandra Klassen had dressed for the weather, bundling herself up in a knee-length wool coat and a cranberry coloured scarf and hat. She was pulling off the thick gloves she wore as David opened the door. Tucking the pair under her arm she offered her hand in his direction, which David shook. Her skin was cold and dry, her grip firm.

"Hello Sandra. Please come in." David stood aside to allow the woman access to the moderately sized office.

She pulled off her coat, which David took and hung on the hook beside the door. She kept her purse and the small tote bag she had carried in.

"Can I get you a cup of coffee?" he asked, coming back across the room.

"Yes, please. Cream, two sugars."

David took his time, allowing the woman a few moments to settle herself. After placing her cup before her, he took his seat. She took a small sip and smiled, making polite noises about how good it tasted.

Sandra Klassen was on the far side of fifty, and had done nothing to stop or hide the signs of aging. Her hair was the colour of steel wool, thick and cut to the length of her chin. She wore no makeup, her complexion ruddy and lightly dotted with freckles. Soft wrinkles spread out from her eyes and the corners of her mouth. For the meeting she'd dressed in beige cotton pants and a dark sweater, neither piece following the modern fashion trends. She looked exactly like what she was—someone's mother.

"So, I believe you're familiar with my son's case?" Her words were solid, neither sad nor defensive.

"I am. I remember hearing about it at the time, of course. And since your call I've gone back over some of the details." He sat back in his chair, thoughtful.

She took another sip of her coffee before continuing. "Then you know my son and the other boys are innocent."

"I know they've always insisted they were innocent and after reviewing the case I have to acknowledge there were a lot of missing pieces."

"The holes in the province's case were so big I could have driven my car through them. They didn't have any witnesses, no murder weapons, and no motive. The police hung my son and his buddies because they were troublemakers, not because they actually killed those boys. They needed to charge someone, the public was angry at the lack of progress in the case."

David remembered the lengthy investigation and the public outcry. He also knew it was best to allow the woman to tell the story her way. "The evidence was pretty sketchy."

"Now I'm the first to admit that Nathan was doing some questionable things at the time, and to be honest I had my hands full trying to keep him in line, but there is no way he could have ever murdered anyone, especially a couple of kids."

"What do you mean by questionable things?"

"He was smoking pot, doing badly in school. He'd been

picked up by the police a couple of times for underage drinking and stealing. That kind of stuff."

"Nothing violent though."

"No, nothing like that."

David opened the file on his desk, flipping past several pages until he found what he was looking for. "But one of the boys, ah… Alex Snider, had been charged for assaulting his sister. You must have been aware of that."

"Of course. I know Alex very well. His mother is an alcoholic, his sister not much better. They both liked to pick on Alex and one night he'd had enough and smacked the girl back. It probably wasn't the smartest thing to do, but I could understand why he acted the way he did."

David let that sink in. "All right. So what is it that you'd like me to do, Sandra?"

"I want you to take another look at the case. Someone did this terrible crime, and there must be evidence somewhere. Find it so I can get my boy out of jail."

"I'm happy to poke around and see what turns up, but I can't make any promises."

"Listen, I've heard good things about you David. I want you on this. A fresh set of eyes and someone dedicated to proving the guys innocent is what we need."

"All right, then we need to talk about the fees involved. With something like this I'd have to ask for at least a five-thousand-dollar retainer up front. I charge seventy dollars an hour plus expenses, and with a case this complicated and with so much time passed the hours are going to add up quickly."

She pulled a small envelope from her purse. "I got a bank draft for ten thousand dollars. We have a donation fund we've been collecting for years, and everyone involved agreed this is the way to go."

David took the envelope from her, peeking inside to verify the contents. It contained a draft in the amount stated with his name on it, just as she'd said. He put it down to grab a contract from the desk drawer. They took a few minutes to fill it in. Once signed, Sandra grabbed the tote bag and pulled out several file folders bulging with paperwork. She handed them across to David.

"That's everything I've collected over the years. Articles, police reports, pictures, you name it. I've also included the names and contact information of everyone even remotely related to the case. If I've missed anything, let me know. I most likely have it somewhere."

David felt that delicious itch start in his brain, like he always did at the beginning of an interesting case that came his way. "Fantastic. Thank you."

"Well, I'll get going then. I'm sure you'll want to look this stuff over, then you can give me a call to set up another time to talk."

"Sounds good, Sandra. Please be assured this will be my top priority and I'll check in with you on a regular basis."

He walked her to the door, shaking her hand again before she left.

The bulging file folder called to him. Grabbing another cup of coffee he sat down at the desk and cracked it open. On top lay a photo of four teenaged boys, sporting the leather studded attire of the defiant, bad-boy class of a decade earlier. They were sitting about a round dining table, pulled together in an obvious pose. Three were mugging for the camera, the fourth glancing at his companions. Despite the tough front they tried to convey to the photographer, the thing that struck David most poignantly was how young they all looked.

The series of mug shots and newspaper articles that followed helped to identify who the boys were. The fourth boy David concluded was the lucky Sam Miller, though his likeness only appeared in one article, a piece that briefly outlined his connection to the other three, and hinted that he might know more than he was sharing with the authorities. As David leafed back through the articles he noted that none contained any direct quotes or excerpts from interviews with Sam or his family, unlike the others involved with the case. That fact seemed curious, and he made a note to follow up on whether any relatives had spoken publicly about his connection to those who'd been convicted.

The next section held what David suspected would be the hardest part of the case to review. On top lay the grim, clinical autopsy reports for Jake and Robert Gagnon, ages nine and eight respectively. A cold sweat broke out on the small of David's back as he read, his once comfortable sweater becoming restrictively warm. His mouth became so dry it was difficult to swallow. By the end of the final page of the report his eyes were brimming with tears, and he hadn't even viewed the accompanying photos yet. To brace himself he decided to take a quick walk around the block.

The bitter air revitalized him and twenty minutes later he was re-seated at his desk, file folder open and taunting. He felt compelled to continue on, and yet sick with dread over the visual assault he knew to be waiting within. In a nervous gesture he ran his tongue along his lips and raked his hand through his thick dark hair. *C'mon David. Get this over with.*

The first ten photos were tight shots of the of the crime scene, with intense focus on the victims. Two impossibly small bodies lay like discarded garbage on the banks of an almost dried-out creek bed, dark twine wound around the small ankles and wrists. Robert's face had been turned away from the photographer, but Jake's body was in the forefront, his clouded gaze captured in agonizing detail. A deep gash ran from his hairline down the edge of his eye, where he'd obviously been struck with something sharp and heavy. The rest of Jake's multiple wounds seemed less serious than the glaring head injury.

One of Robert's hands was pressed against his battered cheek, pale and with fingers curled toward the palm as though frozen while trying to ward off his attacker. The edges of flesh along the gaping wound across his throat had curled back like a set of grimacing bloodless lips. The torn, dishevelled clothing hid the damage to his torso, though the overlapping bloodstains hinted at the viciousness of the assault. In shorts the oddly twisted line of his lower leg bone could not be missed, but the exact nature of the injury had proved difficult to determine. One lone sneaker sat at the crest of the hollow where the bodies lay like a silent sentinel, imploring the viewer to make sense of the evil that had transpired.

The series of shots that followed showed the bodies from

every possible angle and distance, capturing every violent and disturbing detail. The boys had been laid in the spot where they'd been found, but the actual murders had taken place in another unknown location. This had been determined from the small amount of blood pooling and disturbance to the immediate area. In the latter shots, after the bodies had been turned, it could be seen that their clothing was wet from the small bit of water that had remained in the creek, a cold sluggish flow.

Despite their size disadvantage both boys had put up a struggle, an occurrence that would have drawn the attention of any persons in the vicinity. A gravelled walking path lay not twenty feet from the location of the bodies, certainly too much of a risk for the perpetrator to have gambled with. Jake had been laid on his back, his brother on his side, and there had been no attempt to hide their remains. The ground around the creek bed had been so dry that no clear footsteps were recoverable.

Following these were several of the crime scene and surrounding area, including a number of items discovered in the grid search undertaken by law enforcement. Many of the objects were unrelated to the crime, pieces of garbage and debris typical to any publicly accessed forest area. Those that had remained of interest to the investigators had included a belt buckle, bits of fibre, several cigarette butts, and a gold lighter.

The next grouping of pictures had been bundled together with a thick elastic band, the top one showing that the scene had changed from the outdoor dumping ground to the stainless-steel interior of the coroner's autopsy suite. Coroners in Ontario were medical doctors with specialized training in death investigations, who reported their post-mortem investigation findings to the Office of the Chief Coroner. In the course of their investigation they were required by law to answer the following questions; who was the person, when did they die, where did they die, the medial cause of their death, and the means of their death, namely by natural causes, accident, homicide, suicide, or of an undetermined nature. When any of these answers could not be found the case would proceed to an inquest. The Coroner's review had only been one part of the Gagnon case, which had taken more than two years to pass through the criminal justice system.

David had just removed the band when his phone rang, startling him so intensely that the photos jumped from his grasp. They hit the floor and fanned out in a macabre display around his feet. Up close images of every cut and bruise seemed to glare up at him as he reached across the desk. His stomach lurched.

"Hello," he said.

"David?"

"Yep. Hi Jamie."

"Are you all right? You sound funny."

David took a breath, forcing himself to look away from the photos on the floor. "I'm okay, just a bit sick after going over the Gagnon file. I'm right in the middle of the crime scene photos."

"I see. No more explanation needed. Listen, I just called to let you know I wouldn't be home for dinner tonight. Something's come up and I have to stay late at the office."

"Sure. I still have some stuff to do here and then I think I'll head to the gym. See you when you get home."

"We can talk later. I love you."

"Me too. Bye."

The receiver clanged when he replaced it, sending a spidery sensation up David's arm. With a quick sweep he collected the scattered photos and began a focused scrutiny of each and every one. The injuries to the boys had been extensive, a serious case of overkill. The person responsible had not only wanted to take their lives, he'd wanted to torture and humiliate. Anger and determination raced through David's blood, a reaction so intense it took every ounce of his self-control not to get up and punch a hole in the wall. Instead he let out a stream of expletives, repeating them over and over again until his blood pressure began to ease.

The rest of the file contained miscellaneous photos of the three suspects, notes Sandra had taken during the investigation and trial, and several reports from various labs and lawyer's offices. All in all it didn't add up to much. His client was right, the lack of evidence or motive couldn't be ignored.

A glance at the clock showed it to be just after four o'clock, and David realized he'd worked through lunch. His hunger only added to the irritability being fuelled by the new case. He needed a cheeseburger with heavy pickle and an order of onion rings, stat. Once his food cravings had been satisfied he headed to the gym to burn off some aggression on the treadmill. The whole forty minutes he ran he couldn't shake the image of the two boys lying on the dirt, so frail and defenceless. He knew then it would be a hard case to process on an emotional level, but vowed to channel that indignation and anger into getting at the whole story of two tragic deaths, and possibly three wrongly accused young men.

He was lying on the couch nursing a beer when Jamie finally arrived home. His partner walked into the room, loosening his tie and looking as weary as David felt. The rush of emotion he felt at Jamie's arrival made his chest tighten. After moving to a seated position he put down the bottle and pulled Jamie next to him. His strong arms wrapped around Jamie's narrower frame and he buried his face into the warm skin of his neck. The scent of the other man's cologne touched him and he lingered there, eager for his comfort and a momentary loss of present truths. Nimble fingers unbuttoned Jamie's shirt and their lips met in a hungry, needy kiss.

Hours later he lay in bed, pressed tightly to Jamie's side. The wind howled outside and his mind raced with a thousand what-ifs. Long after Jamie had fallen asleep, his slow, heavy breathing a comfort he had no words for, David remained wide awake.

Though he didn't know it then, the coming months would bring many sleepless nights.

CHAPTER 3

Jamie was gone when David awoke, nearly an hour later than usual. He groaned as he rolled out of bed and shuffled to the shower. Once dressed he grabbed his keys and headed out on the road. At the nearest drive through he bought himself a greasy, overly processed breakfast, bringing it into the office with him. Soon a pot of coffee was brewing, filling the room with its savoury aroma. He scarfed down the food without really tasting it and settled back with a steaming mug.

The file sat on the desk. Just the sight of it made his belly tighten. Today would be the day to plan interviews and other places to source for additional background information. Of course the two men still in jail were key, as were their family and friends. Also Sam Miller and those close to him, plus the police, lawyers, and others involved with the investigation and trial. An hour later he'd compiled an ambitious list of those to speak with, and wondered fleetingly if he hadn't bitten off more than he could chew.

After a couple of hours of hit-and-miss with talking to people who'd made statements against the boys, and a few of their high school counterpoints, David put a call through to Jimmy, his pal on the Toronto police force, but got his voicemail. He dutifully left a message about the reason for his call, and reminded the man of his cell phone number. A call through to the penitentiary, located three hours to the east in Kingston, landed him time to speak to both men on Friday morning. Several more calls proved fruitless and frustrating, garnering many an answering service. The only ones he could get through to were Alex Snider's mother and the lawyer who'd represented

Nathan. The latter could meet him the next morning, while the former said he could come right then. With that offer, he pushed aside the rest of the calls until he could return to the office.

He filled his travel mug with coffee and pulled on his coat. A bitter wind blew across the nearby lake, bringing with it a soft shower of snow. David didn't bother to brush his car off, simply letting his wiper blades clear the glass enough to be able to drive. The roads were sparsely occupied, but slick, making driving a mild ordeal. Thirty minutes later David pulled into a small housing complex where most of the cars were years past their prime and windows were covered with flags and towels tacked to the frames. He tried not to make a snap judgment, but his experience had taught him that stereotypes came about for a reason.

The woman who opened the door could have been forty or sixty. Her lank brown hair and sallow complexion gave her an air of despair or ill health, or perhaps she'd simply given up on worrying about her appearance. She didn't offer her hand to shake, and as David passed he had to keep from gagging at the stench of tobacco that wafted from her. Even though she'd had the time to change she was still wearing flannel pyjamas and a fraying pair of Bart Simpson slippers. As they walked down the hallway David had a clear view of the kitchen where a large bong sat on the kitchen table among the remains of the previous night's meal.

They settled in the family room. Two mismatched couches and a giant television dominated the space. The battered coffee table held several dirty glasses, a stack of papers and magazines, and an overflowing ashtray. David had to shove aside a pile of dirty laundry before he sat. The woman obviously hadn't used the time since his call to tidy up either.

Despite his discomfort he forced himself to be pleasant. "Thank you for taking the time to speak with me Janet. I appreciate it."

She shrugged. "Mind if I smoke?" Before he could answer she'd already whipped out a lighter and had a cigarette clamped between her lips.

He did mind, in fact he hated being around smokers, but

he needed to be seen as an ally to get the woman to open up. "Whatever you need to do. Now like I told you on the phone, Sandra Klassen has paid me to look into the case again. She feels very strongly that Nathan and Alex are innocent. I assume you agree?"

She paused so long David wondered if she was going to answer at all. After a long drag on her cigarette she said, "Sure. Why would they want to kill a couple of kids?" There was a soft slur to her words, whether a natural occurrence or influenced by something, David couldn't be certain.

"That's a good point, actually. There was no real motive outside of the Crown's argument of the boys being involved in some kind of occult practice."

"They said my boy was a Satanist. That they were using the boys for some kind of ritual."

"It was nothing they could prove with any certainty though, aside from a few kids who said they'd heard the boys were into that kind of thing. Hearsay is hardly concrete evidence. You ever see anything that would make you think Alex was into that kind of stuff?"

"Nope. He just tried to act tough, and got himself in trouble. People looked down on him."

David assumed she actually meant that the family as a whole was looked down upon, but he let the matter slide. "People tend to make assumptions."

He looked about the space. The furniture held a sour odour, and the carpet was so worn in places the underlay was visible. The dingy white walls were bare except for a Dalmatians calendar and three framed photos. He stood and moved closer to examine them as Janet continued to smoke. One was of a young boy and girl, the second a group photo, and the last one of Janet and Alex in recent years. David recognized the institutional setting, and the clothing Alex wore.

"That's Alex and Jasmine, his sister. She don't live here anymore. She's in Brampton with her own kids."

"And this one?" He pointed to the middle photo.

"That's over at the Klassen place, summer before the murders. Our boys had been friends since kindergarten and sometimes Sandra invited us all over. Don't think she liked us much, but she made an effort." She stubbed out her butt and came to stand beside David. "That's John's parents there."

David looked at the couple she indicated. They seemed closer to Sandra's class and sensibilities, both dressed nicely and smiling for the camera. John stood beside them, though his attention had drifted away from the photographer. David felt a twinge of sadness at the sight of the boy, knowing he'd taken his own life just a few months prior. He scanned the rest of the people, finding Janet, Nathan, Sandra, Alex, and Sam Miller, plus several strangers.

Returning to the couch he made a note of the photo. Janet's unwavering stare reminded David of a disgruntled cat whose personal space had been invaded. It made his skin crawl. For the life of him he could not think of any kind of small talk to keep the conversation going. When she lit up another cigarette David knew he had to speed things along before the second-hand smoke started to shave time off his life.

"So what has Alex told you about the night the boys were killed?"

"He said that Sam was supposed to drive them to a party, but he got in trouble and his parents grounded him. His dad was always a hard-ass about school and the way he dressed. Alex, John, and Nathan decided to go to Nathan's instead and smoke some pot. His mom worked nights, she's a nurse. They all crashed there, didn't know nothing about it till the police came to the school and wanted to talk with them."

"And Nathan's parents were separated, right?"

"Yep. Guess that's why they liked hanging out there. At the time I had my boyfriend and Jasmine here, so there was no privacy." She stubbed out the remains of her cigarette with yellowed fingers.

"So how'd the police get turned on to these guys as suspects?"

"Through Alex's probation officer. He never liked Alex, always giving him a hard time. He went to the police after he'd heard about the murders and suggested that Alex might be involved in it."

David took a moment to digest the information. Warning bells sounded dimly. A professional would have to be very certain of such a belief before offering it to the police. He made a careful note of the man's name.

"Okay, so how did that drag the rest of them in?"

"They were a tight bunch, always hanging out together. Other kids thought they were a bunch of weirdos and the cops thought that meant they could do something like kill those boys."

David remembered some vague statements from some of the boys' school peers he'd read in the file from Sandra. It had been nothing more than name calling and speculation, but the police had apparently been inclined to take it as truth.

"So how were they have supposed to have lured the boys away?"

"Nathan's girlfriend Tammy used to babysit them, and the suspicion was that she'd helped or had introduced Nathan and the others to the boys so they wouldn't be afraid of them."

"That's very premeditated."

"It never stuck, at least Tammy never got charged or nothing. No one saw her anywhere near the boys or the area that night. I never believed it anyway. Tammy was a nice girl, I mean she's stuck by Nathan all these years."

"Really? She's still in contact?"

"Of course, she's his wife."

"She married Nathan?"

"Uh-huh, 'bout five years ago."

That surprised David. "Well I guess I need to speak with her soon." He made a note to call her again when he got back to the office. "What was your take? I mean, what do you think happened?"

Janet gave another of her vegetative-like stares. The moment lasted so long David had to fight the urge to squirm. "I don't think those boys had anything to do with it. None of them. The police didn't have no good suspects, so they blamed them. It got the investigation closed and the papers off their back, know what I mean?"

"Is there anything else you can think of to tell me?"

"Nope. Truth is I don't know nothing, except that Alex didn't do it. He could be a miserable little punk sometimes, but he'd never kill no one."

As Janet began to wind a lank stand of hair around her finger, David realized that no helpful information would be forthcoming from the woman. Her lack of compassion irritated him no end, as did her lifestyle, but there was no sense in voicing his opinions. He'd met many people like Janet, who'd succumbed to the indifference and futility of life at a constant dead end. The best he could do was get out of the house, and pray he wouldn't have to return.

His cell phone rang as he walked to his car. He pulled it from his inside pocket before easing his lanky frame into the car and closing the door. Just the brief twenty-foot trek had left the tips of his ear stinging and his eyes watering.

He smiled as he saw the number. "Hello, beautiful."

"Right back at ya," Jenny answered. "You still taking me to physio today?"

"Of course. I'll pick you up at one thirty."

"'Kay, see you in a bit."

Back at the office David put in an immediate call to the office of Jonas Vukovic, Probation Officer, getting a harried secretary. She managed to find him a time with the man on Monday morning, but she didn't sound pleased about it. The call was ended with a loud *thunk* as she replaced the receiver. Tammy DeSousa, on the other hand, was very open to meeting with him and suggested they meet later that day.

Like the other night, Jenny all but burst from the door as David pulled into the driveway. Though her demeanour implied annoyance he was glad to see that her gait had improved in steadiness and speed. The cane seemed more like an afterthought than a crucial implement, barely grazing the salt-dusted asphalt.

David didn't comment at her hasty escape, having been on the receiving end of her tart responses on a number of occasions. He'd worked on the streets for most of his career, but she'd still managed to surprise him with some of her more colourful phrases.

The outpatient physiotherapy clinic was located in a building adjacent to the hospital where Jenny had spent the better part of three months recuperating from her injuries. He saw her glance at the building, feeling a palpable wave of tension roll out from her. Again he kept his mouth shut. Like Jenny he liked to let sleeping dogs lie, not one to dwell on past transgressions.

Except for Jeremy Black, he thought sourly.

That unpleasant, though not surprising, thought was abandoned as quickly as it appeared. David made a conscious effort not to let the man into his thoughts, thus preventing the bastard of robbing him of any more of his life than he already had.

As luck would have it, a car pulled away from the curb in front of their destination when David turned the corner. He performed a nifty act of parallel parking with his large SUV, a recent purchase spurred by events of the tumultuous case a few months back. His foot sank into a pocket of icy slush as he stepped down from the vehicle, pulling a brief snarl from his throat. Jenny was already letting herself out as he stepped onto the sidewalk. He offered his arm, which she used for balance instead of the much-hated cane.

Inside they sat and waited, as clients were forced to do in any such clinic of the provincially sponsored health care system. David reminded himself not to complain as the clock crept up on two forty, knowing they'd walk away without any financial repercussions. Jenny flicked through a number of outdated magazines with impatience, while making scarce conversation with David.

When she turned toward him to begin a conversation in earnest the movement startled him. To his chagrin he'd almost nodded off.

"So I decided I'd go take that course," she said.

"Seriously? Fantastic. I'll get you signed up right away."

"This doesn't mean I'm going to work for you forever, you know. And you have to pay me decent." She clung to her stubborn disposition.

"Without question. And you have to dress de-cent-ly," he retorted with a smirk.

His words were awarded a world-class eye roll. When her name was called a few moments later she walked off without another word. David let his gaze wander over the room, taking in the varied assembly of clients waiting for care. He recognized the telltale signs of stroke and injury, triggering memories of his own ordeal of regaining the use of his leg after the attack. He'd spent many hours in a similar clinic, sweating through tortuous exercises while vowing to never give up. His knee still gave him trouble when he pushed too hard, but he walked without a limp. Staying fit would keep the effects of his injuries at bay.

Questions from the case popped up, distracting him from his people-watching. He remained bothered by the explanation that Alex's probation officer had handed the boy over to the police. Also troubling was how easily the public had jumped on the bandwagon of believing such atrocious things about people that most didn't seem to know very well. How many times had he made snap judgments, or assigned qualities to people without any kind of corroboration? As often as most, he supposed. He tried to be open-minded, even after seeing the amount of crap he had. His instincts did tend to be on the money, though even he could be duped on occasion.

Jenny emerged from the treatment area flushed, but smiling. For the first time David really noticed what the girl was wearing. With a quick look about he could tell that several others had noticed also. With her winter coat draped over one arm, her outfit was on full display. A plum- coloured top fit like a second skin, the neck-line scooping so low that as much of her breasts were bared as covered. There was a bare strip of skin above her crotch-length leather skirt, and lacy stockings covered her shapely legs. Only her shoes were what David would call "acceptable," the low heel worn more for stability than fashion, he suspected.

David viewed the girl like a surrogate little sister, feeling the requisite outrage at her clothing choices. He could feel heat crawling up from the collar of his shirt.

"Put your coat on," he snapped.

"What?"

"People are staring. How can you even sit in that skirt?"

Jenny laughed. "Stop acting like an old man. There's nothing wrong with what I'm wearing."

David felt like putting the girl over his knee for a good spanking. God knew, she'd probably enjoy it. "Sorry to burst your bubble. There's no way you're coming to the office dressed like that."

"Oh, really?"

"Yes, really. In fact I'm taking you out right now to get you some new clothes. You're going to need them for school anyway."

Jenny looked as though she was about to put up an argument, then clamped her mouth shut. She put on her winter coat and allowed David to help her back to the car. In retaliation to his criticism of her outfit she played around with the radio until she found a station playing some god-awful heavy metal and cranked it up so loud David thought his ears might bleed. She cast him a petulant grin and settled back in her seat.

Several hours later they emerged from the Eaton Centre laden with bags. David had spent a small fortune, but he'd managed to convince Jenny to go with some nicer, modern pieces that she could mix and match. At least he thought she could, he was hardly a fashion expert. Belatedly he realized he should have brought Jamie along, who had a much better eye for stuff like that than he did. At least with her new items she wouldn't be giving everyone a free show of her perky young assets.

On the way back to his grandmother's he realized he'd almost forgotten about the meeting with Tammy. She lived in an area to the other side of the city and David would never make it on time if he took Jenny home first.

"Ah, can you do me a favour?"

She cocked an eyebrow as she looked his way. "Sure."

"I have an appointment that I need to get to. Can you come along?"

"I guess."

"No funny business. I expect your best professional behaviour. I'm working a case right now."

She burst out laughing. "I think your idea of professional

behaviour and mine are a little different."

"I'm serious. This can be a good test of how you'll be with clients."

She gave him a wide-eyed look, and made the symbol of the cross in front of her chest. "Scouts honour. I will be a Stepford assistant."

David was a bit surprised she understood the Stepford reference, but he often suspected the girl was much smarter than she let on. He knew she liked to read, and she was a whiz on the computer, but her general crudeness often overshadowed these more positive attributes.

David found the address, arriving only ten minutes late. He parked, giving Jenny another look-over before they exited. Thankfully she had kept on one of the tops from the mall, though she still wore the leather skirt and lace stockings. Nothing he could do about that. Jenny waved aside his offer of assistance, walking up the narrow walk unaided. The house was a neat two-story brick, with updated windows and a large two-car garage. A new minivan sat in the driveway, beside two discarded toboggans. A curl of smoke emerged from a chimney to the side of the structure. It looked like a typical suburban home.

Interesting.

Tammy answered the bell with such swiftness, David wondered if she hadn't been waiting for him by the door. She smiled as she ushered the two inside. The front foyer gleamed, as did the rest of the house that David could see. In the distance a television played, an indistinct sound that made him picture some type of cartoon.

After introductions Tammy asked for their coats, hanging them both in the closet. Her brows drew together as she caught sight of Jenny's outfit, but instead of commenting she gave a polite smile.

"Jenny is my assistant. I hope you don't mind that she's accompanied me," David said in his smoothest tone.

"Of course not. I'm not one to tell you how to do your business." She waved them along behind her as she moved down the hallway toward the source of the sound.

The living room had been decorated in shades of chocolate and cranberry, a modern and eye-pleasing combination. Two young girls sat on the dark leather couch watching a cartoon that David wasn't familiar with. They glanced up as the group entered the room, one giving David a cheeky smile that showed her front teeth were missing.

"Scoot you two. Go watch this in the basement."

The older of the two, the one with the missing teeth, gave her mom a look of pure exasperation, then led her younger sibling from the room. David took a seat on the vacated couch with Jenny, taking a moment to look over the expensive furniture and electronics. Personal touches dotted the space; framed portraits, knickknacks, a pile of magazines, but everything had a definite place and purpose.

Both he and Jenny refused the offer of coffee. Tammy settled on the matching loveseat, curling her long legs underneath her. She was a very attractive woman, with golden skin and soft auburn hair. Dressed casually in dark jeans and a chunky knit sweater, she wouldn't have looked out of place on any number of women's magazines, the ideal modern working mom. Even the makeup she'd applied was subtle, something David wished Jenny would get the hang of.

"So you and Nathan are still together after all these years?"

"Yes. Does that surprise you?"

"It does actually. Teenage relationships are tenuous at the best of times, but with a situation like this, I'd have hardly expected it to keep going."

Jenny gave him a quizzical look, making David realize she had no idea what they were talking about. Silently he hoped she'd play along.

"Well I suppose that's true. Really considering the state the two of us were in at the time, if this hadn't have happened I'm sure we would have gone our separate ways."

"I don't follow," David said.

"We were a bunch of stoners back then. I was pretty much failing all my classes, on the path to dropping out. Nathan too. Then this bomb was dropped on us and everything changed. I guess I could have buried my head even further in the sand, but instead I totally turned it around. Once they'd been arrested and they were on their way to trial everything changed for me. I quit drugs, I started working hard at school. I just wanted to be clear-headed and knowledgeable about how things worked."

"Well, you're to be commended for that. You've obviously done well for it," he said, waving a hand to indicate the space about them.

"Yes, I do all right. I put myself through school, got a degree in Criminology. I went on to study forensics, and now I work for the government at their provincial lab."

"Really? No problems with Nathan being in jail?"

A soft blush crept into her cheeks. "We weren't married when I applied so I listed myself as single. Of course the truth came to light in time, but I work hard and keep my nose clean. There's been no valid reason to let me go."

"Any of your co-workers give you a hard time?"

A ghost of a smile appeared on her lips. She settled back in the chair, tucking her long hair behind her ears. "Not at all. Everyone's been very supportive. Some have even donated to the defence fund we have for the guys."

"And the girls are Nathan's?" He had to ask.

"Yes."

David liked her directness. "All right, then let's cut to the chase." He'd brought his notepad, always prepared. You could never tell what bit of information would turn out to be crucial to uncovering the truth. "What do you remember about that night?"

Tammy's eyes fluttered closed, her lips in a tight line. Jenny gave him another look, which he responded to with a shake of his head.

"Well, we'd been planning all week to go to this party. That day after school, ah, Friday, Nathan and I got in a fight and I ended up going to the movies with my friend Joanna. We didn't have cell phones or anything back then, so I didn't talk with him again until the next day. I assumed that he and the others would go to the party without me, which unfortunately didn't happen."

"What did you fight about?"

"Stupid teenage stuff. He thought I was flirting with this other guy."

"Were you?"

"No. It was just some guy I got assigned to work on a project with."

David took a moment to look over the notes he'd made when going through the file. "Now, wasn't there some speculation that you were involved in this somehow? I believe you babysat the boys, so the Crown implied that you might have lured them away or introduced the accused to them."

"Yeah that was the story they came up with. I did babysit the kids, but so did others. Alex's sister Jasmine watched them a few times too. I wasn't a close family friend or anything. They had no real explanation, so they made something up."

"The case was pretty flimsy. No real evidence, no witnesses. Why do you think they were able to make it stick?"

"Because Nathan, John, and Alex were a bunch of misfits. They didn't have a lot of friends, and they had a reputation for doing drugs and getting in trouble. Kids assumed stuff about them, and at the time they were okay with that. We all thought it was cool that other kids thought we were freaks. Plus they had no alibis, except each other."

David remembered the teenage mentality well. Many wanted to be seen as different, others as conformers. The hierarchy of high school popularity and acceptance is always a slippery slope. He wouldn't do it again for all the money in the world.

"Gotcha. But in truth you weren't actually into any of the stuff you were accused of?"

"No. We wore our black clothes and Doc Martens, pierced our noses and stuff like that. Outside of playing with the Ouija board and watching a lot of horror movies, we were hardly practitioners of the dark arts."

"Now John was a couple of years younger than the rest of you. How'd you become friends with him?"

The question caused her to drop her gaze, which had been steady and confident until that point. "John was actually the younger brother of another kid we used to hang out with, named

Blake. He'd died about a year and a half earlier in a car accident. He and Alex had gone out with Jasmine and her boyfriend of the time. The guy had been drunk and wrapped the car around a tree. Blake died, and the boyfriend went to jail. When John started asking if he could hang around us, we couldn't say no. His parents hated it though. Hated Alex and his family."

After having been around Janet for the short time he had, David could understand the Deans' point of view. "So they've lost both sons."

Tammy nodded.

"Do you have any idea who might have done this?"

"Not really. I mean no one specific, but the boys' mom did hang around with a lot of losers. She was on her own. The father of the boys had split years before and didn't pay her any kind of support. She worked at the hospital in housekeeping. To be honest she jumped from guy to guy, and she seems to like the tough-guy, biker type, if you get my meaning. I remember one creep had the nerve to hit on me when I was there to babysit."

"Even lowlifes like that would have a hard time carving up two little boys. For what reason?"

"Do you know how many hours I've spent wondering the very same thing? I don't know why someone would want to do this, except that they were very fucked-up. My best guess is it was simply a case of the wrong place, wrong time and some sicko molester or child killer got them. 'Cause you're right. There is no reason for anyone to do something so horrible." Tammy's voice had risen an octave higher than her normal speaking voice, straining against her anger. Bright spots of red appeared on her cheeks.

"Where do you think they would have come across this kind of person?" David felt his own anxiety rise in kind with Tammy's, but he focused on keeping his tone neutral.

"The park. It backs onto the area where the boys were found, and they liked to play down there. Though they weren't supposed to, I know they sometimes went into the trails, you now, looking for bugs or playing hide-and-seek with other kids. There's several different entrances and it's a public space. Anyone could have been there."

David recalled that early on in the case there had been some speculation about just such a scenario. Apparently in the early morning hours of the day after the boys had gone missing, a middle-aged black man had made a memorable appearance at an all-night diner about ten kilometres from where the bodies had been found. The witnesses described him as having been dirty and wet, with long, matted hair and apparently under the influence of some kind of drug. He'd come to the counter screaming about monsters in human disguise, and then had gone into the washroom where he'd urinated everywhere except in the toilet. As no one had wanted to touch the man, he'd fled before police could arrive. After scouring the area and speaking with several of the local homeless the man was not located.

"...last time you saw the boys? Or their mother?" Jenny's voice cut in, making David realize he'd missed part of the conversation.

"Two weeks earlier. I'd babysat for Erin," Tammy answered.

"Anything unusual happen that night?"

Tammy made a face like she was mulling something over. "Well, maybe not unusual, but it surprised me. Sam stopped by the house. He hadn't realized that Erin was out, and he said he'd come by to fix something. I didn't realize the two knew each other."

"Anything else?" David asked.

"No, just that Erin had another new guy that night. Like I said, she didn't tend to keep them for long."

"Why is that?"

"I think she was just really needy. I mean she always wanted me to stay after she got home, like she couldn't be alone or something. It was kinda sad."

"So if it wasn't some dirtbag that Erin had dated, or a stranger. Any other thoughts on who it could be?"

She shook her head. "Sorry, no."

"And you're positive Nathan, John and Alex had nothing to do with it?"

"One hundred percent."

"What about Erin herself?"

"I really don't think so. She had terrible taste in men, and made some questionable choices, but she loved her kids. I think they were the only things that gave her any real happiness. I just couldn't see her doing it."

"What about the evidence used at the trial, I mean what little there was."

"The only thing that stands out for me is the lighter. I have no idea how it got there."

"Right, I remember that was listed in the effects found at the crime scene."

"Yeah, Nathan has no idea how it got there either. He only knows that he hadn't seen it for a couple of weeks before the murder."

"It was Nathan's lighter?" That was news to David.

"Yeah. At least it looked just like one he had. This gold Zippo he'd bought with some birthday money. He'd lost it a couple of other times before, one time it was just dumb luck he'd found it in the cut-through we used to get to his street. Anyone could have picked it up. He could have even dropped it at the park. We stopped to smoke there at night sometimes."

David didn't like what he'd just heard, and for the second time that afternoon had to consciously stop himself from making a snap decision. Tammy was right, any number of scenarios could have led to the lighter ending up where it had. Assumptions led to oversight, or missed chances for finding the truth. With a case as tough as this one, he needed to keep every avenue open.

"So other than that, nothing conclusively tied them to the boys or the crime scene?"

"Nope. And no witnesses. Even the people with so-called inside information about the crimes recanted or were proved to be lying."

"What's your advice on how to proceed?" David asked.

"Review the new forensic results and find a way to get that before the courts. It may be the only way to get a new trial. I highly doubt after all this time that the real killer or killers are going to come forward."

"No way," Jenny agreed.

"What new evidence?"

"The cigarette butts for one. They were all tested at my insistence, and none could be linked to any of the accused. Also some partial prints on the victims' shoes and Robert's belt. None match," Tammy answered.

Though the new evidence was something, it wasn't a smoking gun either, certainly not without new suspects to test against. David left feeling no better about the situation than when he'd come. As if in commiseration, the temperature had made a sharp drop since their arrival and a considerable amount of snow had fallen. He and Jenny talked little on the way to his grandmother's. After leaving her with a "Burn that skirt!" parting shot, he continued on home. There, darkness and silence met him, which under most circumstances wouldn't have bothered him.

What chance did he have of cracking a case so complex and after such a long period of time?

CHAPTER 4

The offices of Santos & Harvey, home to several high-priced barristers and solicitors, resided in what had once been a grand single-family home in Toronto's "Annex" neighbourhood. The structure sat nearly a quarter kilometre from the road, behind a low limestone fence. At one point in time a metal gate must have blocked accessibility to the property, but it had been removed, most likely due to the amount of traffic in and out. David felt a flash of inadequacy as he parked his vehicle next to a row of Bentleys, BMWs and a snazzy red Jaguar.

The receptionist in the front foyer looked straight out of a business professional's dream; all perky breasts, beautifully coiffed hair, and a winning smile. Her name, David soon learned, was Samantha. She'd graduated from the same school where David intended to register Jenny.

Two nervous-looking individuals sat in the reception area. David smiled in their direction, but remained standing. Within a minute Samantha received the call that Mr. Santos was ready, and she escorted him to the second floor. Once at the lawyer's door she gave a soft tap, and after being acknowledged opened it and waved David inside.

Carl Santos strode across the ample space with his arm raised to meet David in a firm handshake. He was younger than David had expected, or he simply had great genes. The man projected vitality and strength, a commanding persona even in the simple act of greeting. The tanned skin didn't seem manufactured, a warm tone that contrasted with David's much paler complexion.

As he sat down David noted the touches of silver at the

temples of his otherwise thick dark hair. He waited until the other man had settled and gone through the typical niceties of offering coffee.

"So I assume your secretary filled you in on the reason for my appointment?" David said, pulling out his trusty notebook.

Carl watched his actions carefully. "Yes. And I'd be a liar if I said a new investigation came as a surprise. Sandra has been like a bulldog with this since day one."

David agreed. "She's very convincing."

"With good cause. I've been a lawyer for a good number of years, and I've never had a case like this before or since."

"How so?"

"Well, we always want to believe our clients are telling the truth, but this was something else entirely. I was one hundred percent certain of Nathan's innocence."

"I understand he passed a polygraph test, as did John and Alex?"

"Yes, with flying colours. The results are inadmissible of course, though I was able to question Nathan about taking one while on the stand. There was just no motive and no real evidence. I felt the whole thing was a farce."

"Any idea why the police pushed so hard to get this case to court?"

"The crime itself was horrendous and the public was demanding recourse. They wanted someone to be punished."

"Would you say there was any intention by the police or other parties to deflect away from the actual guilty party or parties?"

"A cover up? I wouldn't go so far as to say that. I think there was simply very little to work with, and what there was they bungled badly."

"In what way?"

"Poorly secured crime scene, cross pollution of other sites, and some close relationships between parties involved." He opened a drawer in his desk and withdrew a folder, which he then handed across to David. "These are copies of notes I made while prepping for the case. I've highlighted the areas where procedural mistakes were made."

David scanned over the first few sheets, seeing rows of small, meticulous print. A couple of things leapt out at him, items he'd like to follow up on.

"You have any thoughts about who might have been responsible?" David asked.

Carl sat back in his chair, tapping his fingers together. He gave the question serious thought before answering. "To be honest I always thought there was something off about the mother."

"Really, how so?"

He sighed. "It's not something I can put into words. She just seemed so guarded and defensive. I don't feel as though she helped the case like she could have. Does that make any sense?"

"Sure, I'll keep that in mind when I get a chance to speak with her. So do you think she was actually involved or she knew more than she was saying?"

"I don't think she killed the boys herself, but she might have known who did. You know she didn't even come to the trial. Not any of it."

"That is odd for a mother who's lost both her children."

"I thought so. The shrink we worked with tried to say it was her way of coping, but I couldn't wrap my head around it. If someone had butchered my children, I would want to make sure they got what they deserved."

The mention of a psychiatrist triggered a thought in David's mind that he'd follow up with after his meeting was done. "Me too."

"You have kids, David?"

"Not yet," he said with a smile.

"I have three myself. Two in university, one still in high school."

"You must be a very busy man."

He gave a soft chuckle. "That's one way to put it."

"So, do you have any suggestions on avenues to follow up? Anything that really bothered you?"

"I could write a book about the things that bothered me. I think tracking down the man who was seen in the diner near the dumping site would be helpful. Also the issue with Nathan's lighter has always bothered me. He was asked about it in the polygraph test and he passed when he said he didn't know how it got there. It could mean someone close to him was involved or it might have been entirely random. Maybe he dropped it in the park and some kids got hold of it and went into the wood to mess around. Hard to say, but I think it's worth the effort. And Erin. I think you should dig around in her background."

"Thanks for this. Can I call again if I have more questions?"

"Of course. I'll leave word with my secretary to put you through if I'm in the office, and to make sure I get any messages right away. If there's anything I can do to help, don't hesitate to ask."

David could feel the depth of sincerity in the man's words. His belief in his clients inspired him, helping to shift away the veil of hopelessness from the daunting case. The firm belief of an educated and experienced legal professional like Carl Santos only solidified David's position that justice had gone off the rails in Nathan's case.

"Thank you. I'll keep that in mind."

Carl walked him to the lower level, offering his card with his personal cell phone number and the direct line for his assistant. It was a better start to the day than the one before.

Back at his car he pulled his phone free, scrolling through his contacts until he found the number he wanted. It had been a while since he'd talked with the man, but he knew him to be a trusted resource.

"Good morning, Davenport Clinic," a subdued female voice answered.

"Dr. Garfield please."

"May I ask who's calling?'

"David Lloyd."

"One moment."

He was put on hold without a chance to respond. Soft music played, which he began humming along to without even realizing it.

"Dr. Garfield."

"Oh, hello, it's David Lloyd calling. I wonder if you might have some time to discuss something with me?"

"I'm just on my way out. I do have some time around two. Could you drop by the clinic?"

"Of course. Thank you for fitting me in."

"No problem. See you then."

David didn't feel like heading back to the office just yet. He made a beeline for a place that had once been a second home, where, as per usual, there wasn't a parking spot to be found within three blocks. After snagging a relatively legal spot, he doubled back to the enormous stone building that housed the 51st Division of the Toronto Police Service. It was here that David had spent his last five years of duty.

As he came through the front door he caught the attention of two officers chatting near the information desk. One David recognized from his days on the force, a Sergeant Joe Kennedy. The man raised his hand in greeting and after parting ways with the other man, who David didn't know, came to shake his hand. It was a far cry from his usual treatment in recent years. Since helping to crack a complicated drug and porn ring a few months earlier, and after taking a bullet for his troubles, his status had undergone a significant upsurge.

"Hey, Joe. How's things?"

He smiled. "Good. I think I should be asking you that."

"I'm great. All healed up."

"Good to hear. That was some nice work you did. "

"Thank you."

"I mean it. Maybe I'll run into you some time at The Diamond?"

"Could be. I've been known to turn up there every now and again."

"Okay, then a game of pool and a beer's on me."

"Sure thing. Listen I have a meeting I should get to."

Joe held out his hand, which David shook after a heartbeat's pause. "Nice to see you, David."

When Joe walked away David had a brief moment where his legs didn't seem to be cooperating with his brain. That had certainly been unexpected. At best he thought he might get a couple of nods or a wave, not a handshake *and* an offer for a drink. *Would wonders never cease?*

His luck held. He managed to catch Jimmy at his desk, awkwardly tapping away at his keyboard. Detective Benson was strictly old school, and like many his age he had challenges with new technology. David could see a ring of perspiration about the collar of his dress shirt, a telltale sign that he'd been at it for a while. It was the way he'd always done things. He'd let the so-called paperwork pile up until he couldn't put it off anymore then spend the better part of a shift fighting with his computer to get it inputted.

When David tapped him on the shoulder Jimmy hit lift-off, nearly falling out of his chair. A younger detective standing nearby snickered.

"Jesus, David! That's a sure way to give an old coot like me a heart attack." His face was an alarming shade of red, his words rushed.

"Sorry, Jimmy. You up for a break?"

Jimmy stood. "Take me to lunch and I'm all yours."

David glanced at his watch. "It's only ten thirty."

"I've been here since six o'clock. It's lunchtime to me."

David followed as the older man shrugged into his suit jacket and started toward the stairs. There were a few more hellos from passing police staff, and one man stopped to give him a slap on the back. Jimmy simply shrugged, wearing his bland detective-at-work expression.

They headed to the greasy spoon across the street, where most of the police services staff dined at some time or another. David wasn't surprised to find half the customers were in uniform, with a couple of plain-clothed thrown in for good measure. A booth near the back of the restaurant was unoccupied, which they took. A waitress came with menus and a pot of coffee.

"Thanks for the rescue. I hate doing that shit." Jimmy took a long slurp at his coffee and settled back.

"Sure thing. I owe you a lunch or two by now."

"I never mind helping when I can."

The waitress returned for their orders. David wasn't particularly hungry, but ordered a western sandwich and fries. Jimmy went for the special, something fried and smothered in gravy.

Jimmy looked tired. The pouchy bags under his eyes were the colour of soot, clashing with the red running along his lids. His skin tone didn't seem entirely healthy either, and David was sure he'd lost some weight since the last time he'd seen him.

"You feeling okay?"

Jimmy stared down into the coffee cup clenched in his hand like he might find the meaning of life there. David could be patient when the occasion called for it. He waited while Jimmy mulled over whatever it was that had him troubled. At last he met David's gaze with a look that made his stomach drop.

"It's nothing I want to be talking about just yet."

"Of course. Just know you can talk to me if you need to."

"I appreciate the offer. Now let's get to what you came to pick my brain about. I know this isn't just a social call."

David felt sheepish, but really needed the man's help. "I've been hired to look into the Gagnon case."

Jimmy didn't need further clarification and wasn't surprised. "Sandra Klassen hire you?"

He nodded.

"Well you have been in the papers a fair bit with the whole Barrowman thing. I guess she thought you were up to the job."

"What do you think?"

"Now I've always been a fan, David, you know that, but this case is a tough one. There wasn't any evidence to speak of, no witnesses. I don't want to see you spinning your wheels."

"You think the guys are innocent?"

"I do. This whole business never sat well with me. I know one of the guys who was on the investigation team and it burned him right up. Never was the same after. Took early retirement as soon as he could."

"Have you looked at the file?"

"Once. It was enough to make me sick to my stomach." David remembered his own experience. "Being honest, I can't see how they even got it to court. The boys swore they was innocent, and all the evidence was circumstantial."

"Except the lighter."

Jimmy sighed. "The damn lighter. Yeah, that's what sunk

Nathan, and for whatever reason those three seemed to come as a group deal."

"What are your thoughts on it?"

"Well, it didn't look good, but it could be explained. The lighter was found a fair distance from the dump site. It could have been dropped at an earlier time. Hard to say."

The waitress appeared with their food. Jimmy started shovelling it in as soon as the plate touched the table. David picked at his sandwich, thinking about the questions he wanted to ask.

"You have any theories?"

Jimmy chewed thoughtfully, then laid his fork across his plate. "I do. I always thought there was more to the story of the man who'd appeared at Janko's Diner. I mean what are the chances of someone being so close to the dump site, within the time frame the deaths occurred, who was dirty and bloody and acting the way he did. It always seemed fishy to me that there wasn't a better investigation into it."

"What about the Gagnon boys' mom?"

"Don't know what to think about that. She never showed up to trial, I hear. Could have been too much for her. I never heard of anyone pointing a finger in her direction. She was home with a friend the night they disappeared. The woman stayed all night, waiting with her after they didn't come home and the police were called."

"Maybe she wasn't directly involved. I've been told she hung out with some questionable company."

"I heard she played around some. Don't think anything came of any of her exes though. I can double-check if you like."

"That would be awesome. Any advice on looking for the Janko man?"

"Try the shelters and haunts near the diner where the homeless are known to frequent. I bet you could find someone who knows something."

"Even after all this time?" David wasn't hopeful.

"Some of those folks have been on the streets since before you finished high school. Some go through rotations, you know, clean up a bit or move around. Keep asking and you could luck out."

They finished up their coffee and David asked the waitress for his meal to go. He walked back to the station with Jimmy, itching to demand he come clean. But he knew better than to push the man into talking when he wasn't ready. He'd been down that road himself a time or two, and anyone who'd butted in wouldn't have been well received. He'd have to find a way to keep an eye on things without looking like he was spying.

"You going to The Diamond any time soon?" David asked just before heading on his way.

"Maybe Saturday night. I'm on days. Why?"

"Just wondering. Joe Kennedy mentioned something earlier, and I don't think I've been in since the last time I went with you. Maybe I'll see you there."

"Alrighty then. Talk to you soon."

He watched the man walk back inside, feeling terrible that he couldn't be more helpful.

A quick jaunt down the highway and he was at the turn-off for his building. He brought Carl Santos's file up with him, and with a pot of coffee brewing he sat down to look it over. The man was thorough, he'd give him that. He'd made careful notes of concerns and question of all stages of the investigation, and the players involved. Attached to the page he'd written about the Janko's man was the police report, which David discovered to be incomplete and vague. Also of note was the fact that the two officers who did the follow-up, some seven hours after the incident had been reported, had come straight from the Gagnon crime scene. This was the worst of the cross-contamination that Santos had mentioned.

The original report wasn't much better. The responding officer, a C. Morgan, had come to Janko's Diner about an hour after the initial call, and by then the man was long gone. She did speak with the staff and customers, dutifully recording the names, and took a description. There were also notes about the condition of the bathroom, including the fact that he had urinated on several items, muddy footprints and possible spots of blood. No pictures were taken. At that time the murders were not known, so there was no reason to conclude anything other than the man in question had been high or was mentally ill, and that he had sustained some type of injury, not uncommon in the often-dangerous lifestyle of an indigent.

When the morning manager had come in and been told about the incident with the man in the bathroom, news of the murders had already hit the media. He'd heard about the case on the way to work, and had thought there might be a connection to the man because of the timing and proximity. Of course the bathroom had been cleaned by then, as the first officer had given the okay. When the officers and forensic techs from the murder scene had arrived at the diner, not much of the evidence remained. Combined with the fact that they came wearing the same shoes and clothing from the dump site, made everything they collected unreliable.

In a separate envelope in the back of the file were reports and background checks on all people involved in the case, including police, the coroner's office, the parents of the accused, Jonas Vukovic, Tammy DeSousa, and Erin Gagnon. A sticky note on the front of Vukovic's section indicated he'd been involved with a lab tech at the forensic lab at the time of the investigation, a fact that didn't sit well with Santos. That was a tidbit he'd have to question Vukovic about when he met with him. The rest he'd review more thoroughly at another time.

David sat back, sipping at his coffee. His mind wandered, trying to fit together pieces separated by chasms as wide as the Grand Canyon. Nothing he'd read or heard so far had produced anything new in the case, though his conviction in the men's innocence remained firm.

Yet despite the concrete proof of the atrocities that had been committed he still couldn't wrap his head around why anyone would have done such an awful thing.

Perhaps Dr. Garfield would have an answer for him.

CHAPTER 5

The Davenport Clinic looked just as it had the last time David drove up its winding lane, like something out of Toronto's grand past. The seclusion and perceived tranquility must have been welcomed by those whose issues facilitated the need of visiting such an establishment. He was thankful his owns demons were for the most part under control and that his purpose was information, not treatment.

Carol, the mousy secretary, nodded as he entered. She was busy talking on the phone and typing, but she removed one hand from her keyboard to wave him on. One of the people in the waiting room gave a glance in his direction, eyebrows raised as though thinking of challenging his immediate access.

He walked along the hallway to Dr. Garfield's office, peeking in to all the open doors like the die-hard snoop that he was. No sessions were in progress. In fact that whole section of the building felt like a ghost town. Elsewhere clients would be in their rooms, attending private counselling sessions or group therapy, busy with the art of healing. As the hallway took a sharp bend Dr. Garfield's office came into view, the door ajar with soft music wafting out.

He paused, giving the door a light rap.

"Come in, David," a honey baritone voice called out.

Inside he found Dr. Garfield sitting on the couch at the back of his office, munching on what must have been a late lunch. David took the chair opposite, feeling misplaced, as though their roles had become reversed.

"How are you today, Dr. Garfield?"

"Wonderful actually. My wife and I just got back after three glorious weeks in the South Pacific. I feel very refreshed."

He did look relaxed, and certainly more animated than the last time David had been in his office.

"Have you ever been, David?"

"To the South Pacific? The farthest I've been is to Jamaica and that was more than ten years ago. Now that you mention it I really could use a vacation."

"You must take the time to enjoy life once in a while. We both know how trying it can be sometimes." The doctor smiled, but David understood the seriousness of his words.

"True enough. I should get Jaime to cash in some of that vacation he's stored up."

"Jamie's your partner? I don't think I've heard you mention her before."

"Yes, and Jamie's a him, not a her."

"That's nice. Have you been together long?" he asked.

Dr. Garfield took a bite out of his sandwich and looked David's way, waiting for an answer. He seemed nonchalant and unperturbed, but David instinctively felt defensive. He needed to cure himself of that. "Yes, more than five years now."

The doctor took a sip of his tea, nodding. "Lovely. Now what is it I can help you with?"

"I assume you're familiar with the Gagnon case from about ten years ago?"

"Of course."

"I wonder if you'd be willing to look over the case file and give me an opinion on the type of person or persons who could be responsible for this crime?"

"Off the record?"

"Of course. I value your opinion, and in all honesty, I could use any help I can get."

He handed over the file. Dr. Garfield went straight to the photos and autopsy report, reviewing everything carefully. David understood that reading the police interviews and other information could lead to bias. He needed only to know of the crime itself.

David had read through most of an edition of *Psychology Today* by the time Dr. Garfield was ready to talk. He'd made notes as he read, coming back to the photos several times. Consummate professional that he was, he never flinched or looked away from the horrible images; he studied each photo with careful, clinical detachment.

"Well, I have a few observations that may or may not be helpful. Considering what I remember of the case from the time, I think you might be happy with this."

"Go on."

"The first thing that strikes me is the viciousness of the attack. This is a classic case of overkill, an act committed in a state of fury or complete mental abandon. This person wanted to destroy these children, not just kill them. You understand what I mean by this?" He peered over his glasses at David.

"Yes."

"Also the fact that there was no attempt to conceal the bodies indicates that the killer wanted them to be found; they wanted the maximum impact from their murder."

"Can you give me a guess as to who this might be?"

"The father perhaps? A babysitter, or teacher. I can't say for certain."

David thought about the suggestions. The boys' father had been out of their lives for years, living several provinces away. The only sitter David was aware of was Tammy and Alex's sister Jasmine, whom he had yet to speak with. He wasn't sure how he felt about that.

"Why those suggestions?"

"An attack like this tends to be personally motivated."

"What about a random stranger? Is it possible this could be the work of a serial killer or a simple opportunist? I believe there was speculation the boys had been sexually assaulted before killed."

"Unlikely, but not to be ruled out. Certainly there are people like that, say Clifford Olsen for example. This just seems personal to me. Possibly it's more about the mother than the children. Did she have enemies, or perhaps lived a lifestyle where she could have been putting herself at risk? I'm thinking drugs, gangs, something like that."

"Not that I'm aware of. I've been told she had a couple of

questionable boyfriends, perhaps the biker type. I'll look into that. I'm sure the police would have picked up on something, though. As for drugs I haven't heard anything like that."

"Any trouble with CAS or the school board? Sometimes that's a good indication of what's going on at home."

"Good point. I'll see what I can find."

"Now as for the sexual assault, from what I've read in the reports there was no semen recovered from the bodies or their clothing. There is no bruising or tearing like one would expect with forced penetration on a child. I believe the misconception came about because the boys' anuses were dilated, which was in actuality a result of being laid in water, not an assault. It was most likely the snap assumption of one of the detectives, and the theory stuck. You know how it can be."

He did. Even among the most experienced investigators, incorrect assumptions or a misreading of evidence was known to happen. Human beings are fallible, and often times motivated by emotional responses.

"All right, so your educated guess would be someone close to the mother, with an off-side chance it could be a complete stranger?"

"Yes."

"Motivation being to get the mother where it would hurt the most?"

"Yes, exactly. Unless you have fallen into that five percent margin, where you are in fact dealing with a stranger, some kind of sadist with a penchant for children. Then the motivation is simple: to fulfill said person's urges. Unless the children were stalked, which there doesn't seem to be any indication of, then it was simple happenstance. The boys were in the wrong place at the wrong time."

"What does your instinct tell you?"

"That you should look close to home."

"There is an angle with a man who appeared at a diner the night of the murders, dirty and disoriented. It was the right time frame and very close to the dump site. Could be a homeless person, maybe someone mentally ill, but the police never caught up with him. What do you think about that?"

Dr. Garfield remained quiet for a few minutes as he rifled through the photos again. "It does seem a bit coincidental. I'd check it out, if for no other reason than to wipe it off the books."

"Good advice. Anything you want to add?"

"Not at this time. Would it be all right if I took a copy? I could go through it more thoroughly, see if I've missed anything?"

"Of course."

"This will just take a couple of minutes. You can wait here if you like."

"Do you know if Roberta's in today?"

"Should be. She has an art therapy class at three. You remember the way?" David nodded. "Then I'll have my secretary hold the file at her desk and you can get it on your way out."

David stood and shook the doctor's hand. "I really appreciate this. My gut tells me these boys are innocent, and I'm going to need all the help I can get to prove it."

"I'm glad you thought of me, David. I'm always happy to help when I can."

"Thanks again."

They parted ways a few feet down the hallway. David retuned to the foyer, then continued past, down the hallway to the west side of the building. Ahead he could see the doors to the art room were open, and he hoped there was enough time for a chat before the students arrived.

Like the first time he'd laid eyes on Roberta, she was busy pulling supplies from the immense cabinets located in the back of the room. Her long auburn hair spilled down her back, swaying with her movements. Her baggy jeans were belted at the waist, over a form-fitting navy sweater. The jeans were rolled, exposing the heavy biker boots on her feet. She turned, and as she closed the cabinets her initial surprised expression softened into a smile.

"David! How nice to see you," she said and scurried over to him. She grabbed him in a tight embrace and pressed a kiss to his cheek.

"Ditto," he answered.

There was a brief moment where they both seemed not to know what to say next, which Roberta broke with a soft, throaty chuckle. She was a stunning woman, radiating a confidence that would drop most men to their knees.

"So, what brings you to the clinic? You haven't checked yourself in have you?"

"Nope, nothing like that. I like to think I still have a handle on things."

"Jamie might say otherwise."

Now it was David's turn to laugh. "True enough."

"How is your better half?"

"Good. Really good actually. He's come out at work, and it went a lot better than he expected. "

"Glad to hear it. And you've healed up okay from everything?"

He gave his shoulder a small stretch. "Good as new."

"Stella's doing well too. The dance studio has been a real lifeline for her. And she's started taking art classes here again, and seeing Dr. Garfield."

"I thought she'd pull through okay. She's a tough cookie, that one. And she has her mom to lean on."

"Yes, Marjory's been amazing. So supportive. She's completely cut ties with her son and husband. She's filed for divorce and is going take him for everything he's worth."

"Good. And you two are still friends?"

"Closer than ever."

He let the ambiguous statement lie. What did or didn't go on between two adult women was none of his business.

"You know Jamie and I would love to have you guys over some time."

"Oh, fantastic! Wait." She moved back toward her desk and pulled a piece of paper from her leather bag. She handed it over with a huge smile.

It was an advertisement for a burlesque show hosted at the Scarlett Letter, a high-end strip club in downtown Toronto. The proceeds were going to a charity that David wasn't familiar with.

"It's to raise money to give underprivileged children the chance to take dance lessons. It's very important to Stella. She really wants to make something of the studio, you know, have top notch competition teams, be able to bring in experts for workshops, all that stuff. And she wants to make sure there are no barriers to anyone who has the drive and the talent."

"Sold. Count us in."

"Yeah? Great. Stella will be thrilled when I tell her. And you'll be happy to know we have some men on the agenda as well."

"Something for everyone."

"Exactly."

A couple of students wandered in, taking a seat at one of the tables.

"I guess that's my cue."

"Wait." She took the flier from him and wrote a number on the back. "That's my new cell number. I always have it with me. Keep in touch."

She walked him to the door, passing the table where one of the kids let out a knowing whistle. As he made his way down the hall he heard one of the kids ask, "That your boyfriend, Roberta?"

The answer was lost, but he laughed anyway. Let her explain the nature of their relationship.

The file waited on the desk. He grabbed it with a thank you to Carol, who smiled like he'd said something much more profound. He had that effect on women sometimes.

That thought made him realize he and Jamie were supposed to be going to his grandmother's for dinner in a couple of hours. He raced back to the office, made a few more calls, including one to the CAS and the school board of the deceased boys. Of course, no one was in the office to speak with him personally. He left his name and contact information, jotting down a note to himself to follow up if he hadn't heard anything in a few days. His final call got him in touch with a young woman who had also babysat for Erin Gagnon. Nothing she said shed any light on the case, but it was another confirmation in the mother's terrible choices in male company.

After a call to confirm Jamie could still make the dinner, he pulled out a map of Toronto, zeroing in on the area where the boys lived and their bodies were found. David then located the diner and marked all routes that the Janko's man could have taken. For good measure he also marked the closest shelters, police station, and other areas that were associated with the homeless and drug crime within a twenty kilometre range.

Satisfied he'd put in a good day's work David closed shop and drove over to his grandmother's house. She greeted him at the door with a kiss on the cheek, as she had since he was a small boy. He welcomed the familiarity and the mouth-watering aromas coming from the kitchen, a safe and non-judgmental escape from his day-to-day realities.

"What's cooking?"

"Your better half asked for a lasagna, so I made that. And I have salad and homemade bread."

David's mouth started to water. "Mmmmm."

He followed her into the kitchen, content to watch her putter around, getting the last of the meal together. He loved his grandmother more than he had words for, and knew the feeling was mutual.

"You remember about the plant sale we're having at the Seniors Centre, right?"

"Of course. Week from Saturday."

She brought the salad over to the table, plunking the bowl down in front of him. "Good. We need some muscle. See if you can get Sean to come with you."

"Will do."

Jenny wandered into the room, blowing David a kiss before grabbing herself a can of pop from the refrigerator. He watched her walk from the fridge to the table unaided, her gait tight but steady. She took the seat next to him, where he noted that she was wearing some of the clothes he'd bought for her. The new style softened her, helping to wear down the distance she kept from others.

"Hey, handsome. How's things?"

"Good. No complaints."

"Guess who I heard from today?'

"No idea."

"My mom," she said casually, though he could tell she was trying to gauge his reaction.

"What? After all these months of trying to track her down?"

"I guess she was off drying out. That's what she said anyway."

"Okay. How you feeling about it?"

Rhea joined them. "Why didn't you tell me?"

Jenny shook her head. "I don't know. Still processing it I guess."

"Well, was it a good conversation?" David prompted.

"We didn't fight, so I guess you could call it good. Let's just leave it at that."

The doorbell interrupted any further discussion on the matter. Rhea left to answer it, returning with Jamie in tow.

He gave David a kiss, which made Jenny grin.

"You got off in good time," David said.

"I planned for it since we're hitting the road tonight."

"Where you guys going?" Jenny asked.

"To Kingston. I have an appointment to interview two men in prison there. I thought Jamie might be a help, so I persuaded him to come along."

"This about the case with the murdered kids?"

"Yep."

Jamie gave him a funny look, unaware that Jenny had any knowledge of his current case. "You landed yourself a real doozy this time."

"Can someone help me with this food please?" Rhea asked. Jamie jumped up to help her. "Take them into the dining room would you, dear. Thought we might eat in style tonight."

Jamie did as instructed, carrying off the dish of lasagna with Rhea smiling at his retreating form. "How in the world did you get a man that handsome to give you the time of day, David?"

"Ouch. You saying he's out of my league or something?"

"He's out of everyone's league. Seriously he's like movie-star material. Now if you could just get him out of those stuffy suits once in a while…" Jenny let her words trail off, a dreamy look on her face.

"Hey now. Stop mentally undressing my man."

David couldn't help but laugh when Jenny started to fan herself. Rhea joined him when Jamie returned, totally at a loss as to what the others were talking about.

"Did I miss something?" he asked.

"Just some group admiration, darling," Rhea answered with a cheeky wink.

David grabbed the salad from the table and steered Jamie back into the living room. The ladies' giggles followed them, inspiring David to give Jamie a pat on the butt.

"What has gotten into everyone tonight? You guys drinking before I got here?"

David shook his head, but didn't elaborate. The women joined them, and they spent the next few hours eating and enjoying one another's company. David got caught up on the slowly advancing romance between his grandmother and his neighbour John, and all the gossip of Rhea's inner circle at the Seniors Centre. Jenny let David know she'd made an appointment with the school, and asked if he could go with her. He agreed, pleased she was so receptive to the idea.

After picking up their bags, David and Jamie were on the road. As per his type-A personality, Jamie had brought some files from the office. David left him alone during the three hours it took to get to Kingston from Toronto, using the time to mentally plan out the interviews for the following day.

When they checked in at the hotel the man at the counter seemed a bit stiff in his interactions with them, to David a sign of being uncomfortable with checking two men into a room with a single bed. They didn't often travel together, so it was an event he had little experience with, and he felt somehow ill-prepared to deal with such a situation. Walking away with card in hand he had to wonder if perhaps he'd been reading too much into it. Jamie hadn't seemed to notice anything at all. It surprised him sometimes how much of a hang-up he seemed to carry, a lingering ghost of self-consciousness, and the need to defend his life.

Once inside the room Jamie attempted to unpack his overnight bag, but David had other ideas. He caught his partner about the waist, and turning the man to face him, toppled them both to the bed. With lust-fuelled aggression he undressed Jamie, taking time to kiss and explore several areas of his lover's anatomy along the way. In due course they ended up on the floor, knocking the lamp from the bedside table and spilling the contents of Jamie's bag onto the floor.

"Whoa, cowboy! We're not teenagers anymore," Jamie said. His fair skin had taken on an attractive flush, his words breathy and rushed.

"No reason we can't act like it every once in a while." David lay flat on his back, hands clasped over his chest while he waited for his breathing to resume a normal tempo.

"I guess." Jamie turned to look at him. He met David's gaze, his expression bringing an ache to David's chest, a response that only Jamie could elicit. The intensity of his feelings for Jamie sometimes scared David, making him realize just how lost and empty his life would be without him.

Jamie ran a hand along his cheek, smiling. When he rose from the floor David had a phenomenal view of the man's backside, which he watched all the way until Jamie ducked into the bathroom. Soon the sound of the shower running filtered out, luring David in like a Siren's call. After a long, hot shower the two tumbled into bed.

Content, David slipped into a heavy, dreamless sleep.

CHAPTER 6

Kingston Penitentiary was an impressive fortification of limestone and barbed-wire, and one of the oldest continuously used prisons in the world. It backed onto Lake Ontario with a sheer, multi-story drop that few inmates have tried to use for escape, and for those who have, the results were serious bodily injury or death. It houses the worst of the worst of Canada's penal system, including the infamous Paul Bernardo, who David remembered from the Scarborough Rapist days.

"You ever been to Kingston, Jamie?" David asked as they passed the city's old "hanging tower" and the now defunct Prison for Women.

"Ah, no. I've heard about it from some of the people from the office. Every now and again one of our cases brings someone down this way. You?"

"I did my Law and Security course here."

"Right, I forgot about that. Then you should be able to find us somewhere good for lunch."

"Can do. We're here." He pointed at the building as he pulled the car into the adjacent parking lot.

It took nearly twenty minutes to pass through security and be ushered into the small, nondescript interview room. As they sat on the uncomfortable chairs, waiting for the men to be retrieved from their cells, David took a moment to reflect on the contrasting styles between him and Jamie. The expensive navy suit Jamie wore fit him to perfection, exuding a commanding, professional persona that was a far cry from David's dark jeans and sweater. Even in his intense and conservative lawyer mode Jamie was still one of the best-looking men David had ever seen. Not that he was anything to sneeze at, but he could quite happily admit that Jamie was in a class all of his own.

David was staring at him when Jamie looked up from the file he'd been studying. "Yes?"

The door opened as David started to respond, effectively ending the conversation before it began. Two guards, an older man and an intense young woman, brought the two inmates into the room. Once they'd been seated the guards retreated, locking the door behind them.

The decade behind bars had taken its toll on the two men. In his teenage days Nathan Klassen's hair had been worn shoulder length and dyed jet-black. Now it was cut short, a sandy brown that matched his fair skin tone. He'd gained some weight on the prison diet, but looked as though he was keeping it in check with regular workouts. His shirt had been rolled to the elbows to expose defined forearms.

Alex had also cut his hair, a radical departure from the six-inch Mohawk he'd sported in his mug shot and subsequent media photos. Unlike Nathan his hair was naturally dark, as were his eyes, both nods to some Native ancestry. He was leaner than Nathan, but also looked as though he's been making effort to keep himself physically fit.

It was more than an emotional toll from their incarceration that David suspected had left the deepest effect on the men, one that would last long after their sentence had been carried out. They were so far removed from the boys they'd once been that they could have been two entirely different people. An aura of defeat clung to them, like another presence in the room. Scarred and bitter souls looked back at David through their eyes, the hint of a smile more of an automatic response to the presence of their visitors than for any real hope they may have had of being freed.

"Nathan, Alex, I'm David Lloyd." He reached across the table to shake hands with both of them, meeting each of their gazes in turn.

"I'm Jamie Brennan," Jamie added as he offered his hand as well.

"Are you an investigator too?" Nathan asked.

"No, a lawyer actually. I'm here to help David out if I can."

The men seemed to take the explanation at face value, and didn't ask any further questions about his presence at the meeting.

"All right then, let's get down to business. You know that Sandra has hired me to look into your case with hope that I might find something to exonerate you."

The two men nodded agreement.

"To do this I need total cooperation and honesty, otherwise I might as well forget the whole thing."

"We have nothing to hide. We didn't do this," Nathan answered.

David gave Jamie a questioning look. "I believe you."

"And from a legal standpoint, the case against you is basically nonexistent," Jamie said. "I can't believe it ever made it to trial."

"So I think the best way to start is to have you two tell us in your own words what happened that night."

The two men passed some sort of non-verbal communication between themselves before Nathan turned back to David and Jamie. "No sugar coating, okay? Alex, Sam, John and I were a bunch of idiots back then. The only thing we were worried about was where we'd get our next bag of weed from. We thought it was cool that everyone thought we were weird. No one bothered us that way. I know for me I liked being high so I didn't have to deal with my parents' crap too. They were going through a bad time then, fighting all the time. Alex had an even crappier home life, what with his mom and everything." Alex nodded when Nathan paused. "So that night was no different."

"I totally agree. I mean going to Nathan's to smoke up was the original plan. Sandra was working nights and Mark had moved out a few months earlier, so we had free run of the house. The party came up, and then when Sam got grounded we just went back to hanging out at Nathan's. Really it was a pretty typical Friday night."

"But you had a fight with Tammy earlier, is that right Nathan?"

"Yeah, just me being a bonehead. She got assigned to do this

English report with a jock that I didn't like. I saw her talking with him, and I started a fight with her. Pissed her off good too."

"So Tammy would have been with you guys otherwise?"

"Yeah, most likely. Probably her friend Joanna too. John and Alex didn't have girlfriends at the time, so that would have been it."

"So because of the fight it was only you two and John, right?"

"Right," Nathan answered.

"Did anyone see you that night?"

"I don't think so. My mom was working a seven to seven shift. She's a nurse, so she was already gone by the time we got there after school. That was about five I think?" He looked to Alex who nodded. "We'd stopped off and bought some pot on the way to my place. John and Sam had gone home to eat and stuff. Sam called us around five to say that he'd been grounded and he wasn't going out. John came over to my place around seven and stayed the whole night. Alex and John crashed on the couches in my basement."

"And you guys never went out?"

"Yeah, we popped over to the corner store by my place and bought some chips and stuff. Other than that we were in all night. Just watched some movies and played video games."

David made a note of the trip to the store, not sure if it would be helpful at that point.

"All right. When did you hear about the boys' murder?"

"Monday at school. Tammy told me. She was upset 'cause she'd babysat the boys," Nathan said.

"Same. I was with Nathan when he ran into Tammy on Monday morning."

"When did the police first contact you?"

"Wednesday. Alex and I got pulled from class. The police came to the school to talk with us because our probation officer told them he thought Alex could be involved."

"Do you have any idea why he might have done that?"

Alex had become visibly agitated at the mention of the parole officer, running his fingers through his hair and moving about on his seat. "No. I mean he never liked me. He always gave me a hard time, showed up at my house a few times and was rude to my mom and sister too."

"But aside from this fight with your sister, you never had any trouble with fighting or being violent?"

"No. I mean hitting Jasmine was stupid, but that girl could really push your buttons, you know what I mean. It was just dumb luck that she fell against the cabinet like that. It busted her lip and knocked a tooth out. My mom took her to the emergency and I guess the hospital called the cops. Turned into this big deal that it wasn't."

"I'm going to vouch for Alex here. Jasmine could be a real bitch at the best of times, but ever since Trevor got arrested for the accident she'd been a nightmare. She was high or drunk most of the time, and always trying to pick a fight with Alex," Nathan said.

"Sandra said something similar when I talked with her," David said.

"She'd know. Alex spent many nights on our couch after fights at home. I don't know how many times my mom talked with his trying to reason with the woman."

"The truth is my mom is a drug addict and being a mom totally interfered with her getting high. If I stayed out of her way, things would be okay."

"Okay, so Tammy tells you guys about the murders. What did you think? Did it have any effect on you personally?"

Nathan took a moment to think about the question before answering. "I don't want you to take this the wrong way, but not really. I mean I was a teenage boy. Yeah, I knew the kids. I came babysitting with Tammy once, but I wasn't really close to them."

"Same with me. Jasmine watched them too, and I walked her home a couple of times. We'd seen them at the park and stuff, but there were lots of kids around, you know?"

Something about Alex's statement triggered a thought that David couldn't quite get to form. "Did you live near the park where the boys were found?"

"Yeah, we all did. It was near the high school, and we often walked through there. Also the one side backs onto the complex where Alex lived."

David pulled the map he'd been working on at his office from his bag. "Can you show me?"

Jamie also leaned in as the men pointed out the high school and all the homes of the parties involved, including Tammy and Erin Gagnon's houses. All locations fell within the twenty-kilometer radius he'd marked off for possible origins of the Janko's man.

"You guys obviously heard about the man who showed at Janko's Diner that night?"

"Of course," Nathan said. "My lawyer really thought it meant something. He was pissed that the police never found the guy."

"You have any other thoughts about who else could have been responsible?"

"Like I said I didn't really know the kids or the mom for that matter. Tammy always seemed to think it was someone Erin was involved with, but that was a suspicion. She doesn't have any concrete proof or anything."

"She told me her thoughts about this."

Nathan froze, a pained look on his face. "You saw Tammy? And the girls?"

"Yes, a couple of days ago. They seemed to be doing really well."

"Tammy's been a rock. There was no reason for her to stick by me, but she did."

David could see that Nathan was starting to get emotional, but he needed to keep the men on track. "You have a lot of great people on your side. Now, let's go back to Vukovic, your PO. Alex, you say he set the police on you guys. You think it was a deliberate thing, or something that came out more casually and the cops decided to run with it?"

"The way I heard it, he singled me out. Nothing wishy-washy. He told the police he thought I did it."

"This really gets me. Why would he say such a thing? I mean, without his statement there would have been no reason for the police to have looked at you guys at all."

"Well, I wasn't exactly a favourite of the locals either," Nathan said, looking mildly embarrassed. "I'd been picked up a few times for underage drinking and once for breaking into cars."

"It's a far cry from some stupid teenage petty crime to butchering two boys," Jamie interjected.

"I agree," David said. "Just because you were acting like a punk at the time shouldn't have put you on the police's radar for something like this."

"It wasn't just that. My mom had me going to a therapist. She thought the break-up with my step-dad was upsetting me, and the police really ran with that when they found out. Like I was some nut job or something. The prosecution brought in this psychiatrist that testified against me, made me sound bad."

Another nugget of information that may or may not mean anything in the bigger picture. David looked to Jamie to see if he had anything he wanted to ask. In the moment their gazes met he knew Jamie was completely on his side in the matter.

"What about the lighter, Nathan? That seems to be the only concrete evidence the Crown had against you."

"I've thought about that for ten freaking years and I still don't have an answer. I have no idea where or even exactly when I lost the thing. If it had been in the park any number of people could have found it. I really can't help you with that."

"Is there anything you can think of that might help me out? Did anyone suddenly disappear from your life or perhaps seem to be overly interested in the case? Anyone have it in for you?"

"No, not someone who would kill two kids. This is all a big mistake. Alex and I only came to the attention of the police because of that dick Vukovic, and they only pursued it after what happened with John. I mean that kid was only sixteen years old, he'd lost his brother the year before and those assholes at the police station badgered him until he totally broke down. He would have said anything to get them to stop questioning him."

Jamie and David had gone over the complete police reports before coming to meet with Nathan and Alex, including transcribed segments of the interviews conducted with the three boys. The one to which Nathan referred had occurred shortly after he and Alex had been interviewed by the police at school. When they'd explained their whereabouts on the night in questions, John's name had been mentioned as an additional person to corroborate their story.

John Dean, like his parents, had been shattered by his brother's death. In the months that followed he'd been a walking time bomb of misdirected anger and survivor's guilt, too immature to deal with the overwhelming feelings himself, yet lost in the shuffle of his parents' equally consuming pain. Like many do, he'd turned to denial, feigned indifference and drugs. Even then he'd been known to have sudden crying spells or periods of lethargy that made it difficult to function. Confusing and goading someone in such a state into making suspect statements wouldn't have been difficult for an experienced investigative officer.

Neither of John's parents had accompanied him to the police questioning and they'd taken advantage of his vulnerability. He'd been questioned for five hours straight, subjected to veiled and overt threats and had been accused of lying. In the end they'd managed to get the boy to say he couldn't account for all the time during which the murders would have occurred, and that he'd been stoned to the point of blackout. The lynch pin had been when he'd responded to being asked if they could have done things he didn't remember with, "I guess so." That had been enough for the police.

"So the heat really turned up after this interview with John?" Jamie asked.

"Yeah, after that they were gunning for us. They rounded up kids from school who said we were Satanists and all kinds of crap like that."

"We never blamed John though," Alex said. "This wasn't his fault, it was shitty police work. Him killing himself wasn't guilt over the murders, it was for what happened to all of us. He felt responsible."

David sat back, thinking. *What am I missing?*

Jamie flicked through several pages of reports, reading intently. After a few minutes he pulled one piece of paper free from the file. He scanned it, then handed it over to David.

"What about this report that you and Tammy were seen in

the park around eleven p.m. that night?" Jamie asked Nathan.

"More lies. Tammy was with Joanna at the movies. I never saw her that night at all. I didn't even speak to her until Sunday afternoon, 'cause she was still mad at me for starting the fight."

"Could be just that, Jamie. Kids lie, especially if they're being coached," David said.

Jamie didn't look entirely convinced. "You're right."

"So basically you three came to the police attention because of a false accusation and a somewhat suspicious statement. I don't get it." David felt a rush of heat, a physiological reaction to his building frustration.

"It didn't help that there were no other viable leads, or evidence that pointed in any other plausible direction." Jamie gave David a pained look.

"Our reputations and attitude didn't help either. Like you said we were a bunch of punks back then."

David and Jamie made eye contact, and David knew from his partner's expression that he felt as disheartened as he did. The interview really hadn't shed any new light on the case, only regurgitating known facts and suspicions.

"All right guys. Thanks for your time. I will leave you my card in case you have any questions or think of anything you think I should know."

He handed over the card, which Nathan tucked in the breast pocket of his shirt. For good measure he had the men sign releases, giving him permission to speak with their physicians, therapists, and anyone else who might be resistant to sharing personal information.

"I hope you find something," Alex said. He didn't look hopeful.

"Me too," David answered.

As they watched the men being led back to their cells, David felt his heart drop. He was certain of their innocence, yet at his wits' end in how to go about proving it.

After a leisurely lunch and an intense discussion on the next steps in the investigation David and Jamie hit the 401 highway for the long drive home.

Sleep would be a pipe dream that night.

CHAPTER 7

David gave up on sleep in the wee hours of Saturday morning. He waited it out till six, then headed over to the sparsely populated gym. A hard two-hour workout relieved some of the built-up tension, but the pressure of the case hung on like a bad cold. His success or failure could have a direct impact on whether two men would regain their freedom, not something to take lightly.

He came through his office door a little past eight thirty, bagel and coffee in hand. The blinking light on his phone could be seen from the door and several papers waited on the fax machine. He grabbed the papers on the way to his desk, settling down to read them over his breakfast. A scrawled note filled the first page, an explanation from Jimmy on the attached police reports. He'd run Erin Gagnon and the father of the murdered boys, both of whom produced nothing alarming. The records of two men who were recent exes of the mother had also been sent. Not surprisingly, both men had a few black marks.

Maurice Castroni, thirty-eight, had been arrested twice for drug possession and once for a DUI, though he appeared to have been clean for the past several years. Or he hadn't been caught in any illegal shenanigans anyway. His profession was listed as a cook, his last known place of work was a restaurant David had been to a few times in the past, a nice Italian bistro on the north side of the entertainment district.

The second man, Angus Pierson, had been arrested for domestic violence a number of times against multiple women, the last incident netting him a two-year stay behind bars. He'd been released three years earlier, and his parole officer indicated he'd gone back to school to retrain as a welder and was gainfully employed in a local factory. Last known addresses and phone numbers were listed for both, along with their next-of-kin.

The new names were added to those he had yet to contact, adding to the feeling of futility. Sandra's file sat on the desk, a visual reminder of the stakes he faced. He pulled his notes from the interviews he'd conducted so far, starting his own file to supplement the case history. After making an additional electronic copy, he felt somewhat better about the ground work he'd put in thus far. David pulled out the map, now covered with red dots and notations, from his bag and laid it flat on the desk. After studying it for several minutes the realization that it would be best to trace the routes in real time couldn't be ignored. If his messages and the calls he was about to make didn't net him any further meetings that day he'd head over to the area.

Sandra had called for a check-in and to let him know she was free over the weekend if he wanted to get together. There were also return calls from Sam and his father, John's mother and a Detective Brown, who'd been one of the lead investigators on the case. He made a mental note to check out the guy with Jimmy. The last message was from Mark Ester, Nathan's step-father. His tone indicated he wasn't pleased about being contacted, but had left a good time to get in touch. The only delinquent return caller was Jasmine Snider, which from her depiction by others didn't surprise David in the least.

The clock sat at five past ten, not the greatest time to be trying to reach people. Of those to try he figured Sandra to be the best candidate. As he suspected she answered right away, open to meeting with him at any time. He managed to connect with Sam's father, who offered him a time the next afternoon, but Sam, Erin and Chuck Gagnon, the Deans, and Detective Brown didn't pick up. Jasmine Snider also didn't answer, so he left another message stressing the importance of her getting back to him. Mark Ester had said he'd be away until Sunday evening, so David had no choice but to wait to speak with the man.

After a number of confusing calls David figured out that

Maurice Castroni had been killed in a car accident about five years earlier. A conversation with his mother, who'd been listed as his next-of-kin, let him know that the man had not been in contact with Erin for some time before the murders, and that the time they'd dated had been only a few weeks. It seemed like a dead end, but David would make sure to verify the particulars with Erin when he got a hold of her. Angus Pierson didn't answer and didn't have voice mail. He jotted down the man's address in case there was time to make a personal visit.

He'd wasted enough time that he figured he could rationalize lunch so he hit a McDonald's on the way to Sandra's house, an action he enjoyed in the present, but would most likely regret later in the day. The overindulgence of fat and salt gave his mood a much-appreciated boost, and he justified the calories with the intense workout he'd endured earlier. Scarfing down the messy meal had been challenging while driving the busy streets of downtown Toronto, but he'd managed the feat without spilling anything in his lap. Bully for him.

The Klassen house sat on the outmost edge of the area David had marked out on his map. Once parked along the curb he reviewed the map again, noting the close proximity to the high school and the crosswalk that cut through the southern end of the park area, the non-forested space where a large playground, two soccer fields, and a pond were located. Going north the space turned into conservation land, with several kilometers of walking trails and wooded land. It was off one of these trails that the boys' bodies had been dumped and the infamous lighter found. All this public space was neatly hidden by residential neighbourhoods on all sides, making it somewhat of a hidden gem for the local inhabitants.

The local police station lay several blocks to the south, covering one of the smaller areas in the Greater Metro Toronto area. David had passed the building on his way in to Sandra's, also catching a glimpse of the playground end of the Simcoe Park, where the boys had been found. A few kids and parents had been milling about, and he noted that a city hockey rink had been erected to be used over the winter months.

Sandra must have spotted his car, as the front door opened

and he could see the woman squinting in his direction. He returned the map to his bag and stepped out of the car. With a quick wave he came up the neatly shoveled walk, shaking hands with the woman before entering the house. A wave of warmth and the strong scent of cinnamon hit him as he stepped inside. The sound of children's laughter came dancing into the foyer.

"You have company?" he asked.

"Tammy's here with the girls. I understand you've met already?" she asked. She held out her hands for his coat.

"Yes, the other day. I don't want to interrupt..."

"No, don't be silly. This is important, and we're just making some cookies. C'mon in. I have coffee on the go." She hung the coat and turned to duck into a doorway to David's right.

He followed, finding Tammy and the two girls coated with various cookie dough ingredients. A fresh batch sat on the counter, close to the area being used to prepare them. Tammy smiled as he entered, prompting the two girls to turn their attention his way. The younger one giggled, the older girl giving David a look that was a combination of smirk and scowl.

"Weren't you at our house the other day?" the older girl asked.

"Yes I was. I'm David."

Without responding the girl turned back to the cookie she'd been spooning copious amounts of icing onto.

"David, this is Scarlett and Jenna."

"Nice to meet you," he said. He didn't have the greatest success in interactions with children.

Still giggling, the younger girl, Jenna, started licking the icing from the spoon she'd been using. Sandra joined him with mugs of coffee and indicated that he should sit at the table. Tammy ushered the girls out, letting them take a couple of the cookies with them.

"So, how are things going, David?" Sandra asked, fixing her coffee to her liking.

David helped himself to the sugar and cream sitting on top of the oak table. "Slowly, to be honest."

"I figured as much. It's been almost ten years after all."

"Now that's not for trying, or a lack of support I must say. And hey, we're only a week in, so it's not like the investigation is closing up shop anytime soon."

Tammy returned to the kitchen. She grabbed a cup of coffee and took the seat beside David. The sun poured in through the uncovered front window, manifesting as a rainbow-tinted halo about Sandra's form and highlighting the grain of the wood furniture. Under other circumstances the setting and conditions would have been inviting, though in truth frustration burned at the back of David's throat like a bad case of indigestion.

"Don't let me interrupt," Tammy said. A fine dusting of flour still coated the lower portions of her arms.

"You're not interrupting. There's not much to report at this time I'm afraid. I was hoping that we might brainstorm a bit and come up with some new avenues to look into."

"Sure, fine with me," Tammy answered.

"All right then." David pulled his file from his bag and opened it on the table. "I've connected with Carl Santos, Janet Snider, and Nathan and Alex. I've also talked with a police friend of mine and a psychiatrist, both of whom have doubts that the murders were committed by a group of teenage boys. The psychiatrist in fact thinks the nature of the crime, specifically the viciousness of the attack, seems very personal and might in fact be directed at the mother and not the boys themselves."

"Like one of the idiots she'd been sleeping with. Like I told you," Tammy said. Her eyes searched David face expectantly, looking for confirmation.

"Could be, though I'd be remiss to make such a conclusion without the evidence to back it up. I need to have my eyes wide open here, so to speak. Jumping to conclusions could have a negative outcome."

"Right, right. I get ya." She took a sip of her coffee and slipped her mother-in-law a pained look.

"I'm sure you can understand how stressful this is for Tammy and me. We eat, sleep and breathe this mess every day."

"Of course. I don't mean to be insensitive, just practical. You've hired me to do a job and I want to do it to the best of my abilities. I also think Nathan and Alex are innocent, and I want to find the person who is responsible and get them behind bars."

Sandra laid her hand on top of David's, meeting his gaze. "We all want the same thing. So let's do this."

David passed around his notes, giving the women a few minutes to go over them, and answered any questions they had. There were two scenarios the conversation kept returning to; that the murders had been committed by a complete stranger or in some type of retaliation against the mother. David had to agree that either was plausible, given the amount of time and resources that had been poured into the investigation. The only problem was that no meaningful evidence had been uncovered to support such scenarios.

"It's driving me crazy that more wasn't uncovered during the investigation. I mean all the players, and at least the dump site for the victims, are within a relatively small area. Someone must have seen or heard something. I assume the neighbourhood was canvassed?" David asked.

"Yes, the night the boys went missing and again during the murder investigation," Sandra said.

"And this homeless man, the one from Janko's, I would think he's not the only one in the area. Has there ever been any problems with transients, you know with begging or trespassing, anything like that?"

"Not really. I mean nothing comes to mind and I've lived here since before Nathan was born. I'm sure things have happened over the years, but nothing that stands out."

"I know you've done your research. Did you go over newspaper reports from before and around the time of the murders?"

"Of course." Sandra said.

David's cell phone rang, interrupting the passionate conversation. He pulled the phone from his pocket, finding an unfamiliar number on the display. "Hello."

"Yes, is this David Lloyd?"

"It is."

"Hello. My name is Erin Gagnon. I'm returning your call."

"Yes, Erin, thank you for getting back to me."

Both women tensed at the mention Erin's name. Tammy leaned forward, almost touching David, though he doubted she was aware of invading his personal space.

"Can you let me know what this is about? I don't quite understand from your message. Are you a police officer?"

"No, a private investigator actually. I've been hired to look into the deaths of your boys and I hope I would be able to speak with you?"

There was a pause long enough to make David wonder if she'd hung up. "The murders you mean. Who hired you to look into this?"

"Sandra Klassen."

"I should have guessed. That woman just won't give up on this." Anger made Erin's words hard and deliberate.

"Will you speak with me?"

She sighed. "Sure. Why not? May as well get it over with and then you can leave me alone."

"Thank you, Erin. I appreciate it, and I promise to handle this with the utmost respect."

"Right. Listen, I'm at work. I get off at seven. I can meet you after that."

They agreed to meet at a coffee shop close to the hospital. David knew it well after the many weeks he'd spent visiting Jenny.

He returned his attention to the women, neither able to conceal their curiosity.

"I'm going to speak with her tonight."

"Good. Listen I know her kids were murdered and that's probably one of the most horrible things any person could go through, but I know she's holding back. Don't let her off just because of the empathy factor."

"I won't, don't worry. I have an excellent bullshit radar, and when I get wind of something off I follow it through till I'm satisfied."

"Good. Sorry to sound like such a heartless bitch, but something is off with her. I know it." Tammy had a look like she'd swallowed something bitter.

"You agree, Sandra?" David asked.

"I always thought it was strange she never showed at the trial, but I don't have the same conviction that Tammy does. That doesn't mean she's not right. Maybe the woman does know something. Maybe she's afraid, I don't know. Could be a lot of things going on, and it's worth looking into."

"I agree. Now, do you have any photos of Nathan from that time? You never know when it might come in handy and the ones in the file are either group ones or grainy newspaper clippings."

"Sure. Give me a sec."

As Sandra left the room David found himself under Tammy's scrutiny. The woman's anger could not be denied, and with good reason, but David had learned from personal experience that hanging on to that kind of hatred never boded well for anyone. It drained one's spirit, and often inspired such tunnel vision that truth and resolution tended to fall by the wayside. The power of her feelings prickled along David's side, making him want to flee as quickly as he could without being rude.

"So Sandra tells me you got shot a few months back while working another case. That right?"

"Yes, that's true. Not something that happens often in my line of work, thank God, but every now and again I stir up enough trouble for someone that they resort to violence."

"That worry you taking on this case? I mean you could turn up something that will send someone else to jail." She took a sip of her coffee, waiting for his reply.

"I hadn't thought about it, to be honest."

"You married?"

The question took him by surprise. "Ah, no. Involved, but not married."

"I bet your girlfriend isn't too keen on you taking on a dangerous situation again, especially so close to this shooting you went through. I wouldn't like it, I know that."

"Jamie and I have a good relationship, and he knows I can handle myself. I mean he worries, but he doesn't sweat all the details."

The change in her demeanor couldn't have been more obvious if it had set off a neon sign. Her eyes narrowed and the cup she held connected sharply with the table. "He? You're gay you mean?"

"Yep. Is that a problem?"

She blinked a few times. "No, I mean I guess it doesn't make any difference in you doing your job."

"Right."

She shifted awkwardly in her chair. "I'm going to go check on the girls. I'll talk with you later." She made a hasty exit, almost knocking into Sandra, who carried a couple of photo albums with her.

She took the seat Tammy had vacated and opened the top album. Inside were photos of a Sandra as a young woman, the man David took to be her husband, and a small baby of indeterminate sex. She flipped through it in quick succession, a smile frozen on her lips. Her hand trembled as she turned the pages. David could feel her reaction to the picture as though it were his own. The poignancy of the moment moved through the room like a burst of chilled air.

"Wrong one. This is Nathan as a child."

David stopped her from closing the album, sensing she needed an empathetic ear, even just for a few minutes. "Is this Nathan's father?"

"Yes, Bill. My first husband. He died when Nathan was three. Cancer."

"I'm sorry."

"Me too. He was a great man, would have been a wonderful father."

"So Mark was your second husband?"

"Yes, we got married when Nathan was about eight. He was a good guy too, but he was very rigid, and despite the years he was in Nathan's life he never quite slipped into the role of father, you know what I mean?'

"Did he and Nathan not get along?"

"Well, they didn't fight, I mean no more than normal families do. Mark never was abusive or anything like that, it's just like he couldn't quite connect the way he should have. I guess that's why we never had children of our own. Though he was good to Nathan, you know went to soccer games, paid for things, I never fully believed he wanted to be a dad."

"Is that why you broke up?"

"More or less. He seemed to be pulling away from our life, and the family, like we weren't important any more. It just wasn't working. Then the more we tried to make it work, the worse it got. The last year we were together all we did was argue. It was hard on all of us, and then he decided to end things. It hurt, but it was for the best." She pulled out another album, rifling through some pages till she found what she was looking for. "That's Mark."

David studied the photo of a man who appeared to be in his early to mid-thirties, attractive in a bland "every man" sort of way. He had short dark hair and a mustache, and stood several inches taller than Sandra. The next picture caught him preparing a meal over a roaring fire, with camping equipment and a blur of green foliage in the background. A young Nathan sat at his side, smiling toward the camera.

"Happier times?" David said.

"Yes. Mark loves the outdoors. Hiking, boating, camping, you name it. Comes from his father I guess. He used to take Mark on camping and hunting trips with him, right from a young age."

"And what does Mark do?"

"He's a physical therapist. Back then he worked at a hospital, now he works in a Sports Injury clinic."

There were a number of hospitals in Toronto and the surrounding area, but he made an educated guess. "He worked at the same place as Erin and Sam Miller's mother?"

"Yes, actually. Well, for a brief overlap anyway. It's close by, which is why some people move to this neighbourhood I'd guess."

David made a note of the information, which he was certain had already been investigated by the police and legal teams. Staring at the photos he felt antsy, almost angry, as though he'd already stumbled across the answer, but had yet to process it.

Sandra handed a couple of pictures to him. He glanced at them briefly before tucking them in the front of his file. "I'll make copies and bring them back. You have any pictures of anyone else around that time, the other boys or their parents, Tammy, Mark?"

"Of course." She flipped through two other albums, making a small pile of photos. "Is there anything else I can do?"

"Not right now. I'll keep in touch about anything important I turn up."

Sandra smiled. "I don't want to be a hindrance David. I trust that you're working hard at this. Just keep me in the loop as you feel I need to be. I don't want to slow things down for you."

"I am working hard, and I'll do everything I can to turn up some new evidence."

Sandra gave a quick nod, accompanied by a pained smile. David knew there was so much more she wanted to say, but understood that continuing to unleash her private pain and speculations was useless. Action was the only way to go. Only digging up witnesses and concrete evidence would set things right.

He bid Sandra good bye, pretending to be oblivious to the sounds of Tammy and her daughters in the background. The slap of cold air on the front step came as a relief.

To help clear his head, and also to orient himself to the area where the accused and victims lived, David took a drive. He made a large circle of the neighbourhood, visually hitting the highlights; Nathan's house, Simcoe Park, and Janko's Diner. He parked across the street from the restaurant, taking in the adjacent businesses, the traffic and the cross-section of humanity walking along the snow-dusted street. A glance at the map showed a homeless shelter some ten blocks to the west, but nonetheless a direct shoot to the restaurant.

During one mistaken turn David had passed Belisle Street, a name that instantly sent up a red flag. Pulling his notes from earlier in the day he realized that it was the place where Angus Pierson currently resided, a welcome coincidence. He wondered if the proximity to his ex-girlfriend's residence had even crossed the man's mind. On impulse David doubled back.

A dark sedan sat in the driveway, covered in a light coating of snow. It didn't appear that the vehicle had been moved recently, but that also didn't mean Angus was at home. David parked on the street and approached the front door.

The bell gave an unexpectedly loud chirp when he pressed it, instigating a series of hollow echoes, like the home wasn't adequately furnished. He waited a few moments, letting his gaze wander over the quiet, middle-class neighbourhood. Most homes had at least one vehicle in the driveway, and puffs of warm mist were being emitted from the dryer vent of the house directly across from where he stood. Two young boys were building some type of fort in the impressive pile of snow deposited at the edge of their property by a passing plough. The sight brought a memory of Sean and him acting in a similar fashion in their younger days.

The sound of the door opening caught his attention, followed by a suspicious, "What do you want?"

David turned back to the house to find a man he pegged to be in the northern ranges of forty, dressed only in a pair of flannel pajama bottoms. His eyes were bloodshot and his hair disheveled, clearly having been interrupted from sleep.

"Angus Pierson?"

"Yeah. Who's asking?"

"My name is David Lloyd. I'm a private investigator looking into the Gagnon murders. I'm wondering if you'd be willing to speak with me?"

Still standing behind the house's outer door, the man peered out at David like he'd suddenly grown a second head. It took several minutes before understanding seemed to dawn on the man, draining away his angry scowl. "Like Erin's kids you mean?"

"Yes, exactly. I can come back if this isn't a good time."

"Don't matter the time. You just caught me off guard there. C'mon in." He pushed the screen door open, holding it to allow David to enter.

The home reeked of tobacco and grease. David was fairly certain that anything he touched would leave a grimy residue so he made sure to keep his hands in his pockets as he followed Angus down a central hallway. They ended in the kitchen where the scent of oil was the strongest. Evidence of its use coated the stove top and the surrounding counter space and walls. Angus started a pot of coffee before grabbing a pack of cigarettes from the pocket of a coat draped over the back of one of the room's vinyl chairs. He lit up and leaned back against the counter, eyeing David.

David sat, pushing back from the table so he wouldn't be tempted to rest his arms on its surface. "So, thanks for letting me in. I won't take up too much of your time."

"You got a card or something?" Angus asked after passing a stream of smoke through his nose.

"Yes, of course." He rooted about in his pocket until he found the small cache he always kept on him. He handed one over.

Angus squinted at the card for a few minutes, his lips pursed. David wondered if he were having difficulty seeing, or perhaps reading it. Finally Angus gave a shrug and laid the card on the counter. He grabbed the pot and poured himself a cup with no offer to David.

"So what does this stuff about Erin's kids have to do with me?"

David laid his notebook on his lap. "I understand you were dating Erin at the time the murders happened?"

The question garnered a lopsided grin. "I don't know about dating. We hooked up every now and again. Girl could be clingy though."

"By hooked up, you mean you were having sex with Erin?"

"Yep. A real spitfire in the sack, but she wanted more than I was looking for."

David ignored the crass comment. "How long did this go on and when did it end?"

He took a slurp of coffee. "A few months, like four tops. It ended right after the kids were killed. I didn't want to deal with the drama."

A real humanitarian. "So did you speak or see one another after the murders?"

"Yeah, she called a few times, but like I said I didn't want no part in it."

"Have you seen her since?"

"Just on the TV. Never in person again."

He tossed back the remainder of the coffee, and stood watching David with his meaty arms crossed over his chest. He had a crude attractiveness, though he was starting to go a bit soft around the middle. His hair was thick, and only lightly peppered with grey. His eyes continued to draw David's attention as they were an intense green, a shade more commonly seen in the feline species.

"Is there anything you can tell me about Erin in that time that might shed light on what happened? Did she have any enemies, any strange things happen that could have been hints of things to come?"

"Not that I remember. We didn't talk much, you know. I came around to get laid, not deal with her shit."

"Gotcha. So nothing comes to mind?"

"Nope. Once the cops were involved I split. I have my own problems, and I didn't need getting mixed up in hers, especially a friggin' murder investigation. And anyway it's not like I was the only guy she was seeing."

"You mean Maurice Castroni?"

"That fat piece of crap was one of them. He stopped by one night when I was there. Guess he didn't understand she'd dumped his ass."

"One of them? So there were more?"

"Yeah, bitch got around. I knew there was someone else 'cause she got calls a couple of times, like where she acted real weird, you know, like she didn't want me to know who she was talking too."

"Any idea who it was?"

"Nah. Didn't care either. I was seeing other chicks too. As long as I kept it wrapped I didn't really care where she'd been." Angus made a gesture toward his neither region that made bile race up the back of David's throat. He'd need a shower when he got out of that place.

"Anything else?"

He hesitated, taking a leisurely amount of time to light up another cigarette. "Well, now I can't be sure about this, but one time I came over and this young guy came out of her bedroom. I'm talking like not-legal young. Erin said he was just there to do some work or some shit, but she sure looked guilty as hell."

The nugget of information caught David off guard. Surely if the encounter had been sexual in nature Erin would not have wanted the information to come to light. It would have offered her up to possible criminal charges and a certain scrutiny of her morality during the investigation. It was bad enough she'd been with men like Angus, who had no redeeming qualities whatsoever, except perhaps between the sheets. But the validity of the statement was not to be taken at face value considering the source.

"I will look into that. Now if you think of anything that might help, please get in touch. I'll let myself out."

He made it out of the house as quickly as possible and was pulling onto the street when his cell phone rang. He looked at the number. "Hey, Jenny."

"Hey, yourself. You up to anything tonight?"

"Maybe some work. Not sure. I can pick you up in a few hours.

"Please. I've got major cabin fever."

"Okay. See you then."

CHAPTER 8

A visit to the police station didn't fare any better than his earlier phone call. Detective Brown was off shift, due to start his new rotation the next day. David left his card with the reception clerk.

The only other angle he could see pursuing right at that moment was the Janko's man. He ended up taking the long way round to the restaurant, which caused him to pass the Harbour Light shelter, another destination he'd marked on his trusty map. A free parking spot offered itself on the next block, so he decided to take his chances that a staff member might be available without notice. A discreet sign marked the building so as not to draw unnecessary attention from the public. David climbed the steps and pushed the bell.

A female voice spoke through the intercom. "We're not open until six."

"I'm not a client. I'm a private investigator and I wondered if I could speak with anyone about someone that may have stayed here?"

"Just a moment please."

A few minutes later a woman with thick eyebrows and hair pulled into an untidy knot at the back of her head opened the front door and gave David a blatant appraisal. He handed her a card, which she did little more than glance at.

"What is this about?" she asked.

He offered his hand, which she shook. "I'm David Lloyd and I've been hired to look into a murder case that happened some years back. There has been a suggestion that a homeless man known to frequent this area may be involved or could be a witness."

She stuck her head out further, looking about as though others might be waiting to accost her. She frowned. "Come on in. It's too cold to speak on the step."

He followed her in, noting the security cameras and the panic button worn about her neck. She led him to a small office.

"Sorry, I don't mean to seem rude, but we get those trying to pull a fast one. My name is Erica."

"No problem. I didn't call, so I imagine I took you by surprise."

She nodded. "So this is about a client of ours? You know I can't divulge personal information."

"Of course. I would just like to give a description and if you think it might fit one of your clients, then perhaps you could speak with him?"

"All right." She didn't sound convinced.

"This would have been in May of 1991. The person of interest is a middle-aged black man, possibly with mental health issues. Sorry, not much of a description."

"You're talking about the Gagnon murders, those little boys."

"Yes." David didn't see any reason to hold back.

"Well, the first problem is that this shelter has only been here for five years. The other is that isn't much of a description. The population that comes through here is transient. Some come on a regular basis, some in cycles. Others move about from city to city, sometimes gone for years at a time. The other issue is that most don't give a proper name."

It had been a long shot. "I understand. Just thought it couldn't hurt to ask."

"Now, I can tell you that before we were here some of the homeless liked to camp out in Simcoe Park or in the abandoned buildings on Chelsea. Some of those buildings have been put back in use, but a couple are still empty. Also there's the Salvation Army up a few blocks. They have a meal drop in three times a week, and a free clothing room once a month. They've been here for about thirty years, so they might have more answers for you. Also there's Janko's. It's a twenty-four-hour diner, so if enough money can be scraped up for a cup of coffee you can sit in there for some time to get warm."

He didn't know if she realized it but her short speech had set off a firework of possibilities in his mind. His heart gave a weird, off-tempo thump in connection to his excitement. *Hot diggity!*

"Now the bigger problem will be getting any of these folks to talk with you. They're notoriously private and suspicious. And of those that will talk, you have to wonder if what they're telling you is true. Many lie and others are so mentally unwell they couldn't relate the truth to save their lives."

Back to square one. "I appreciate the information. It's very helpful."

"You're welcome, though I have to say I really hope one of our guys isn't involved in something so awful."

"Like I said, they could simply be a witness. Now you have my card, so please feel free to contact me if you think of anything else."

David thought back to his call with Jenny. She'd be the perfect ally to approach the population in question. He knew from experience that the homeless, low-level drug traffickers and those working in prostitution often overlapped, whether it be a simple territory issue or in different barter and exchange situations. Those on the streets were often more likely to speak with someone they saw as being in the same realm, certainly over any kind of perceived authority. He imagined he'd be lumped in with police when it came to trust.

Next stop Janko's. In the odd hours between standard meal times, restaurant occupancy often thins out, as was the case at Janko's. There was a couple in a booth near the back, a few patrons at the counter and one family at a table. David approached a young woman standing at the host station. She looked bored, and was idly flipping through a magazine.

"Hello. I wonder if the owner or the manager might be available?" David asked with his most winning smile.

The girl looked up, making a face that indicated she liked what she saw. David felt decidedly icky about being checked out by a girl young enough to be his daughter.

"You'd want Manny, my uncle. He's working in his office."

"Could you ask him if he has a minute to speak with me?" David asked, handing across his card.

The girl took it, taking time to read it over. "A PI for real? Cool."

"Yeah, cool."

"Just give me a sec." She came around the front of her station, giving David an obvious mental undressing as she walked past.

He waited, taking the opportunity to check out the layout of the restaurant. He noted there was only one entrance, and the location of the washrooms. The space was essentially rectangular, with the off-centre front doors and host station dividing the establishment into two halves. To the right the bigger space boasted the kitchen and counter, with numerous free-standing tables and booths lining the windows. To the left were the washrooms and an area consisting entirely of booths meant for parties of four or less.

The young woman reappeared, accompanied by an older man with a shock of white hair. He was thin, of medium height and sported a neatly trimmed mustache. She pointed in David's direction, and as the man turned his attention away from her she gave David a flirty wink. He tried not to react, instead concentrating on the man coming toward him with his hand outstretched.

They shook. "Thank you for meeting with me. Manny, is it?"

"Yes, no problem. Now what is this about?"

"Is there somewhere we can talk?" David felt itchy under the unwavering scrutiny of the young woman.

"Yeah, sure. C'mon back to my office."

His "office" had most likely been a storage room in its original inception. The space was barely wide enough to fit the man's desk and small filing cabinet. David sat on the one other chair in the room, a piece that would have been more at home in some type of Victorian manor.

"So, I wanted to touch base with you about an event that happened here about a decade ago. Would you have been the owner then?"

"Yep, been the owner for twenty-three years. Took over

from my pop when he got too old to handle the long hours."

"Oh, a family business then?"

"Yep. Janko's my last name. Same as a few who work here. Like Lila up front there."

David experienced a flash of discomfort at the girl's name, as though she could be still watching him through the wall. "Great. So you are probably very familiar with the night I'm looking to ask about. This is to do with the man who came in here on the same night that two boys were murdered. You know what I'm talking about?"

"Of course. I wasn't here that night. Our evening manager was in, guy named Mike Snell. There was a cook and one waitress on also. My son-in-law Randy called the police back the next morning after he heard about them murders on the radio."

"You have problems with the any of the homeless people in the area?"

"Not for the most part. Every now and again some poor bugger comes in here three sheets to the wind and we have to ask them to leave. In those cases it's 'cause they're being too loud, or maybe they got sick in the washroom. Never had any violence though." The man's words were thoughtful, implying a sensitivity to the unfortunate people he was referring to.

"The man in this case, had he ever come in before?"

"Hard to say. There's several guys that fit the description, both past customers and current. Thing that stuck out most for Mike was the stuff the man was saying, you know about monsters and stealing children's souls. That and the fact he was bloody and covered in dirt. He seemed very disturbed and Mike thought he might have hurt himself, but he wouldn't let anyone near him and he wasn't making a lick of sense."

"You have a phone number I can reach Mike at?"

Manny pulled open a drawer in his file cabinet, rooting around until he found what he was looking for. He jotted down the number and handed it to David.

"Thanks for this. Could you also ask Randy to give me a call?" David passed the man his card.

They walked back out together, parting ways as they entered

the main area of the restaurant. David figured he may as well grab something for dinner since he was there, so he sidled up the counter to take a look at the menu. He found the usual diner fare, with some welcomed Mediterranean touches. He ordered three chicken souvlakis on pitas, with sides of fries and salad. The smell when it came caused instant salivation, followed by a painful gurgle from his stomach.

With bag in hand he moved toward the front door, concentrating on not making eye contact again with Lila. She had other ideas. She stepped out from the host station, intentionally blocking his trajectory. She grabbed his free hand, as though to shake it, but instead pressed a piece of paper into it. He shoved it into his pocket without looking.

Almost as though not of his own free will, he glanced back as he pushed open the door, finding the girl watching him. She blew him a kiss and he made a beeline for his car.

He and Jenny pulled into the driveway about thirty minutes later. One of the windows in the kitchen was open, allowing music to escape into the otherwise quiet darkness. They entered through the side door, into the combination mud and laundry room, a space that opened directly onto the kitchen.

"David, that you?' Jamie called from out of sight.

"Yep, and Jenny." He came into the room, after removing his shoes and coat, to find that Jamie had been busy while he was gone. Most of the kitchen had been painted a curious shade of green, much like a Granny Smith apple. It looked sharp with the dark wood cabinetry.

"Looks good," Jenny commented before grabbing the bag of food and heading to the living room.

"What she said," David said and gave Jamie a quick kiss. "Wash up and come join us for grub."

Jenny was already eating when David came into the room. He dropped his bag beside the coffee table and took his container of food. Jamie arrived a few minutes later with three beers in hand. He sat beside Jenny.

After a few bites Jamie pointed to the bag, asking, "Janko's Diner? You sure like to bring your work home with you."

"I stopped by there to talk with the owner, see if anyone

still worked there who might have seen the man. Food looked good."

"It's yummy," Jenny mumbled with her mouth full.

"Anything new?" Jamie asked.

David pulled his notebook from his bag, in the process dumping a number of loose papers onto the carpet. He flipped through till he found his notes from earlier and handed them across to Jamie. Jenny reached over to pick up the papers, stopping at a particular one. A huge grin spread across her face.

"You dog. You actually going to this?" She held up the flier for the burlesque show Roberta had given him earlier in the week.

Jamie laughed. "The Scarlett Letter? Let me guess, Roberta?"

"And Stella. It's a fundraiser for her dance studio, to help kids who can't afford lessons."

"So you're considering it from a purely charitable standpoint," Jamie chided.

"Of course."

"We have to go!" Jenny said.

"Why not? Should be fun," Jamie said.

"All right then, people. Pencil it into your social calendars for next weekend."

He let the rest of the meal go on without bringing up an idea that had been itching at him since his conversation at the homeless shelter. When in the midst of a case he hated to let his guard down, or be idle in the progress. Even though it was a Saturday night he planned on getting some work done.

Jamie left to dump the containers and check on his painting, perfectionist that he was. Jenny lay down on the coach, rubbing her belly.

"Full?"

"Totally."

"So, listen, I wanted to ask your help on something?"

She turned her head in his direction, giving him a look out of the corner of her eye. "Do tell."

"I need to speak with some of the homeless people down around Chelsea, and I wondered if you'd help me out. You know how those types are, they may not talk to me 'cause they'll consider me like a cop."

"My area of expertise, so to speak, isn't homeless people, its hookers. And pimps. Some drug dealers." She rattled of the list like it was the most common thing in the world.

"But those working in the area would at least be familiar with those on the streets, right? Like through drugs and other things not entirely legal."

"Sure, I mean I knew the regulars in my area. At least by sight, some by their name. There's gossip in the streets too, just like any walk of life. We like to look out for each other as far as the cops and any creeps that might be going around ripping people off, or hurting them."

As grim and seedy as the implication of her words were, it also encouraged David that they might make some headway. "So you'll help me?"

"I can try. When ya thinking?"

"Tonight."

"Tonight? Seriously?"

Jamie came back into the room. "What's tonight?"

"David wants to go out and speak with some homeless people to see if they know anything about the man he's looking for."

"I'm game," Jamie answered, taking David by surprise.

"Up for a walk through Simcoe Park too?"

"For sure, the only way to top off such an evening. You better buy us some drinks after."

Jenny laughed, but David could tell she was secretly delighted he'd turned to her for help. Little by little he seemed to be chipping away at the wall she'd lived behind for so long. Soon he'd be not only ingrained in her life, but hopefully her heart as well.

First stop, the café to speak with Erin Gagnon.

CHAPTER 9

Jenny took no offense at being asked to sit the meeting out, and decided to go and visit a few of the staff who had cared for her while at the hospital. Though she still had anxiety from the situation that landed her there, she was grateful for the kindness and concern she'd been shown by the hard-working staff. They made arrangements to pick her up in an hour's time. David watched until she had safely made her way through the front doors before driving a couple of blocks farther up the street. A parking spot was open on a narrow side street and they were in the café in a matter of minutes.

Erin had already arrived. She sat with her hands wrapped about a mug of coffee, hair pulled back in a low ponytail. She looked much like she had in the photos on the case file; small, olive-toned skin. Time had been kind. She could have easily passed for her early twenties, when in reality was closer to her mid-thirties. David nodded in her direction and Jamie followed him to the table.

"Erin? I'm David Lloyd. This is my partner Jamie Brennan. I hope you don't mind if he joins us?"

Erin looked up from her coffee, her expression sullen. "Why not?"

The men sat across the table from her. They both ordered a coffee when the waitress appeared.

"So I may as well jump right in. We don't need to be wasting either of our time here. Like I said on the phone I've been hired to look into the circumstances around the arrest of Nathan Klassen, John Dean, and Alex Snider. As you're aware the men have always maintained that they are not guilty of murdering…

your boys." Erin made a pained expression at the mention of her sons. "I am trying to be sensitive, Erin. I can understand how stressful this must be for you."

"No you can't. Unless you've been through what I have, there's no way to understand. My boys were killed, butchered. I've done everything I can to make my peace with that and get on with my life."

"You're right, I, we can't understand how you feel, but our intention is not to upset you. We only want to make sure the guilty parties have been found and are punished. I'm going to be blunt and say I really don't think these guys did it."

Erin rubbed her lips together, eyes staring into her cup as though she might conjure the truth from the depths of its content. "Why?"

"A lot of reasons. Motive for one. Why would three teenage boys want to kill a couple of kids? Also where did it happen?"

"They were druggies and delinquents from what I heard."

"And they don't deny that. But smoking dope and shoplifting is a far cry from a crime like this."

She was quiet again, thoughtful. "How come the police never found any other suspects?"

"That's part of what I'm trying to determine. It seems like the case against these guys was shoved along the judicial system without merit. Frankly I think it stinks."

"You really think the killer is still out there?" She paled as the words left her mouth, the very idea enough to affect her physically.

"Unless they've been picked up for some other reason or they're dead, yes."

She sighed. "What do you want from me?"

"Just some information."

The coffees arrived and the men took a moment to fix them to their liking, while Erin studied them one at a time. Her expression didn't betray any opinion she may have formulated about the two.

"So ask," she said.

"Well I guess the most obvious question is do you have any thoughts on who might have done this?"

She took a moment and then shook her head. Something about the action set David's radar into action. "I can't think of why anyone would want to do this."

"You weren't having any trouble with anyone. Say the boys' dad or an ex-boyfriend? Any odd people seen around the neighborhood."

She shifted in her seat, not looking at either of the men. Something was off. The look on Jamie's face confirmed the tickle of suspicion David was experiencing.

"I already answered these same questions for the police. Several times. How can answering them again help anything?" she asked. Tears brimmed along the lower lids of her dark eyes.

"Sometimes time gives us better clarity," David answered, trying to not to sound harsh.

"No, I wasn't having trouble with anyone." Her tone had slipped from irritation to defensiveness.

Jamie cut in. "We understand you were dating a couple of different men at the time?"

"So? That's not a crime."

"Of course not, but these guys had records and perhaps kept company with types that might be capable of such a vicious crime. I have to ask if there may have been drugs involved? Perhaps money owing or something like that?"

Erin shook her head, bright circles of pink appearing on both cheeks. "No, nothing like that. At least as far as I was concerned. What they did on their own time was not under my control."

"I spoke with Angus earlier," David said, the statement triggering a flash of something dark across Erin's features. "He let on that you might have had something going on with a young guy, possibly someone underage."

Her cup rattled against the table as her hands began to tremble. "Excuse me? I don't think so. He really said that?" Then she mumbled something that sounded like "fucking jerk."

"Okay, so you don't think anyone you were dating might have been involved. What about your ex-husband?"

She shook her head.

David looked to Jamie, raising an eyebrow.

"No threats, no suspicious behaviour around the neighbourhood or your work?" Jamie asked.

"Nope, nothing like that."

"And you were working at the hospital then?" David asked.

"Yep. Had been there about a year. I used to work for a cleaning company, but I made peanuts. When I got on at the hospital my pay more than doubled. Been there ever since."

"Did you know any of the parties before they became suspects?" David asked, knowing full well that Tammy had babysat for Erin.

"Well, I knew Nathan through Tammy. He came with her a couple of times when she babysat."

"Didn't Jasmine also babysit?"

The question made the spots of colour on Erin's cheeks spread. "Ah, yep. She came a couple of times."

David pressed. "So did you know Alex?"

"I guess. He came and walked her home once."

"John Dean or Sam Miller?"

She took a sip of her coffee. "Not John himself, but his mom also worked at the hospital. She was a secretary. Sam I never heard of till the investigation." Her words lacked conviction.

"Really? I thought someone told me that Sam had come by your place before?" David said.

"Nope, got your facts wrong there."

She looked David in the eye, a vague smile on her lips, but her outward calmness seemed forced, insincere. David couldn't quite put his finger on what is was she was lying about or withholding, but he had no doubt she wasn't being completely truthful.

"Anything else you feel important to share with us?" Jamie asked.

"I don't think so."

"All right. Well, we might be in touch at a later time, but I guess that's all for now," David said.

Jamie nodded agreement. Erin made an abrupt departure after saying goodbye, walking quickly to the exit without looking back.

"What the hell was that about?" Jamie asked.

"I don't know, but it was sure fishy."

"I don't get the angle though. Why would she not want to help find the person responsible? They were her kids after all."

"Dunno. Maybe she got herself mixed up in something bad. Maybe someone was threatening her. Maybe she wanted the kids out of the way. I don't know what to make of this."

"It could just be she's really pissed off that someone is opening this up again. You and I both know that sometimes innocent people come across badly when under stress. Some act like robots, and say things they don't mean. I had one woman who laughed like a hyena the whole time she was being questioned about her sister's death, and it was just her reaction to the shock."

"Yeah, but it's been ten years."

"I don't think anyone would ever get over something like this."

"Maybe."

David made notes of the conversation, certain there was more to the story than they'd been privy to.

Thirty minutes later David and company were exiting the car he'd parked at the southern end of Chelsea, with the intention of making their way up to the top cross street, Redmond Avenue. This would be the street that Janko's was located on, about ten blocks west, in essence having navigated two sides of the box of streets surrounding Simcoe Park. Despite the fact that she'd passed many a winter night dressed in hot pants and a thin leather jacket, David made Jenny dress for the elements. She looked about fifteen years old in her puffy winter coat and toque.

They'd entered the quiet residential end of the street, passing the road to Sam's teenage home, and the cut-through that Nathan indicated he used to get to and from school. Soon the high school came into view, a shadowy monstrosity of a building with a large field as black and still as a calm stretch of ocean. The three took a brief tour, seeing nothing alarming and crossing paths only with a middle-aged man walking his dog.

Jenny mashed up a handful of snow, nailing David square in the chest with a pretty decent throw. He retaliated, an act that reduced them all to prepubescent behaviour for the better part of thirty minutes.

After dusting off the evidence of their bout in the snow they returned to Chelsea Street, making their way up several more blocks. Quite quickly the neighbourhood changed from residential to a run-down industrial region, lousy with wide, multi-story warehouses and processing facilities. Many had the telltale signs of disuse, including broken windows, padlocks on entranceways, and overlapping layers of graffiti. David could see how the sites would be a draw for the homeless, especially during the harsh winter months. Any roof over your head was better than none.

As if on cue, two men came shuffling out from the back of a squat building with a large rolling door across the front that must have been the access for commercial vehicles during its working heyday. One had his arm about the other as though helping his friend stay upright. From the distance David couldn't tell if the man receiving assistance was elderly, disabled, or simply intoxicated. The leader darted a look about, on the alert for trouble. He spotted their group, bringing the movement of the two to an abrupt stop. As he pointed in their direction the other man looked their way, then turned back to his friend, pressing against his chest as though for comfort.

When they started to turn back the way they'd come David called out, "Wait! Please, we'd like to speak with you."

They two shuffled along for about another twenty yards, with David, Jamie, and Jenny quickly closing the gap between the parties. As they seemed to realize that attempting to escape was futile they stopped walking, with the more dominant of the two keeping the other pressed tightly against him, obscuring his companion's features. He watched the three step closer with beady black eyes, barely visible under the tangle of dark hair and an odd Pepto-Bismol-pink-and-green striped hat pulled low on his head. The rest of his outfit consisted of garments in varying shades of grey and black, making the hat even more garish and out of place.

"Whadya want?" he demanded in a deep voice, with a surprising melodic quality to it.

"First of all we're not cops, or social workers. Nothing like that. We just want to ask you a few questions about someone you may know." David kept a respectable distance, careful to keep a smile on his face and his voice neutral.

The second man dared a peek out from where he was pressed against his friend's side. The face had the appearance of a dried apple doll, with a dark complexion and deep runs of wrinkles, like a toy David's grandmother had as a child. A pale pink tongue snaked out, running along the non-existent lips, and exposing a mouth devoid of teeth. Rheumy eyes tracked each of their three faces in turn before the gaze dropped to the snow-crusted pavement. What David had taken to be a man was in truth a woman, with an estimated two decades on her protective companion. David had to wonder if they were mother and son.

The man flicked a suspicious look in Jenny's direction. "What's it worth to ya?"

David had suspected he'd be asked for some compensation, having hit the bank machine on their way down. He pulled out a twenty and handed it over.

The man snatched it from his hand and tucked in an outer pocket in his worn jacket. "Ask."

"We're looking for a man, black, probably in his fifties, who used to be in this area about ten years ago. He may have liked to talk about monsters, or things stealing souls. Can you think of anyone like that?"

The man made a silent inquiry of his female partner. They locked eyes for about thirty seconds, until she gave a quick shake of her head. He thought about the question a bit longer before finally answering. "I don't think so. Selena and I been round here longer than that, but we don't talk with other people much. We keep to ourselves."

David pulled out the copies of the photos he'd made, handing then over to the man. "Do you recognize any of these people?"

He looked at them slowly, studying each face though he had no visible reaction to any. "Nope."

"Okay, thanks for talking with us." He left his card with the man, not expecting the effort to net any further information.

Irritated, but still a long way from discouraged, David led the other two back to the street. They made a few more stops at other buildings with similar results. In several instances the parties were reluctant to speak with them, though after being left alone with Jenny for a few minutes they changed their tune. A few were familiar with the case though had no direct knowledge that could help them. One man thought the person they were looking for might have been named Joseph, but didn't know where he was or how long it had been since he last saw the man, many years at least. By the time they'd travelled to the top of Chelsea, David had handed out about twenty cards and was down almost two hundred dollars.

After a brief stop to warm up over cups of coffee they headed east along Redmond, passing a bustling Janko's before taking a left down Juniper. This street ran parallel to Chelsea, and if followed far enough would lead them past the cross street to Sandra's, the housing complex where Alex had lived and his mother still did, and even the local police station. The pink elephant at the heart of their travels was, of course, Simcoe Park, at that time of night a dark, desolate space holding tightly to its secrets.

The three passed Ridgewood Place, the housing complex, and continued walking for another two blocks before reaching the eastern end of the crosswalk that cut through the park, a straight shot back to Chelsea and the nearby high school. They took the walk only as far as the deserted playground at the southern tip of the park. Several hundred yards beyond this lay the forested area with walking trails where the bodies of the young Gagnon brothers had been discovered. At night this area was nothing more than an indistinct haze of shadows and darkness.

"This is creepy," Jenny said, breaking an uncomfortable silence.

"Yeah, but necessary. I want to see the place at night, like it would have been when whoever killed the boys came to dump their bodies."

David pulled out the map and a small penlight from his pocket. He'd carefully marked out the walking trails and the site where the bodies were found. They passed the unoccupied swings and the ice-coated jungle gym, footsteps making a soft crackling over the fresh snow. The layer of white thinned to hard, frozen ground as they entered the woods, the towering trees making a canopy of sorts that helped to block a large accumulation of snow. Jamie took David's hand as they walked deeper into the darkness.

As the anxiety around their mission swelled, their collective breathing began to sound like Darth Vader, a notion that brought an inappropriate chuckle to David's lips. Jamie tugged at his hand, questioning his reaction. He shook his head.

A fork in the road came into view, the trail to the right leading to a small Guardian shed, abandoned at that time of the year. Several hundred yards beyond that and off the main trial would be the area they had come to view. A lump appeared in his throat as David passed the darkened shed. As they continued he noted a depression in the ground running alongside the path, what he took to be creek bed. He knew this waterway was shallow and easily passable at the best of times, but in the summer season when the boys had been found it had contained enough water to affect forensic testing.

A small cross with the name Gagnon had been nailed to a tree at the edge of the trail, indicating the location that no doubt drew countless visits from those affected by the crime and others with a simple morbid fascination. David gave his head a small toss in the direction of the woods, and Jamie nodded his acquiescence. He broke his hold on David's hand to help Jenny down the mild slope, which was partially impeded by trees and tangled shrub. Another twenty feet in and the main trail was barely visible any longer.

A second, larger cross materialized, stark and somber against the pale ground and skeletal trees. Ribbons and other offerings had been left on and about the marker, striking an emotional chord with David. He'd seen the terrible photos and read the gruesome autopsy report, but seeing the site of two young lives cut short and dumped like garbage on a forest floor cut deep. Jamie looked equally troubled, eyes wide and with a hand cupped about his mouth.

Jenny shot David a hard look, pointing to an area behind where he stood. He turned, squinting, but not seeing what had grabbed her attention. As he began to turn his attention back to his companions a blur of motion pulled his gaze back. A crackling sound shot through the night, triggering a cold rush of adrenaline. David took off running.

Behind him David could hear Jamie telling Jenny to stay put. His breathing sounded amplified, exiting in great icy bursts. More than once a tree limb or clump of frozen shrubbery slapped him or caught on his clothing, attempting to slow him down. Jamie was close on his tail, calling out his name. His small flashlight did little to penetrate the thick darkness of the woods, managing only to flash a tiny beam in a jerky arc before him as he ran, but was enough to catch the movement of his target. He briefly caught sight of a pair of military style boots and the edge of a long dark coat, flapping as the wearer moved at impressive speed.

David pushed ahead, sensing more than seeing when he should dive to halt the chase. He collided with another body, prompting a grunt of pain and a string of expletives. Hands grabbed at him, trying to wrestle out of his grasp. The strength of the other party surprised him. He thought he had the upper hand until something large and heavy crashed into the back of his skull.

The other person stood, with David drawing on his last bit of strength to hang on to their legs. His head throbbed and he felt dangerously close to throwing up. He felt his grip slip as a wave of nausea hit him. Just then Jamie came crashing through the mess of brush and barreled into the object of David's pursuit. The two hit the snow-crusted ground, and it was enough for David to take a breath and push on to assist his partner. Between the two of them they managed to hold man down.

David flicked the light over the face of the man they held, surprised to find such a youthful presence looking back at him. "Listen, I don't want to hurt you. I just want to ask why you're out here."

The young man looked from David to Jamie, and back again. "You cops?"

"No, we're not. We're not going to arrest you or tell you to leave, though I can't imagine this is the best place to be on a night like this." David sat back, removing his grip from the man's arm.

Jamie did likewise, letting David take the lead. The young man let out a breath, seeming to relax.

"Why do you care if I'm out here?"

"I don't, except it's right near the spot where two boys were murdered."

"So?"

"So, why are you out here? You like stuff like that? Hanging out at murder sites?"

The man grimaced. "Jesus, no. I just needed somewhere to sleep. I was going to break into the old work cabin."

"The cabin's up by the trail, a ways back," Jamie said.

"Not the new one, the old one."

"Show us," David said, not letting on his surprise.

The three doubled back, finding a none-too-pleased Jenny standing in the same spot they'd left her. She joined them as the young man led them about fifteen yards deeper in from the spot where they'd first seen him, on the other side of the waterless creek bed. The cabin was a skeleton of a building, unable to provide more than basic shelter, certainly not warmth.

Despite their best efforts they couldn't manage to convince the man to go to a shelter or even a motel, so they had no choice but to leave him there. They said little on the walk back to the car.

Inside the clock on the dashboard showed it to be nearly eleven pm. David's head throbbed like a massive hangover, and he felt more than a little disheartened after the complete lack of advancement in the case. Everyone was in agreement to call it a night. They dropped Jenny off before heading home.

"Thanks for a lovely night, fellas," Jenny said, giving a mock salute.

"Well, that was a bust." David felt tired and weary.

Jamie turned to look his way. "Maybe not."

"How so?"

"Well, we've been wondering about this man, right? Thinking he knew something about the murders. Maybe he saw something that night. What if he had been in the cabin or on his way there and saw the boys' bodies being dumped? Could explain his hysteria, maybe even the blood if he'd touched them."

"That's a lot of maybes."

"Yeah. Still, it's worth considering."

"Not much to consider if I can't find the guy. No one seemed to know who he was."

"Well, you still have other avenues to pursue right? You haven't talked to everyone on the list. We need to poke into the mother's story a bit more. God, we haven't even sunk to desperation yet, where we might start hitting Jimmy up to run every molester, rapist and other weirdo active around that time."

"You sure know how to cheer a guy up," he responded, chuckling.

Back home they made a beeline to the bedroom, neither interested in anything more than a quick roll in the hay and some sleep. As David pulled his damp jeans off a crumpled bit of paper fell from his pocket. Jamie grabbed it from the bed where it had landed. He held it up. "This important?"

David suddenly realized what it was and felt his cheeks flame. "Jesus, don't look at that."

Jamie laughed. "No way after you say something like that." He unrolled the paper, eyes flicking across the words. "Who's Lila and should I be worried that she wants to…"

David snatched the paper and tossed it in the waste basket. "She's some girl from Janko's dinner. Arguments about cheating aside, if I even thought about going out with her I should be shot. She's about sixteen. I didn't know what to do when she handed me that, so I shoved it in my pocket and got my ass out the door."

Jamie's brows arched with surprise. "Wow, girls are pretty forward these days."

"I can be pretty forward too."

He jumped on the bed, pulling the rest of Jamie's clothing from his body. He spent the next ten minutes licking his way along his partner's naked form. The craziness of the case faded away, and there was only the warmth of Jamie's body and his soft moans of pleasure.

CHAPTER 10

Soft light filtered in, hailing the gentle arrival of Sunday morning. David peeked at the clock, groaning when he saw it was only ten past seven. He rolled over, wrapping his arm around Jamie, and nuzzled into his sleep-induced warmth. Jamie murmured, not quite awake. The next thing he knew there were noises from downstairs and three hours had passed.

When he sat up his head protested the movement, giving an urgent pulse of pressure. He touched the back of his head, feeling a bump the size of a walnut and sighed. *That's what you get for tackling a homeless man in the woods, idiot.*

Jamie sat at the kitchen table in a t-shirt and cut-off sweats reading the paper, a cup of coffee within reach. He smiled when David entered. After grabbing a cup of coffee loaded with cream and sugar he joined Jamie at the table. He didn't speak until half the cup had been consumed, and with the number of years they'd been together Jamie knew better then to try and engage David in conversation.

When he put his cup down he reached out and placed his hand on top of Jamie's.

"Good morning."

"You too. There's a couple messages for you."

"Yeah, from who?"

"Mark Ester and some guy named Mike."

"Nice, I wasn't expecting Mark until tonight."

"Yeah, I wrote the number down for you."

"Thanks." He walked over to the phone, noting Jamie's neat handwriting on the pad beside it. His hand had just touched the receiver when it rang, making David jump. "Hello?"

"Hi, can I speak with David Lloyd?" an unfamiliar male asked.

"This is David."

"Oh, great I caught you. This is Sam Miller. I'm returning your call."

"Right, thanks for getting back to me. Like I said in the message I'd like to set up a time to speak with you about the Gagnon murders."

"Yeah, sure. Of course. I knew Sandra had been thinking about hiring an investigator. Don't know how much help I can be but I'm happy to talk with you."

"Okay. Well I'm actually meeting with your father at around one. Can I come after I'm done there?"

He paused. "Ah, today's not good actually. I'm leaving in a little bit for a business trip. I'll be back Wednesday. Could we meet then?"

"Sure thing. What time works?"

"Evening would be better." He rattled off an address which David dutifully recorded then hung up.

With his second call he got Mark, who said he would be free around dinner time. Mike was working the evening shift and was happy to talk with David if he could stop by.

"Might be my lucky day," David said when he was done with his calls.

"You want company?"

"I think I'm okay. I can always call you if things get sticky."

"Sure. Lord knows I have my own work I should be paying attention to."

"You feel like hitting the gym first?"

"Sure. Why not."

"'Kay, I'll give Sean a call."

An hour later the three were sweating their way through cardio and a circuit of weight training exercises. They joked about, Sean ribbing David about his age and health even though he could still press more than Sean had ever managed. Jamie had only been accompanying the brothers for the past couple of months, and still held some reservation about the other male members knowing that he and David were a couple, and not just buddies. David let the matter go, knowing that Jamie being there was a huge leap forward from where they'd been in their relationship some six months earlier.

The three men decided to grab lunch at a restaurant near the gym, a habit of Sean and David's. As usual the place was busy, those in the know drawn by the home-cooking of Betty and Chester, the married couple who'd owned the place for close to forty years. There were no pretenses at ambience, and the lighting made everyone look as though they were suffering from a mild case of jaundice, but the food was not to be forgotten.

One of Betty and Chester's granddaughters came to take their order. David and Sean hadn't even looked at the menu; both going for the house special, a skillet filled with eggs, bacon, sausage, and cheese and served with home fries and thick Texas toast. Jamie had gone for an order of pancakes and a side of fruit, for which Sean and David ribbed him good-naturedly.

David was about halfway through his lunch when the familiar prickle of being watched came over him. He cast a quick peek about the restaurant, the tight quarters and heavy flow of customers making it difficult to get clear view. A man at the counter gave a quick side wave, the movement drawing David's attention. It took about five seconds for the understanding to sink in. Jamie had stopped eating, following David's line of sight. When he saw who David had spotted a sour looked crossed his face.

Jeremy Black.

"What's that bastard doing here?" Sean asked.

The question pulled David's attention back to his table. "I don't know. Not like this is an exclusive place or anything."

"Does he know you guys like to come here?" Jamie asked in a tone he reserved for those of the lowest standing, like the men and women who crossed his path in court.

"Could be. It's not a secret."

"He's leaving," Sean said.

All watched as Jeremy walked to the door, where he stopped to give a mock tip of a hat in their direction. Then he was gone.

"That's enough to make me lose my appetite," Jamie said. He pushed his plate toward the middle of the table.

"Not me," Sean said, taking another generous mouthful. "The guy's one of the nastiest pricks to walk the face of the earth, but he certainly isn't worth missing a meal over."

David laughed, despite his mood being far from amused. He also started eating again, though with much less enthusiasm than prior to seeing Jeremy. A few minutes later they settled up the bill and David and Jamie parted ways with Sean. After a quick shower at home and some fresh clothes, David was back on the road.

Samuel Miller, Sr. lived in the same house he had when the murders had been committed. For the third time in a week David pulled into the now-familiar neighbourhood, passing several places with significance to the case. The Miller house was located on a cul-de-sac, just north of the police station. David parked and walked up the neatly cleared driveway and front steps. A leftover Christmas wreath still hung on the door.

David rapped on the door, which was opened a few minutes later by a nice-looking older man dressed in gray flannel pants and a forest green sweater. He shook hands with David and invited him inside. They settled in a small den just off the foyer. A small television sat in one corner, a desk with computer and files on the opposite side of the room. A small conversational area had been set up under a large window that allowed a generous stream of sunlight to penetrate the space.

"Please sit down. To be honest I'm happy for the break from work," Samuel said, making a motion in the general direction of the desk.

"What is it that you do?" David asked.

"I'm a mortgage broker. I tend to do most of my work from home these days. The wonder of email and faxes and all that."

"It's nice to set your own schedule though," David offered, a sentiment equally applicable to his own career.

"Sure. Now you didn't come here to jibber-jabber about my job. Take a seat and let's chat."

David liked the man's easygoing nature. He took a seat on a wing-back leather chair, sturdy and kind to his lanky frame. "Thanks. Every bit of insight I get is helpful."

"You know I was never a big fan of either Nathan or Alex, at least I wasn't too keen on the way they were acting back then, but this whole case against them was a crock of horse shit. Those boys weren't murderers. They were immature, selfish little pecker heads, and they did some things that I certainly don't approve of, but they weren't capable of something like this."

David laughed. "I appreciate the candidness. So you were aware of the drugs and other stuff the boys were up to."

"Of course. Sam was involved on more than one occasion. They'd been caught drinking underage, trespassing, cutting school, even shoplifting. Luckily Sam wasn't with Nathan when he got caught breaking into cars. That's the one that got him charged. They were a pack of delinquents, but not violent."

"And John?"

"He was a tagalong. He'd never have got up to anything much without the older boys' example."

"What did you think when you'd heard that Nathan and Alex's probation officer was the one who turned them in?"

"I couldn't believe it. I'd heard the boys complain that the guy had it in for them, but I thought they were just being immature, you know, not accepting the consequences of their behaviour."

"You think there was a motive for him going to the police?"

"He must have really thought they did it. Can't say I understand the reasoning, but he is a professional after all."

"What were your thoughts on what happened?"

He gave a low whistle. "Now that's a stumper. At the time my immediate thought was they ran into some sicko, wrong place, wrong time. After some time passed, though, and I heard from Evelyn about how Erin Gagnon was acting, I had to reconsider my assumptions."

"Evelyn is your wife?"

"Was. She passed about five years ago. Had a massive stroke."

"I'm sorry."

"No worries. I've made my peace by now. San took it hard. They were very close."

David let that slide for the moment. "So did Evelyn know Erin?"

"Yeah, from the hospital. They weren't friends per say, but they knew who each other were." *Another hospital tie.*

"And what did she say about Erin?"

"Well the woman didn't take more than a week off work after the kids were killed. She never talked about it. She didn't go to the trial. She continued getting around, if you know what I mean. Just seemed real cold, like unmoved by the whole thing."

"Could have been just an act. Maybe she was going home every night and crying herself to sleep, or drowning her sorrows in a bottle."

"Could have been I guess. Don't know. It just never sat well with me."

"To be honest I've heard the same thoughts from others in the case. I spoke with her myself last night, and there was definitely something off with her. Now what about Sam? How was he during this whole time?"

"He was real upset of course. These were his best buddies and they were having their lives taken away from them. The whole thing scared him straight, truthfully. He changed school for his senior year, really buckled down on his studies and got himself into university. He did his MBA, and he ended up working for a company that designs and manufactures medical equipment."

"Wow, good for him."

"Yeah, in a sick way it was the best thing that could have happened to him."

"Now, he didn't know Erin or the boys, right?"

"Not as far as I'm aware."

"What were his feelings on what happened?"

"He thought the boys ran into some creep at the park. He was adamant that Alex, Nathan, and John had stayed at Nathan's smoking dope and watching movies all night. He even talked with them on the phone couple of times."

"And there's no way he could have snuck out."

"Nope. I had the alarm on, and after a few instances with him I'd cancelled his code, so he had no way of turning it off. If he'd opened the door or a window the alarm would have gone off."

David took a moment to process the conversation, wanting to make sure he didn't miss anything important to ask the man. So far, he'd been the most articulate and forthcoming person he'd interviewed. "Now this might seem like a strange aside, but do you recall any trouble around this area with indigents, you know maybe trespassing or theft. Maybe sleeping in the park?"

"Well the park is always a mecca for that type. And kids wanting to smoke dope and have sex. I'm sure over the years some have been picked up, but nothing specific comes to mind. You thinking about that man who went to the diner that night? Up there at Janko's?" His thick eyebrows drew together, resembling a giant silver caterpillar crawling along the man's forehead.

"Yes. I keep coming back to that, and a coincidence like that really seems to be pushing it."

"I've though that myself. But the police never found the guy, so it seems like a dead end. Unless you managed to track him down?"

"I wish. No luck there though. Funny, I feel like a dog with a bone with this. I just don't want to let go."

"With the kind of work you're in you must have honed your senses and pick up on things others don't. I imagine it'll become clear to you soon."

"I suppose. Is there anything else you can think of that might help."

"I wish I had more to tell you. I really do. I feel awful about those men sitting in jail."

David handed over a card. "Feel free to call me anytime if you think of something."

"Will do."

David left feeling slightly unsettled, as though he'd just been told something important that had escaped his understanding.

David pulled up to the Dean's house, dread a stone in his stomach. He couldn't even begin to imagine the pain they must be in, having so recently lost the second of their two sons. No parent should have to bury a child, let alone two.

Like Erin Gagnon.

He parked the car and let that association settle on his brain, a thought that pushed aside the hostility and suspicion he'd been holding onto against the woman. Regardless of what kind of person she'd been, or how loose her morals might have run, she had still been a mother. A mother who'd had her two innocent boys taken from her in the most violent, soul-shattering way.

The Deans had moved from the suburban Toronto area they'd raised John and Blake into an adjacent borough that offered modern condos with built-in gyms and gourmet kitchens. David knew these were the types of buildings that quietly discouraged children, or are at least prescribed to the old adage of them being "seen, but not heard." There was ample guest parking in the front of their particular building, which David helped himself to.

He was buzzed in after one ring. Something about the promptness unsettled him even further. He really didn't want to speak with these people, though he knew in the onus of being thorough he had to. They at least had to be cleared of needing any further scrutiny, like all the parents did.

Mr. Dean answered his knock, ushering David in to the immaculate living rom. Mrs. Dean sat on an overstuffed navy suede chair. She rose as he entered, coming to shake his hand. Her grip was firm and cool, and she seemed quite calm until David looked into her eyes. One glimpse chilled him to the core. Her pain shimmered in the pale blue colour, a drowning and unforgettable agony that transferred to all that crossed her path. The ghost of her lost children hovered about her, a shroud of remorse so encompassing as to not be overlooked. She smiled, but the effort wasn't lost on David. No attempts at pleasantry or normalness could erase what he'd seen.

"Thank you for taking the time to meet with me," David said. He took a seat on the matching couch after the husband had made a gesture in its direction. "I can't even imagine what this has been like for you two. I am sorry, though I know words won't make up for what you've lost."

Mrs. Dean, who'd introduced herself as Melanie, made a sound low in her throat before regaining her composure. She sat down again in the chair she'd risen from. Jeffery Dean stood beside his wife, leaning on the side of the chair. Both sets of eyes looking at David made him desperately want to fidget.

"All right, I would like to make this as quick and painless as possible, so I'll just dive right in. As you know Sandra has hired me to re-examine the Gagnon murders, in hope of exonerating Nathan, Alex, and John. I fully believe in their innocence, let me assure you that. So I have to ask, do you have any idea who might have done this?"

"We think it has something to do with this so-called Janko's man," Jeffery said. "It never sat well with either one of us that something like that could be completely unrelated to what happened to the boys. That would be quite the coincidence." His wife nodded her agreement.

"I've thought the same thing. I haven't yet connected with the main police investigator on the case, but I'm hoping he can shed some light on this. I only have the bare bones of what may have gone on in the investigation of this angle."

"What happened to those boys is a terrible, awful thing. Only someone very disturbed could have done this. That certainly wasn't our John. He may have stumbled a bit after Blake died, but he was kind-hearted. He wouldn't have hurt a fly, let alone be able to butcher two little boys. It's sick that anyone could have thought such a thing of any of those kids. That man must have done it." Melanie blanched at the thought of what had happened. She blinked back tears. David could almost hear her thought process: *I will not cry. I will not cry.*

David wasn't sure he'd jump to that conclusion yet, but he felt fairly certain he must have at least been there. It could have been a case of dumb luck, in that the poor guy had simply stumbled onto the bodies after they'd been dumped. Maybe he'd become bloody trying to see if they were still alive?

"He could be guilty, that's something I'm going to look into. The big stumbling block of course, is that no one knows who this guy is. I have to consider he may simply be a witness. Either way it's important to get a lead on this man."

"I have wondered about the mother. She didn't seem quite right when all of this was happening," Jeffery said.

"I've heard the same sentiment from others. I met with her

myself last night, and I'm inclined to agree. I think she's hiding something. Whether it has something to do with this directly or not is still to be determined."

"I don't know what else we can tell you, David," Melanie said.

"What are your feelings on the other boys? You're certain of their innocence?"

"Of course. John insisted they were together all night, and we know he didn't do this."

"Now he did say that he'd been intoxicated to the point of passing out. Any thoughts that the other two might have slipped out without him?" David didn't really think this was a possibility, but it didn't hurt to provoke responses in others.

"Not a chance. Those two boys were being idiots, and I can honestly say I'm glad they weren't my boys acting like they were, but they sure weren't killers," Jeffery answered.

"I second that."

"Okay, so any thought on the hardcore attempts by the police to pin this on the boys?"

"It was that parole officer, Jonas Vukovic. He put a bug in their collective ear, and then it seemed like the whole investigation stopped considering anyone else."

"Yes. What an asshole that man is, pardon my French, but he just makes my blood boil. A pompous, self-righteous creep. Once that suggestion came from him it turned gospel." Melanie had leaned forward, her body tense. The outburst had manifested itself in a change of posture and demeanor.

"Yes, then when those idiot kids started making comments about the boys and their friends being witches, and Satanists, and whatever other baloney they were spewing, it was a done deal," Jeffery added.

David flipped back through his notes. "Ah, Jake Allen and Alicia Marsten. Is that who you're referring to?"

"Names ring a bell. There were others I think, but there was this one couple who was really vocal about the whole thing. They made official statements and everything."

Hmmm, interesting.

"Any other suggestions?"

"I don't think so." Melanie looked to her husband for confirmation. He shook his head.

"So how do you feel about Sandra going through a private investigator?"

"I don't know that there was any other choice. Not even after John's…suicide. We've tried everything to get this officially reopened, a new trial, anything. Nothing's worked."

"Yeah, Sandra needs this as much as we do. Poor woman. She'd been so strong and so positive after everything that's happened to her."

The statement tickled David's curiosity. "More than the stuff with Nathan?"

"Oh, yes. Well, I mean there was the unfortunate business with her first husband. Cancer I think it was. Then Mark. What a piece of work he turned out to be. You wouldn't know it now, but Sandra was quite the looker. Mark liked pretty women. He was always flirting, even after they got married. I guess it wasn't a surprise that he strayed."

This was new. "So he cheated on her?"

"More than once I think. Got really nasty there at the end." Melanie's lips curled down, indicating her distaste.

"Any idea who with?"

"Well at least one gal from the hospital. One of the nurses."

David backtracked. "Did either of you work at the hospital?"

"I did back then. I was a ward clerk. Now I work in a private medical office. Jeffery's an orthodontist."

"So is that how you knew Sandra?"

"Yes. That and our sons went to the same school. We became friendly over the years."

A common story over the past few days. "Anything else you want to add to this?"

Melanie scrunched her nose. "I don't think so. I don't see how Sandra's personal problems could have anything to do with the murders."

In David's experience things that seemed inconsequential or unrelated many times turned out to be the key to finding the truth, or at least might turn the investigation in the right direction. He'd have to follow up on the information with

Sandra. Who knew, maybe Nathan was guilty, just not the other boys. Maybe he'd been in some kind of rage, which when fuelled by the drugs had made him completely lose control. After all, he only had the boys' word that they were just smoking pot. Maybe they've been into something else.

After leaving the Deans, David took a jaunt over to Janko's Diner, hoping to have a chance to speak with Mike, the night manager. He parked, not surprised to find the lot nearly full. Inside Lila stood at the hostess station. As soon as she caught sight of David she smiled, then gave a quick peek about to see if anyone was looking in her direction. Once she'd ascertained that she wasn't the object of anyone's attention she made a gesture in his direction that left no doubt about what she'd like to do to him. He'd never been so flustered in his life. Luckily a couple walked in the door behind him, forcing Lila to abandon her crude attempt at seduction. As she greeted the customers David moved past to the main counter and asked the waitress picking up her order if Mike was available.

The man in question came out from the kitchen door, taking a quick scan until he settled on David. After he gave a nod of confirmation the man came to sit on the stool next to him.

"David?"

"Yes. Thanks for meeting with me."

"No problem. Glad to help if I can."

"I guess the most helpful thing is just a description of the event as best you can recall."

Mike screwed up his face, nose scrunched into a series of furrows, as though having a difficult time retrieving the memory. The look was so intense David thought the man might pull something.

"Well, it was real late. After midnight anyway. The restaurant was quiet, only a couple people in. That time of night we don't have a hostess, people just come in and seat themselves. I was sitting at the counter with Martha Van Koughnett, who was the evening cook back then. This man busts in, eyes crazy and shrieking like a banshee. About scared the pants off me, truth be told. He raced right up to us screaming and shaking his hands about. I tried to talk to him, but he wasn't having none of it. Ran off to the bathroom. I left him alone for about fifteen minutes then went and checked on him. He'd made a right mess in the bathroom, peed all over the place and left bloody handprints on the sink. I confronted him and he took off again."

"Can you describe the man?"

Mike squeezed his eyes shut, thinking. "Um, like maybe in his forties. Black guy, grey hair, real bushy. Skinny face, beard. He was dressed in sweat pants and big winter coat, boots I think."

"Would you recognize him again? Like if I had a picture?" A thought had begun to form in David's mind, one that might lead to nothing, but it was worth a shot.

"I think so. Yep, pretty sure. Cops tried that though. Had me look at some photos."

"Had you seen him before that night?"

"Pretty sure he'd been in a couple of times before, but I'm positive he never came around after that night. Not when I was in anyway."

"Now tell me what you heard the man saying."

"A lot of it was mumbo-jumbo, between moaning, crying. The things that I heard clearly was 'monsters in the woods' and 'stealing those kids' souls.'"

"Well that's not stuff you hear everyone say."

Mike shook his head, looking solemn. "I have to tell ya, it wasn't only what he was saying, it was how he was talking. He was spooked, like really scared. The sound of his voice made the hair on my arms stand up. Real freaky."

"Okay then. I'll be in touch."

Mike walked him to the door. He mulled the past week over in his mind, certain the truth had at least been hinted at, yet remained unable to make sense of it.

Mark Ester would be his last stop on a day that had drained him in both an emotional and physical sense. Further fuelling the lingering veil of negativity was the newly uncovered information that Mark Ester had been unfaithful to Sandra. He had no respect for cheaters. It was something he'd never do or put up with, and couldn't for the life of him understand how anyone could do something so disrespectful to a loved one.

He parked on the road as the drive to Mark's house held

a car and a large pickup truck with a hard cover for the cab. The truck also had chains on the tires, indicating it was used to travel to areas more rugged than urban Toronto. The house itself was small, a bungalow with minimal adornment.

Mark hollered from inside after David had pushed the bell. A few minutes passed before the man came to open the door. He was still in the midst of tucking in his shirt as he stepped aside to let David enter. Mark's hair was damp and David smelled mint and lemons, he assumed from a very recent shower. He was the same height as David, but leaner, more the body type of a runner or swimmer.

"Sorry, I got in a bit later than I expected."

"Oh, I thought you were at home when I called earlier."

"No, my cell phone. Has a Toronto area code."

"Right, I guess that's why I assumed you were here."

"I was up at the cabin. I go there most weekends."

The mention of a cabin made David recollect the conversation he'd had with Sandra. She'd mentioned that Mark was an outdoor enthusiast.

"Cabin?" David asked as Mark led him to the living room.

"Yeah, was my dad's. He left it to me when he passed a few years back. Good for fishing and hunting in the warmer months, and skiing and snowmobiling this time of the year."

"Must be nice to have somewhere to get away."

"I love it. I can't keep myself cooped up all the time."

A woman came into the room dressed in pajama bottoms and an old sweatshirt. Her damp hair had been pulled back into a low ponytail. Apparently, Mark hadn't been alone in the shower.

"David this is Carmine, my girlfriend."

She shook David's hand before perching on the arm of the chair where Mark sat.

"You're all right with having Carmine here for this interview?"

"Of course. She knows about what happened."

Carmine gave a small nod and made eye contact with David. He pegged her to be in her late twenties, at least fifteen years younger than her significant other.

"Okay then. So as I told you on the phone Sandra has hired me to look into the case to see if I can't find something to help exonerate the men, or at least get them a new trial."

"Waste of time and money if you ask me. The cops never found anything the first time around."

David took an immediate dislike to the man's attitude. "Well that's the point really. There was little evidence to speak of and no motive. The boys basically got hung on bad reputations and the suggestion of the parole officer. Do you really think they were guilty of this crime?"

"Well I didn't say that, though you're right about Nathan and his buddies being class-A punks back then. There was a number of years of trouble before this happened."

"But nothing violent, I mean nothing to suggest that Nathan could be capable of such a horrible act."

Mark gave him a look that had him fighting back a shudder. Carmine didn't seem to notice anything amiss, but David could have sworn the temperature had suddenly dropped ten degrees. The hair on the back of his neck prickled.

"I guess not. But people can be responsible for shocking things sometimes. I see that in my work all the time." To David he sounded bitter, angry.

Mark then smiled in Carmine's direction and all traces of whatever monster had been lurking vanished completely. He seemed mild, harmless, yet something about the way the man had looked at him reminded him of another personality chameleon he'd encountered on a recent case.

"Right, you worked in the hospital."

"That's right, about five years. Now I'm private."

"I work there now. I'm a registration clerk." Carmine offered.

David smiled, unable to shake the feeling of unease. "Right. Thanks. So Mark, do you have any ideas on who might be responsible?"

"I've always wondered about that homeless man situation. That seemed a bit too coincidental."

"Most people I've talked to feel that same way. I've been out looking for leads to help identify the man, but no luck so far."

"Well I guess that's not surprising with the type of people

and the number of years that've passed."

"True. Can't hurt to poke around though."

The look returned, turning David's blood to ice. "Of course."

"Okay, any thoughts on Erin Gagnon?"

"What do you mean?" Mark asked.

He and Carmine shared a look that David didn't understand.

"I've heard different opinions on the woman. I just wondered what you thought. You do know her. right? I mean you worked in the same hospital and it is her kids that Nathan has been convicted of killing."

"Of course I know her. All I can say really is she's a different kind of nut. Real hot and cold. That, and she gets around."

"She's a slut," Carmine happily clarified.

Wow, this is quite the pair.

Carmine continued to grin as though they weren't discussing such a distasteful topic as the murder of children. Mark looked almost blank, as if the conversation was starting to bore him.

"All right. What do you think about Jonas Vukovic?"

Mark shrugged. "He's kind of an ass, but I assume he knows his job. I mean I never heard of any backlash toward the man over his statement. Unless I've missed something?"

"No, not that I'm aware of. Just seems like quite a leap from vandalizing some cars to butchering kids."

As if in response to the mental image David's words invoked, Mark's eyebrows gave a shaky dance. "I can see where you're coming from. Again, I didn't say I agreed with the man, just that he is a professional and the police seemed to take his word as golden."

"Yep, does seem suspect though. I don't like the fact he was dating a tech that worked at the forensic lab either."

"That sounds like politics to me. I mean, people might think Carmine and I shouldn't be dating either 'cause we work at the same place."

David let the matter drop. "So things being what they are what does your gut tell you about this case?"

"Obviously some sicko child molester got a hold of those poor boys," Carmine cut in.

Mark paused for a heartbeat. "What she said."

David didn't see any point in asking about the infidelity issue with Carmine present. No doubt Mark would simply lie or at least be less than forthcoming with information. He'd have to try him another time. By then he was annoyed, cranky and plain tired of people talking bullshit. "Okay, well this has been very helpful. I'll be in touch if I need to ask anything further."

"You know where to find me."

Mark walked him to the door. The air slapped against his skin, itchy with the intensity of the cold. *Asshole.*

Jamie's car wasn't in the driveway when he pulled in. He parked, feeling a spark of gratitude for a bit of time alone to digest everything he'd just heard.

Inside he flicked on the light in the mudroom, depositing his damp boots on the utility carpet. As he passed through the kitchen he dropped his coat on the back of a chair and deposited his keys on the spotless counter. Jamie had obviously had a go-through of the room. Everything had been wiped, cleared and put away, just as his partner liked it. He grabbed a beer from the fridge and chugged down half the contents in one swallow. He leaned back against the counter to polish it off.

As he turned to place the bottle in the sink the light came on. The action surprised him so much that he launched into a defensive charge as he turned. When Jenny came into view he skidded to a stop, a sheepish grin pulling at his lips.

"Jesus, girl. I could have knocked your teeth out."

"Sorry, I used my key. Didn't think you'd mind if I came over," she answered. She seem distracted, a pale version of the spunky, and often inappropriate girl he'd come to know.

"What's going on?"

She looked right at him and he could tell that she'd been crying. "My mom showed up."

"Holy crap. Really?" The news surprised him.

"Yeah. I told you she called. Well, it wasn't the best conversation. We've never exactly had a great relationship. She was gone a lot, doing drugs and men, whatever had her attention at the time. I finally left when I was fourteen and I've only seen her a few times since then."

"Right, so I can understand your being skeptical about her being cleaned up."

Jenny smiled then, a real smile that lit up her face. It wasn't something David had seen more than once or twice in all the months he'd known her. "Thank you. Rhea didn't see it the same way when I talked to her. She thought I should give her the benefit of the doubt just 'cause she'd given birth to me."

David could see that his grandmother would have reacted like that; it sounded like her. "She's only saying that to try and help. She thinks all kids deserve to have their parents in their life. I totally get that sometimes that's the worst thing that could happen."

"I know she means well, but she just doesn't get what that woman is like. She can't imagine how I grew up. Jesus Christ, when I was eleven years old my mom let some guy fuck me so she could score some coke. Anyone who could do that doesn't deserve to be a mother."

The tough persona Jenny had adopted to distance herself from the pain she'd been subjected to over the course of her short life crumbled. The unmasking left her raw and vulnerable, a young woman used and abused on a scale that most couldn't even begin to fathom. Tears poured down her cheeks. A sob, seemingly years in the making, escaped her trembling lips. Her anguish erupted in a primal, urgent rush that would not be stopped. David could do nothing but pull her into his arms and cradle her against his chest.

They stood that way for the better part of fifteen minutes, the intensity of her outburst enough to drain David's own spirit. The poignancy of the moment left him breathless, unsettled to the point he feared he would collapse under the emotional burden. His cheeks began to sting, a sensation that alerted him to the fact that he was also openly crying. Her sobs had soaked though his sweater, leaving a moist, warm film on his skin.

Neither one of them heard the back door opening or the footsteps moving in their direction. When Jamie laid a hand on David's arm he gave a little jump of surprise. His heart flew into his throat and his head throbbed without mercy, but he had never been so glad to see the man in all his life. Jamie eased Jenny out of his arms, seamlessly taking over the role of caregiver. David took several deep breaths and grabbed a paper towel to mop up his tears.

Enough time passed for Jenny to settle to the point that she could speak, though her words were shaky and without strength. "Wow, I don't know what it is about you guys. I've never felt so safe with anyone before. I know you understand and you don't judge...and, and that means more to me than anything."

"I'm at a loss here as to what set this off," Jamie said, "but you have to know we love you like a sister, or even our own kid. We will help you any way we can."

David rejoined them, pulling them both into a bone-crushing embrace. "Screw everyone else. We have our own perfect family right here."

CHAPTER 11

The bed was empty when he awoke the next morning. His lids peeled away from his eyes like they'd been lined with sandpaper. The crying jag, which had repeated itself after he'd retired to bed with Jamie, left him with a feeling close to a hangover. His mouth was dry, his head sore and the overall lethargy indicated the start of a terrible day.

The shower washed away some of the persistent melancholia, but the dull grey sky he saw on the way to the car reflected his mood to a tee. Even the fact that the temperature had jumped above zero from the day previous did little to assuage his foul mood. He ignored every thought about the case on the way to the office, much like the scenery blurring past his window. He needed a large dose of caffeine before he'd be ready to dive back into the mess the Gagnon case had turned out to be.

He hit a Tim Hortons drive thru on the way downtown, grabbing the largest coffee they had. He'd finished it by the time he parked. Once inside his office he flipped on his computer and opened his appointment book. The light blinked on the answering machine and he had several messages in his inbox. Everything would have to wait as he realized he needed to be at his meeting with Jonas Vukovic in fifteen minutes. *Shit.*

David had yet to process everything he'd learned about the infamous parole officer, and he certainly didn't feel up to interviewing the man. He'd have to keep a tight hold on his emotions so as not to let on what he knew.

He arrived at the squat, institutional building with no time to spare. After locking the door he raced up the front steps, scanning the board next the elevators to find the location of

Vukovic's office. As luck would have it he was located on the first floor, just inside the interior set of doors. The door to the waiting area stood ajar. A young woman sat at the desk, slipping papers into a large file cabinet behind her workspace. She looked up as David entered, her Coke-bottle lenses magnifying her eyes to cartoonish proportions. The room was empty except for the two of them.

"Can I help you?" she asked.

"I'm David Lloyd. I have an appointment with Mr. Vukovic."

She put down the pile of paper and glanced at the day planner on her desk. David scanned the series of appointments for the four officers in the office as she did, seeing his neatly penciled in name.

"Right. I'll just let him know you're here."

David smiled and remained standing. He may as well have taken a seat because the man kept him waiting nearly twenty minutes after the secretary had announced his presence. She continued with her work, humming along with a light rock station. David paced back and forth, feeling his temper come to life. He hated being kept waiting.

At last a door opened at the back of the waiting area and a man headed in David's direction. The secretary looked up and the two made brief eye contact. He stopped at David's side, hand outstretched. He shook, perhaps with more force than was necessary, and made what he hoped was a pleasant smile. The man stared back with a bland expression.

"Mr. Vukovic?"

"That's right. I assume you're David Lloyd?"

"Yes."

"Well then, let's go to my office where we can speak privately." He turned without waiting for an answer, striding back toward the open door.

David didn't know what he'd expected, but the man's appearance took him by surprise. He was tall, handsome, and, from what he could make out of the body under the dark pants and sweater, in great shape. His colouring hinted at a Western European heritage, though the name definitely had origins farther to the east. He had a thick head of dark hair threaded with silver, and sported a gold band on his left hand.

The door led to a narrow hallway with several offices. They passed two closed doors before Vukovic stopped and indicated they'd come to their destination. David ducked inside with the other man on his heels. Something about the man being behind him gave David a colossal case of the heebie-jeebies. It took everything in him not to shudder.

As he sat Vukovic closed the door and made his way around the side of his desk. Like any government service the working space was utilitarian and overflowing with paperwork. It was also devoid of any personal touches, including pictures of either a spouse or children, though the man's framed certificate for his Master's of Social Work hung on the wall behind the desk. David could see that the man had pulled Alex and Nathan's folders in preparation for the meeting. He opened Alex's and briefly scanned the front page before giving David his attention.

"Now what is it I can help you with?" His manner was direct and professional, with an undercurrent of snideness.

"I've been hired to look into the case against Nathan Klassen and Alex Snider, and I hoped that you might be able to shed some light on this matter. I understand that at the time of the murders both boys were a part of your case load."

"That's true. The two had been convicted on separate issues, the ones that landed them with me at any rate. They had been picked up together on a number of other occasions." His condescending tone left no doubt about his opinions of the two.

David continued. "I believe Nathan had been arrested for breaking into some cars, while Alex had come to the courts over the assault of his sister."

"That's right."

"Can you explain to me why you felt these two would be capable of such a violent crime? It seems to be quite a leap from theft and shoving a sibling to butchering two children."

Vukovic met David's gaze with eyes as dead as any he'd ever seen. "Those two were a couple of creeps. They were messing around with a lot of stuff back then."

"Can you elaborate on 'stuff'?"

"Well drugs for one. Witchcraft and the occult for another."

"And you learned about this how?"

"I visited both the boys at their homes. They both had all kinds of occult paraphernalia, knives, Ouija boards, books. You name it. And it was a well-known fact around the high school that their group participated in orgies and blood ceremonies. It was only a matter of time before they did something like this."

The man seemed oddly passionless about two individuals he supposedly believed to be cold-blooded killers. "So you would have met the boys' family members then? The parents, Alex's sister Jasmine?"

Vukovic didn't so much as blink. "Of course."

The man was a cold bastard, that much David could tell. Whether this was by nature or after too many years working in the system, David couldn't speculate.

"Those boys had been on the wrong path for some time."

David bit back the retort that came to mind. "That seems to be a matter of some debate. Alex and Nathan both acknowledge that their behaviour was not the best, but I haven't heard anyone speak of them in terms like you're presenting."

"Perhaps you haven't spoken with the right parties yet."

"Perhaps." David knew there was no way he'd get anything out of the man. He was as closed off as they came. "Now could I ask you about your relationship with Nerine Minniker?"

"Excuse me? What does that have to do with this case?"

"I understand Nerine worked at the lab responsible for the forensic testing on the case, which seems to be somewhat of a conflict of interest if you were also involved."

Vukovic's eyes narrowed. "Hardly. Nerine didn't work on this case. Besides that both of us were consummate professionals and would never allow a personal situation to have bearing on our work."

"So you were involved with her?"

"We were dating at the time, yes."

"But not any longer."

"No, we ended our relationship after a few months. It was never anything serious."

The man is a rock, but there is something off.

"I see. Well I suppose that's all I need at this point. I may need to touch base again in the future."

"You know where I am."

David let himself out.

David spent the remainder of the morning on the phone. He spoke with the Children's Aid Society and the school board, neither organization having anything bad to report on Erin Gagnon, and Nathan's counselor, who was happy to forward the boy's records to Dr. Garfield once David had the release faxed over to him. He also connected with Detective Brown and made arrangements to meet with him later that afternoon. Jasmine didn't answer again, and he failed to reach either of the people who'd testified to the "occult" connections of the accused. He drowned his frustration at the lack of progress in copious amounts of coffee.

The phone rang, jolting David from his intense focus on the work at hand. "Hello?"

"Hey, Dave, Jimmy here. There's a bunch of us heading to The Diamond tonight. You up for a drink?"

"Sure I guess. I'll check with Jamie and get back to you."

Jimmy chuckled. "You on a short leash now?"

"Just trying to stay out of the dog house. You know how it is."

"Do I. The Mrs. and I been married thirty-five years in June."

"You deserve a medal."

"Smart ass. I'll talk to ya later."

He then placed a call to Jenny, who'd spent the night at his place. She sounded in much better spirits and promised to talk through the situation with her counselor, who she was meeting at two. She reminded him of the intake appointment for the school on Thursday and promised to call if she needed anything else.

His stomach growled, causing a peek at the clock. It was past one, and he had just enough time to grab some lunch before meeting with Detective Brown at two thirty. The Indian restaurant on the corner would do the trick, though he expected flak from Jamie for the inevitable case of flatulence that would hit him later in the day. The butter chicken was heaven to his tongue; the entrée washed down with basmati rice and mixed veggies.

With all the spices and calories working their way through his system David made his way over to the station, where Detective Brown had agreed to see him. There was even a spot left in the visitor parking, shortening his voyage across the messy lot full of icy puddles brought on by the quick thaw. His shoes were only mildly damp when he reached the front steps.

Like any active police station there was an odd assortment of people milling about, many working in various law enforcement capacities and those who'd deviated from the straight and narrow. The overlapping waves of noise and conversation and endless shifting bodies would be enough to drive any mad, but he knew how well adapted police officers become at filtering out background noise. David marched up to the desk officer and let the man know who he was there to see.

A few minutes later Detective Brown arrived to usher David into a secure area of the building. He was just as David had pictured from their brief phone conversation; middle-aged and starting to slide from meaty to overweight. The beard was a surprise. He had the hard eyes of one with a long-standing career on the force, and a solid, confident stride as he led the way back to his office.

His office was a space shared with five others, of which three desks were currently occupied. None of those in the room even batted an eye as they entered. Detective Brown had pulled the files; one lay open on top a desk cluttered with reports, computer equipment, and an impressive collection of empty coffee cups. He pointed at a chair near the desk, which David took as his cue to sit.

"So Sandra Klassen hired you to look into this mess again?" he said as he lowered himself into the well-worn office chair.

"That's right Detective. She and the parents of the other boys are certain of their sons' innocence."

"Mmm-hmmm." His eyes flicked to the case file on the desk, then back to David's face. "Call me Art. No need to be formal."

"Right. Thanks Art. Now I really appreciate you taking this time to talk with me. I used to work on the force myself, so I know there's never enough time in the day."

"No worries. I planned on being at the desk today. Got a ton of paperwork to catch up on."

The comment reminded David of Jimmy, and he had to fight the urge to smirk. "All right let's jump right in so I can get out of your hair. Now I understand you were the lead officer on the case?"

"Yep, me and Lester Racelli. He retired soon after this case went to trial. I could get you in touch if you need."

"That might be helpful, thanks. So let's make this easy. You tell it to me in your own words and if I have any questions I'll jump in. Sound good?"

The man turned out to be more than obliging, and, David soon discovered, a darn good investigator. He went through the case step by step, right from the initial call when the bodies were discovered. He shared official transcripts of interviews, forensic reports and even a few photos that David hadn't seen before. There were no earth-shattering revelations, but David was intrigued by the comments from the two high school students and the anonymous call about seeing Nathan and Tammy in the park the night of the murders.

"So what's your opinion on the validity of the statements from Jake Allen and Alicia Marsten?" David asked when the man had come to the end of his tale.

"I think those two kids wouldn't have known their own ass from a hole in the ground. Couple of stoners, but they stuck to their story."

"So you think these supposed Satanic gatherings never happened?"

"If they did it was only in their drug-soaked brains. The boy ended up in jail, but the girl had straightened out, last I heard."

"But their testimony damaged the boys' case."

"Yep, that along with their bad attitudes. And that SOB Vukovic."

That made David perk up. "I had the displeasure of meeting the man this morning. He's a real prick."

"My sentiments exactly. I've crossed paths with him a few times over the years with different cases, and he's always acting mightier-than-thou, only seeming to be available to help when it strikes his fancy. I don't have time for that kind of nonsense."

"I hear you. So did you have issue with his statement? This is what brought the boys to the attention of the police in the first place, correct?"

Art leaned back in his chair, nodding deeply. "It did. Vukovic apparently put in a call to one of the officers here who he chums around with a bit, and he brought the boys' names to me."

"What's the officer's name?"

"Rob LeClair."

David had never heard of the man, but he made a note of it. Something to follow up on later.

"What about the Janko's man angle?"

"Now that was a bugger of a situation," he said. He gave a deep sigh before continuing. "I spent many, many hours trying to track that individual down and I never uncovered a solid lead. I even had a man work undercover as a homeless person for several weeks, but he never turned up a thing. Like the man was a ghost."

"Yet there were several witnesses at the diner."

"Yep."

"You ran through old mug shots and reports I'm assuming?"

"Yeah we showed some photos around to the Janko's staff and through the shelters and people on the street. Didn't get us anywhere."

"Be nice to have a name."

"Preaching to the choir. That's a dead end, I'm afraid."

The two settled into a thoughtful silence. *Think, David. Think.*

"Do you think the boys were guilty?"

"I was never entirely convinced, but we had a lack of alibi except for the boys themselves, the reports of weird behaviour and that damn lighter. The boys did nothing to make themselves look innocent neither, always being difficult and mouthy. Wasn't much, but the Attorney General went with it. After that it was out of my hands."

"But you didn't like it?"

"Not a bit. I think we all have one of those in our career, a case that just didn't pan out like we'd expected." He'd begun showing signs of agitation, tapping his fingers and shifting in his chair.

"You like the mother for this? Or maybe one of her questionable companions."

"The thought did cross my mind, but nothing ever gelled. She dated some scumbags for sure, but all had tight alibis, and in the God's honest truth none seemed likely candidates. If this had come from some kind of fight in the Gagnon home, I could see one of the kids having got in the way, or maybe tried to defend their mom from taking a beating. Not like this though."

An idea struck, one that seemed as enlightened as implausible. "Have you run the description of the Janko's man through the system for incidents after the murders?" David asked, grasping at straws.

"No, but I can if you want me to."

"Why not. If anything turns up I can canvas again, see if anyone recognizes the guy. Who knows maybe he isn't gone, or maybe he's come and gone again. You know these guys often travel about, sometimes dodging the law."

"Seems farfetched, but I'll take a look."

"All right. Any comments on the crime scene contamination issues?"

David could just about feel the man's blood pressure rise at the question. Art's face flushed. "Didn't happen on my watch I can tell you that. I was off the night the bodies were found, got called in from a fishing trip. After I heard what happened I had the people involved reprimanded. The mess-up on our end haunts me to this day. If we'd ever found that Janko's man, we wouldn't have been able to prove any evidence came from him and not our own team."

"Was there evidence? The way I heard it the Janko's staff cleaned the bathroom after being given the okay from the responding officer. When the police followed up the next morning after finding the bodies there was nothing left."

"True enough. The forensic team did take swabs anyway. Never came to anything, but like I said it would have been a tough sell in court in any case."

There didn't seem to be any more to say. David handed over

his card. "Call me anytime. There's my fax number on there too if you find anything that you want to share."

Art stood and offered his hand cross the desk. "Good to meet you, David. Hope you can shake something loose. I don't like the feeling of thinking I helped put some innocent kids behind bars."

"I appreciate your time. I'll be in touch."

His grandmother had called while he was in the station. She needed help moving some items from the basement she wanted to donate. Ever the dutiful grandson, he swung by and carried them to the main level for her. Once she sorted through everything he'd come back and cart it to the donation centre. For his troubles he left with a tin full of homemade oatmeal cookies, his favourite.

He had a few more stops to make before heading home, and didn't pull into the driveway till after five o'clock. The house was dark and Jamie's car was still gone. He made a few trips into the house with groceries and other assorted items from his errands. With the radio on, David bustled about the kitchen until he pulled together a passable meal and popped it in the oven. Continuing his domestic streak he threw in a load of laundry and made a pass through the main level with the vacuum. By the time Jamie arrived home the house looked better than it had in a couple of days.

David heard Jamie before he saw him; the sound of the door opening, the soft shuffling of him hanging his coat. He came around the corner into the kitchen with his briefcase in one hand, loosening his tie with the other. He stopped short when he found David putting their dinner on plates.

"Grab a seat. Dinner is served."

Jamie obliged, dropping the briefcase and tossing the tie on the counter. David placed the plate before him and took seat across the table. He'd already poured wine and cut a few slices of bread from the loaf he'd picked up at the Portuguese bakery.

"To what do I owe the honour?" Jamie asked between mouthfuls.

"Dunno, just being nice. I am capable of that every once in a while."

"Okay. How was your day?"

"Pretty good. I did a few more interviews."

"Anything turn up?"

"Not yet, but I'm getting close. I can feel it."

"I'm sure you'll get to the truth. You're like a dog with a bone when you get set on something."

"Is that a compliment?"

Jamie laughed. "Absolutely."

"'Kay, well eat up, we've got plans tonight."

"What?"

"Jimmy asked me out for a drink at The Diamond and I thought we could both go."

"The Diamond? Isn't that the dive out by your old precinct?"

"Yep, Jimmy and some of his buddies are heading there after shift."

"And you want me to come?"

"Why not? We're out and proud and all that crap now right? Plus, it's good to stay in the good graces of our men in blue." He gave Jamie his most winning smile.

"All right, give me an hour to get some work done and I'll go."

About ninety minutes later David and Jamie set out on the road. On the way there David had a sudden urge to swing by Erin Gagnon's house, which Jamie made no protests to. They drove through the quiet neighbourhood, found the woman's street and headed down it at a diminished speed. The house was dark and the driveway empty. No luck.

The side trip added less than twenty minutes to their travel time and soon they pulled into the pothole-riddled lot of The Diamond. For a Monday night the place was jumping. Most of the lot was full, and a glance at the aging neon sign advertised a band that David had never heard of. That would explain the turnout. Free entertainment always attracted a good crowd.

As they made their way across the lot Jamie cast a wary look about the outside of the establishment. "Really? This is somewhere you like to hang out?"

David grinned. "It's not as bad as it looks. Anyway it's the company, not the ambience."

Inside the band was in full swing, the bass thumping so loudly the vibrations could be felt through the floor. Instinctively David's hand rose to touch his left ear, even though the music had yet to make his hearing aid whine. Jamie gave a look of reassurance and he let his hand drop, fingers brushing his partner's.

Like usual the murky lighting lent an air of neglect, the overlapping sections of darkness punctured by flashing beer signs and the red fluorescent tubing that travelled along the wooden hood over the bar. David led the way through the milling crowd, passing a few familiar faces. There were a few stops for congratulations with people he'd barely spoken to in recent years, a strange but satisfying series of interactions. He caught sight of Jimmy and a few of his counterpoints sitting at a table, most likely waiting for one of the pool tables to become free. Jimmy saw them approaching and raised a hand in greeting.

He stood to shake hands with David, and after a pause of surprise at seeing Jamie had accompanied him, turned and shook hands with the other man. "David, nice to see you. Jamie, you still with this old dog?"

"Hey now. Who you calling old, gramps?" David shot back.

Jimmy took the liberty of introducing Jamie to the three other officers at the table. A waitress stopped and David placed an order for a couple of beers. He felt the tiniest bit self-conscious, though none of the other men showed discomfort with him having brought Jamie along. In fact Marco Arabetta and Jamie had launched into an intense discussion on a current case, one that Jamie had been newly assigned to.

The beers were delivered and David took a hearty chug while looking about. He nodded and smiled at a few people, for the most part simply scanning the place to get a feel for the crowd. A number of patrons had gathered before the small stage, clapping and tapping their feet to the blast of classic rock. A few individuals made awkward, drunken attempts at dancing, looking for the most part as though they were experiencing some kind of loss in muscle control. One older man was desperately trying to keep up with a perky twenty-something female in tight jeans and a halter top, a sight that made David chuckle.

A hand on his shoulder drew his attention back from the crowd. He turned to find Joe Kennedy standing beside him.

"They're pretty terrible, huh?" he asked, tapping his beer bottle in the direction of the band.

David scanned the group again, who all looked to be under twenty-one. "They're really loud."

"I can remember the days when I would have thought this kind of shit was good music."

"Me too. Hey Joe, I'd like to introduce you to my partner, Jamie," he said.

Joe reached across the table to shake Jamie's hand. "I'm Joe Kennedy. Used to work with David." He leaned close and spoke loudly to be heard over the rumbling music.

"Nice to meet you Joe. I think we might have crossed paths in court before?"

"Yes, you're right. About eight months ago. The Landon case. Geez, that was messy." Turning to David he added, "Jamie here really nailed the asshole on the stand. It was beautiful."

"He has a way with that. He looks mild-mannered, but in court he's a shark."

Joe nodded. "Can I get you guys another drink?"

"Sure," David answered, holding up the bottle of Canadian to show his preference.

"Be right back." Joe headed to the bar.

David started to relax. He gave in to the music, as grating and forced as it was. The space exuded merriment, with laughter, loud conversation and comical attempts to pick up coming at him from every direction. When a table opened up he and Jimmy moved off to play a game. Jamie gave him a smile to let him know he was fine. He turned his attention back to Marco and the others at the table as David walked away.

Jimmy might have been older than David, but he certainly hadn't lost his skills. Even though he still looked somewhat under the weather and had lost weight, Jimmy played a mean game. He won with an impressive rebound shot that seemed to defy the laws of physics. David conceded the loss by buying his friend another drink.

Joe had wandered back to the table he'd come from, which held a group of rowdy officers with an impressive collection of beer bottles and shot glasses. He knew how important it was to let off some steam when working in a physically demanding and stressful occupation like law enforcement. He also knew the statistics about how many went too far with their vices, leading to performance problems, marital upsets, and health issues. He was thankful he'd managed to keep a good head on his shoulders, especially after all the crap life had thrown his way.

Jimmy and David changed places with Marco and John Rimmel. The band had finished their set and the pre-programmed music filtered through at a more tolerable level. They spent the better part of an hour chatting with various people who came by the table, several of whom had come to congratulate David on the case he'd solved before Christmas. Much of the evidence he'd uncovered was still being investigated and prepared to bring a number of people to trial. It was nice to have some appreciation for his hard work, and the fact that he had nearly been killed while doing it.

They decided to call it a night. David had an ongoing case and Jamie had regular office hours to keep the next day, so midnight seemed a good time to bow out. They received an enthusiastic send-off, and Jimmy promised to keep in touch about the case.

The cool night air embraced the men as they stepped from the building, a welcomed sensation after the endless, biting cold of the previous few weeks. The mildness continued to erase the signs of winter, leaving the air damp and pungent, the asphalt a slushy mess. Beyond a ten-foot radius the lot was a blanket of darkness, the sign a lighthouse beacon in a sea of indistinct vehicle-shaped masses. Once the door closed behind them the music came to an abrupt halt, replaced with the soft *shwoosh* of nearby traffic. He had the vague awareness of a car door closing.

He leaned in to give Jamie a quick peck on the cheek, something he would never have dared earlier inside the bar. Jamie had a strict aversion to public affection, something David hoped would lessen with time. Not that he would ever be openly demonstrative, but never touching one another in public seemed too far to the other end of the spectrum.

A person passed to David's left side. "Fucking queer," a male voice said.

"'S'cuse me?" David asked. Jamie pulled at his arm, shaking his head.

The man turned. "Hey there, David. Having a date night, are we?"

The sight of Jeremy Black's sneering amusement at his own comments curdled the beer in David's stomach. His hands curled into fists. The vein in his neck throbbed, in tempo with the hot burst of adrenaline coursing through his body.

"Leave it, David," Jamie said.

"You heard, pretty boy. Leave it alone."

"Why don't you shut the fuck up, Black!" His voice was oddly flat, barely audible above the violent buzzing in his ears.

"You wanna try and make me?" Black smirked and took a step closer to David.

David stood his ground. He cast Jamie a sideways look, catching his shrug. He felt more than saw Jamie step away from the two of them.

"You're not so tough on your own, you fucking pathetic piece of shit. Get out of my face or you'll be eating your next meal through a straw."

"Right. Two pansies are going get the better or me? I don't think so."

"Not two, one. See I told you he was a pussy, Jamie."

That did it. Jeremy took a swing a David, catching him in the jaw. Jamie gave a bark of surprise. The pain seemed a secondary concern to the fury that erupted from David, surging out from the place in his brain where it had been tightly locked away for so long. Fire raced over his skin, feeding his anger and pushing him to violence that he would not have been capable of under different circumstances.

He barreled into Jeremy with the instincts of his old football days, taking the man to the ground. He heard the crack as Jeremy's skull smashed against the pavement, as bright and startling as a gunshot. Jeremy struggled, punching from his restricted position, and flailing his legs about in an ineffective attempt to cast David off. With one hand about the man's throat David unleashed a brutal pounding about Jeremy's face and upper torso.

David paused, looking down on the bloody and already swelling face of the man that he had loathed for so long, thinking he'd feel some type of release from what had happened, instead finding emptiness. Some people had come out of the bar during the fight, their proximity momentarily distracting David. Jeremy took advantage of the loss of attention, throwing David off and scrambling to his feet. He kicked out, taking David in the side, but it was not a solid connection. David jumped to his feet and turned about, swinging at Jeremy with all his might. The two continued to fight for a few more minutes before others intervened. As he was pulled away David realized it was Jimmy and Marco.

"What the hell is going on David?" Jimmy asked. His eyes were bright and his breath reeked of alcohol and cigarettes.

He didn't answer. His breathing filled the night, and the only thing he could see was Jeremy, broken and sagging against the wall of the bar.

"He started it," Jamie said.

"I don't fucking doubt it, but he's still a police officer." Jimmy walked off to talk with the small group who had assembled around Jeremy.

"Jesus Christ, David. You really lost it," Jamie said.

"I know. I just couldn't take the high road anymore. He's a piece of shit." The blast of adrenaline has started to reside, hitting him with dizziness and a sudden chill. He wiped a hand across his mouth, finding blood. He hadn't even realized Jeremy had hurt him.

Marco came to stand with him and Jamie, and turning his back broke out in a huge grin. "I'm so glad that asshole finally got what was coming to him. Only wish I'd been able to get a few hits in myself."

"Don't encourage him," Jamie said, even though he too was smiling.

"You kicked his ass!" Marco giggled.

Jimmy returned. "He's not going to report anything. He knows you could press charges just as easily as he could. There's no certainty how things would play out. You know he's got some excessive force charges already."

"You could still press charges, David. I mean you have a parking lot full of cops here," Marco offered.

He looked at Jamie, who had gotten very quiet. He cocked an eyebrow, but didn't comment. David looked back at Jeremy, who had one of the waitresses wiping at his wounds with a damp towel. He glared in David's direction, to which he gave a mock salute.

"I'm good. I'm going take that fucker down and I'm not going to do it in a way that he might be able to weasel out of."

The crowd began to disperse, most going back inside to continue drinking. David and Jamie went home, with an unspoken agreement not to discuss the situation at that time.

Jeremy Black was the least of his worries, at least for the time being.

CHAPTER 12

Tuesday started with a series of surprises, none of which had anything to do with the case at hand. As usual for a weekday, Jamie had left long before David pulled his weary butt from bed. That particular morning consciousness came with a throbbing head and tight ache that seemed to radiate to all areas of his body. For a moment he couldn't put the discomfort in context, then the events from the previous evening flooded back. He shuffled into the bathroom, letting the shower run until it was hot enough to coat the mirror with humidity. He hadn't liked the sight of his reflection anyway. The scab on his lip and the crescent of purple bruising about his left eye only reminded him of that fact he'd sunk to Black's level the night before. Now he felt like a thug, in addition to his anger.

The scalding water pounded down on him, alerting him to the areas of his torso affected in the fight. His knuckles screamed in pain when touched by the stream of water. He knew by midday they'd be crusted over and tight, making mundane movements difficult. In frustration he swore a blue streak until he couldn't think of any additional phrases.

In the kitchen David got the coffee pot brewing and grabbed a bowl of cereal to take with him to the table. He allowed himself a few minutes to eat and sip at his coffee while he read the morning paper. Humanity at large had not become less vile or depraved while he slept. A glance at the clock showed it was after nine, and he needed to get his butt in gear. As he gathered up his stuff the telephone rang. He thought about letting it go to voicemail, but the number on the call display surprised him.

"Hello," David said.

"Oh hi, David. Good I caught you," Susan answered. He could not think of a reason for Jamie's mother to be calling him.

"Yep. Slow start this morning. So what can I do for you?"

Thirty seconds of silence passed. "Well I was hoping that you and Jamie would be able to come over and have dinner with...Richard and me on Friday?"

David was stunned. It had been nearly four months since Susan had told Richard about Jamie being gay, and the fact that he had a long-time boyfriend. Though Susan and Jamie's two sisters had come around to the news pretty quickly, Richard had not. There had been a couple of tense phone conversations between father and son since the truth had come to light, but they had not spent a minute in each other's presence. David knew that Susan had been trying to get Richard to come around, and he appreciated her support, but he knew from personal experience that people had to come to terms with their own feelings on their own time.

"Is Richard aware that this is going to happen?"

"Yes. He'd like to meet you. I've invited Samantha and Caroline too, so there'll be plenty of friendly faces."

"Why ask me? Shouldn't you be talking with Jamie about this?"

"I did last week and he's not too keen. I thought you might be able to persuade him. I don't want this to go on any longer, it's been terrible. I'm not saying Richard is on board yet, but he's trying. I know he loves his son and he misses him. He wants to be there for him, and that has to count for something, right?" A note of desperation had crept into her voice.

David pinched the bridge of his nose with his fingers, fighting off the return of the headache. He really didn't need family drama in the midst of everything else, but he knew he had to do everything he could to help Jamie and Richard's relationship. "Of course it counts. I just don't want to do anything to make the situation worse. What if this blows up?"

"It won't I promise. This is a baby step."

"All right then. What time do you want us over?"

"How about six?"

"Sounds good. See you then."

"Thanks David. You know I really am glad Jamie has you in his life."

David chuckled. "No need for flattery. I already said yes."

"I mean it David. You're a special guy. I'll see you Friday."

David hung up and grabbed his coat. He wasn't sure how he felt about the upcoming family dinner, but he knew that Jamie and his dad needed to start somewhere. On a whim he took a cruise past Erin's house, this time finding her at home. There were two cars in the driveway, prompting him to park and observe. Less than an hour later two people came to the door: Erin dressed in a long t-shirt, and a man David didn't recognize. They kissed and basically dry humped for a few minutes before the man walked to one of the cars, got in and drove away. *Guess she's still up to her old tricks.*

He waited about thirty minutes longer and Erin reappeared, this time dressed, and got into her own vehicle. She pulled out and drove in the opposite direction of the hospital. After a decent drive they arrived at a cemetery and Erin pulled into the front gates. David didn't need to see her visiting the graves of her murdered children so he continued on to the office.

Once driving again thoughts of Jamie's family issues flooded back. The uncertainty of how to broach the subject with Jamie plagued him the entire way to the office, until he made a conscious decision to push the issue aside and get back on track with the case.

Fate had other ideas.

The streets had been packed, with a parking spot not to be found for three blocks. The rise in temperature had left the sidewalks running with chilly water, fed by the slowly melting ice clinging to the edges of the long line of office buildings. David's socks were damp by the time he made it to his building and he cursed himself for the decision to wear regular shoes instead of something more waterproof. As he stepped from the elevator he spotted a woman sitting on the bench near his door. She looked up, making eyes contact. She seemed vaguely familiar though he was sure he'd never seen the woman before.

She stood as he closed the distance to his door. Once right

in front of the woman he could see how tiny she was, no more than five foot. She gave him a tentative smile, but seemed to lose the nerve to look him in the face. Her gaze darted about as though expecting some type of ambush. She smelled of citrus and cigarettes.

"Can I help you?" David asked while opening the door.

"Are you David Lloyd?"

"The one and only."

"My name is Sharon. I guess you're a friend of my daughter's?"

David took a few seconds to process her words. "Jenny?"

She nodded and cast another furtive glance about the hallway. Now David understood why the woman seemed familiar. She had the same body type as her daughter, and shared the same sandy brown colour of hair, though hers was gently streaked with grey. Her good looks were fading, aided by the rough life she'd lived. The drugs had taken their toll, aging her before her time. Where Jenny's complexion was peaches and cream, her mother's looked sallow, further marred with dark bags and lines pulling at her eyes and mouth. Though she was thin, it seemed unnaturally so, her skin pulled tight across every angular thrust of her bones.

"Can I speak with you? Please."

David shrugged and stepped back to allow her to pass into the office. He went about his usual opening shop procedures, putting on the coffee and checking the phone and fax machine. He needed a few minutes to process the appearance of the woman, a specter of Jenny's past until she'd arrived in the flesh. He loathed the woman just from the few stories Jenny had shared, sure that he would have ripped her a new one if he ever crossed paths with her. Now that she was there he hesitated. Maybe the call from Susan had him rattled. Or maybe it had made him see things with family in a new light. He decided he would at least hear her out.

"Coffee?" he offered when the pot had filed.

"No thanks. I don't want to put you out." Her words had a soft, Maritime lilt.

He poured himself a cup and sat at the desk. Sharon fidgeted with the strap on her purse. David did nothing to try and ease her discomfort.

"So what can I do for you, Sharon?"

"I suppose Jenny's told you about me. You know what she went through as a kid?"

"She's told me some. Enough to get you guys weren't the Brady bunch."

"Yeah, well she had it rough. I make no bones about that. I was a shit mother."

"So what do you want from me?"

"I just want to know how she is. She won't talk to me. Keeps slamming the phone down every time I call."

"So you came all the way out here to see her in person?" David was incredulous at the thought.

"Yep. That didn't work neither. She told me to fuck off and slammed the door in my face."

"Can't blame her for that. She'd been through hell."

"But you're her friend, right? Way I hear it you got her off the streets and been helping her get her life better. Sounds like she trust you."

David sat back, thinking. Sharon sounded like she'd been told about their relationship. The conversation was too forward to be guesswork.

"How do you even know about me? Where'd you get Jenny's number anyway?"

"The hospital got hold of me a few months ago. Guess I was listed as her next-of-kin or something. Some nurse gave me this number." She recited his grandmother's phone number.

"Let me guess. You talked with Rhea?"

"Yeah. She was real nice, you know. She encouraged me to keep trying with Jenny. She suggested I might talk with you, see if you could help. Rhea says Jenny's really close with you, has all kinds of respect for you, so I figured it couldn't hurt."

David knew she meant well, but he could have rung his grandmother's neck at that moment. Jenny spoke very rarely of her mother to David, and he suspected she mentioned her even less to Rhea. The woman really had no idea about the conditions in which Jenny had grown up, or how much responsibility

Sharon had in her daughter's abuse. Jenny was on the mend to recovery in both body and mind, and if she wasn't ready or willing to face her mother at that point, no one had the right to force the issue. Just because someone was family, it didn't mean they deserved a place in your life no matter what. In reality the ones closest to you often instigated the most hurt.

"I'll be blunt Sharon. I love your daughter like a little sister, and I'd do just about anything to protect her. She's doing really well now, even getting ready to go back to school. And she's made it very clear to me that you don't have a place in her life, not right now at any rate. I think if you push it, she'll cut you out for good. You know what you did to her, and it was a pretty bitter pill to swallow for a kid. Jenny may never get over it. I suspect she'll make peace with her past, and if I have any say in it she'll keep her life on the upward climb it is now, but she'll always be scarred. You need to let her come to you, if or when she'd ready."

Sharon's eyes brimmed with tears, but she didn't utter a sound. After a few minutes she nodded. "I guess I have that coming. I appreciate the honesty."

"I don't play games, and I don't take kindly to those who do. You get my meaning?"

She sighed. "Yep, I do. Loud and clear. I'll back off." She stood, clinging to the purse like a lifeline. "Will you at least tell her I stopped by, and that I'm sorry. I don't deserve her love, I know that, but I have cleaned my act up. I've been sober for over a year now."

"I'll tell her."

"Okay." She left without another word.

Dave leaned back in his chair, overwhelmed by a rush of emotion. He fought through anger, frustration, and uncertainty. Could anything else fall in his lap?

The light on his phone had been blinking, so he picked up the receiver and checked the messages. Jimmy had called to check in. So had Sandra Klassen, who he didn't have anything to report to at the moment. There were a couple of hang-ups and an offer to clean his carpets before a garbled and abruptly ended message played out. At first the words were difficult to make out, as though the caller had the receiver pulled away from their mouth or obscured in some other way. The voice was female, slurred and distraught.

"...don't want to get into this again...too many years...the pain (crying)...just want to run away from it all...I'm so sorry, sorry ever met him...(more crying)...sorry..." followed by a loud bang as though the phone had dropped, and the call ended.

What the fuck?

He replayed the message three more times, but it didn't make any more sense than the first. Though the timing was suspicious David couldn't even conclude that it had to do with the Gagnon murders. It could have been about one of his other open cases, or even a voice form the past. Jesus, it could have been a wrong number.

Yet something about the call chilled him. He couldn't explain why, but he was certain he'd hit a nerve. Someone knew something, and the passing of a decade had done little to assuage their guilt, or fear.

He'd accomplished nothing through the passing of the morning, except for getting himself embroiled in a couple of sticky situations. He now had two "talks" to undertake, neither of which he wanted to touch with a ten-foot pole. He could probably ease Jamie into the conversation, but Jenny wouldn't buy it. She'd be on him in a heartbeat if he tried to butter her up.

To distract himself he wrote down the bits of the message he could understand and made an audio copy with his handheld recorder. After that he came to a standstill.

As he sat there sipping at his coffee and willing his brain to think of some path he'd yet to pursue the phone started ringing. When he leaned over to grab the receiver his fax machine began squawking and spitting out paper.

"Hello," he said.

"David? It's Dr. Garfield calling. You have a minute?"

"Yes, of course. Always glad to speak with my friendly neighbourhood psychiatrist."

Dr. Garfield chuckled. "If only I had that response from everyone."

"I expect we have about the same effect on people, namely suspicion and disdain."

The man actually laughed. "I'd have to agree. So let me get to the point here. I've reviewed the notes from Nathan Klassen's counselor and there is nothing to support the boy being capable of such violence. He presented a mild case of depression and some anxiety from the death of his father. The condition was treatable and would have eventually subsided or eased completely in my professional opinion. Just thought you might want to know."

"I appreciate the time you've spent on this, Dr. Garfield."

"Maybe I'll have a favour to ask in return some time."

"Of course. Now has anything else come to you about the manner of the boys' deaths that might help me out?"

"I'm sorry David, I don't have anything else to offer you on this. I do stand by my statement that this is a personal crime. I firmly believe you're looking for someone who knew the boys, or someone close to them."

"That's the feeling I have too, but I can't seem to find anything to back it up."

"Keep looking. You'll find your answers."

"Thanks. Keep in touch."

As soon as the phone had been replaced David snatched the papers from the fax machine. The first page was a hand-scrawled note from Detective Brown explaining that he's sent over the booking photos of any men who matched the Janko's man description that had been picked up in the years since the crime. David scanned the pictures, knowing he was really grasping at straws. Even worse was the realization that he'd have to hit the streets again.

After scarfing down a cheese steak hoagie for lunch he turned his attention back to the strange call he'd received. He made a list of all females involved in the case, those he'd spoken to and those he'd yet to connect with. He ran through them systematically, eliminating each in turn, until the only names remaining were Jasmine Snider, Erin Gagnon, and Alicia Marsten. Jasmine and Alicia didn't answer, so he left messages. Erin picked up after a long series of rings.

"Hello," Erin said, sounded as though she'd just woken.

"Erin, this is David Lloyd."

"What do you want?"

"I received a strange call last night and I'm trying to determine who it was from. Any chance it was you?"

Click. She hung up.

Nice. Her reaction made it seem likely she'd been the caller, but what did it mean? Who was she sorry she'd met?

Out of sheer exasperation David reviewed the file again, along with his own notes. Nothing he read, nor re-read, in any way pointed to the boys' guilt. If anything all that he'd discovered clearly showed the utter lack of case against them, and even more annoying was the fact that no other clear suspects had been shaken loose. It seemed a toss-up between Erin Gagnon and the Janko's man, though no motive or evidence for either being responsible had been established.

David returned Jimmy's call, thanking him for the concern. He took the opportunity to ask the man to run a search for any crimes similar to the Gagnon murders that had occurred in the years since the crime. He expressed what David had already surmised, that such a search would be fruitless and a colossal waste of time, but agreed to do it anyway. After another unanswered call to Jasmine and Alicia, David headed to the library.

Two hours later the only thing he'd accomplished was getting his headache to return. He'd reviewed newspaper articles and case studies of any crime involving children in the past twenty years. Though he'd found some cases with comparable circumstances, none had enough in common to seriously consider being the work of one killer. Still he printed off copies of everything, and packed it in with his other files. He'd check it against whatever Jimmy found.

At four o'clock he gave up. The day had been fruitless. With the fight, the call from Jamie's mother, and the appearance of Jenny's mother, there was no way he could continue on. He drove straight to the gym, where he put in a grueling two hours. With his body exhausted and aching, and a thin coat of sweat covering his skin, he went to sit in the sauna. The humid box was one of the few places where David was able to completely relax. He leaned back against the wooden bench, letting his eyes slip closed. His breathing slowed, lungs warmed by the dense air. Images from the files and snippets of conversations from the past week filtered through his brain, spinning by like the roll of microfiche at the library. What if he couldn't find the truth? Nathan and Alex would surely spend the rest of their lives behind bars if something new wasn't uncovered.

A shudder rocked his body. The cold reality of the case infiltrated the perceived safety of the sauna, somewhere he'd always been able to leave his worries behind. David burned with anger, mostly at himself, though he knew he'd been dogged about pursuing every aspect of the case, no matter how slim the chance in bringing him closer to the truth. He left not feeling much better than when he'd come.

At home, Jamie's car sat in the driveway. After parking he sat for a few minutes in the damp cold, trying to figure out the best approach to speaking with Jamie about the upcoming dinner with his parents. The car door slammed shut, the sound echoing through the quiet night.

"You all right there?" a man's voice called.

David turned and looked across the street, not surprised to find Mr. Albert standing at the end of his driveway. "Yeah. Just a crummy day."

"Gotcha. Had a few of those myself before."

"How's things going with Rhea?"

"Wonderful. She's one heck of a lady."

"Good to hear. Listen I need to get inside. I'll talk with you later."

"Good night, David. Give my best to that fella of yours."

"Will do."

He stepped in the back door to find Jamie peeling off his shirt and dumping it in the washer. He smiled as David entered and gave him the once over.

"Do you greet everyone half-naked these days?" David teased.

"I spilt something on my shirt and I didn't want it to stain."

He hung up his coat and wrapped his arms around Jamie,

pressing him against the humming machine.

"Jesus, your hands are cold," Jamie said and tried to pull away.

"Not so fast." David pressed his mouth against Jamie's. Jamie tensed, resisting the embrace, then melted against David's chest.

David helped remove the rest of Jamie's clothes, allowing himself to be lost in the pleasure he gave to his partner. The monsters in the dark receded, leaving only warmth and a connection David knew he would never want to live without.

The fire alarm began to shriek in the kitchen. Both men suddenly became aware that a cloud of smoke had drifted into the room. Jamie jumped down from the washer, grabbing his boxers from the floor and skidded around the corner.

Davis followed. Jamie had pulled a pan from the stove top, which continued to spit and smoke from the sink. The acrid stench burned David's nostrils. He popped open a window to allow the smoke to dissipate, then came to help Jamie with the mess.

"Jesus, I was sautéing some veggies for a sauce when you came in. I totally forgot what I was doing..." He gave David a sheepish look.

"I can be very distracting when I want to be," David said. "Let's just order a pizza or something."

"Sure, go ahead. I'm gonna grab some clothes." Jamie made a beeline out of the kitchen.

"I like you how you are," David called after him.

He called in an order and grabbed some plates and glasses from the cupboard. Almost against his will he retrieved his bag from the mud room and pulled out the Gagnon files. With a sigh he opened the top one and started to peruse the contents. When Jamie returned in pyjama bottoms and a Maple Leafs sweatshirt, he joined David. He grabbed another file and started reading. Every so often Jamie would jot down a note on a lined pad that was sitting on the table.

The pizza arrived and the two men continued with their review in a comfortable silence. When David couldn't read anymore he pulled the packs of photos free and spread them out before him. He scanned them, seeing nothing new.

"You want a beer?" he asked Jamie.

"No, I'm good."

David grabbed himself one and leaned against the counter to drink it. Jamie continued to look at the photos, bent over to scrutinize them closely. David smiled at his intensity.

"So anything jump out at you?"

"Not really. Most of the items collected at the scene were cleared. It's pretty standard stuff found in any public area. Mostly garbage. The two items that stand out are the lighter and the belt buckle."

"Nathan's never denied that the lighter was his. He just doesn't know how or when it got there. The belt buckle was never attributed to anyone, but that doesn't mean anything. It could have come from anyone. Who knows how long it was sitting there. "

"Well, it's not covered or particularly dirty, so I'd say it had been dropped some time close to the murders. But you're right, it's a public park. People are through the area every day."

"Really, there was no forensic evidence to speak of."

"It's a tough case, David. It was then, it's even worse now after all this time."

David tipped back the last of his beer. He placed the bottle in the sink with a soft clack. "Listen I need a break from this. Why don't we go watch a movie or something?"

"Fine by me."

They passed the next few hours without talk of murders or any of the unseemliness their work brought into their lives. When the movie ended David turned the television off and made eye contact with Jamie. He felt heavy and electrified with anxiety.

"Your mom called this morning."

"What did she want?"

No sense beating around the bush. "She wants us to have dinner with her and your dad on Friday."

Jamie started to say something, then clamped his mouth shut. He scrunched down on the couch.

"I told her we'd come."

"Why? The man's been a total ass about all of this. I don't think I want to do this right now. And I already told her that when she called me about it."

"I get it, I do. My dad was the same way, but it's a place to start. It's an olive branch. Why don't we go and if you're not happy with how things are going we'll leave?"

"I guess…"

"C'mon, I'll be right there with you. How bad could it be?"

Jamie looked at him sideways, lips pulled down. "You're kidding right? This has the potential for a major disaster."

"Be positive."

"Since when are you Mr. Sunshine?"

David sighed. "I'm not. I fully expect life to kick me in the ass at every turn. I'm just trying to be supportive here. Isn't that what I'm supposed to be doing?"

"Who are you, and what have you done with David?"

"Shut up. Give me a break. I'm not good at this crap."

"You're right. I'm sorry. I appreciate the effort. Okay, we'll go and see what happens. You need to take me out for a drink afterwards though."

"I'll take you out for ten."

They moved to bed soon after. Jamie read while David lay thinking about his next best course of action. With the wind whispering past the windows David fell into an uneasy sleep.

CHAPTER 13

David wasted most of Wednesday with mundane chores and activities clearly divorced from his professional life. In addition to helping Rhea deliver the items to the donation centre, he took her grocery shopping and dropped her off at her monthly bridge game. Afterwards, he finished up the trim in the basement and carted off the empty paint cans to the recycling depot. The last item on his list had been to hit the copy centre, where he made multiple reproductions of the photos Detective Brown had faxed him in preparation for another evening canvassing the lower echelons of society. This time David planned on expanding his search, making sure to hit not only the neighbourhood in question, but all areas where the homeless were known to congregate in the Greater Toronto Area.

Six o'clock snuck up on him, and before he knew it David was on the road to his appointment with Sam Miller. The man now lived in a high-priced condominium near Lake Ontario that must have set him back a cool million dollars or more, a far cry from his modest childhood home.

David pressed the buzzer, to be promptly answered. The lock was released and he took the elevator to the sixth floor. The plush royal-blue carpet looked clean enough to eat off of, and the paint had nary a scuff or chip anywhere in view. He found the number he was looking for and knocked.

The door opened and Sam Miller invited David inside. Sam took David's coat, and as he entered he could smell freshly brewed coffee and a hint of vanilla. He was led into the living room, then left alone as Sam went to retrieve the coffee. He experienced a terrible urge to snoop, but knew he didn't have enough to time to make it worth his while. He scanned the space instead.

The furniture was dark leather, formidable and expensive. One wall of the room consisted of floor-to-ceiling windows, which with the curtains open gave an impressive view of the lake. An expensive stereo system and a large television dominated the far end of the room. A black lacquer shelf held several hundred DVDs. The space radiated a very masculine feel. Davis suspected that Sam was single, or at least didn't cohabitate with anyone of the opposite sex.

Sam returned with two mugs, handing one to David. When the liquid touched his tongue he could have moaned. It was bar none the best coffee he'd ever tasted.

There was a striking resemblance between father and son, though Sam's hair was dark where his father's had settled into a nice silver hue. Both were tall, of medium build and slightly stoop-shouldered. Small indents on the man's lobes indicted he'd had them pierced once upon a time. He wore his hair longer than average, but it suited his bone structure and casual manner. Time and circumstances had been kind to Sam; he looked healthy and well-groomed, comfortable with himself.

David sat, enjoying the coffee. Sam picked up a remote and hit a button. Alternative music that David didn't recognize filtered out, the sound low and unobtrusive. "Hope you don't mind?" Sam asked.

"Not at all. And thanks for making this time to meet with me. I know this isn't a pleasant subject for you." As he adjusted his position the couch made a noise like he'd passed wind.

"Of course. Glad to help if I can."

"So I know you were best buddies with these guys, and I assume you believe they're innocent." Sam nodded, so David continued. "And you're positive they did exactly what they say they did, stayed at Nathan's place to get high and watch movies."

"I'd bet my life on it."

"Are you still in touch?"

"Of course. I go down to visit them at least once a month."

"Any idea why they were targeted?"

Sam made a face like he'd just sucked a lemon. "Not at all."

"You have any ideas on who might have done it?"

"I honestly think it was some random guy the boys ran into at or near the park. I've run the scenario over and over again and it's the only thing that makes sense."

"Most people would agree with you, but there are still some who think it could be connected to the mother."

Sam gave a blank look.

"Erin Gagnon had a reputation for hanging around some rough characters."

A tension that David hadn't picked up on until that moment seemed to drain from Sam at his statement. "Right. I'd heard that."

"But you didn't know the woman yourself?"

"Not really." His shoulders hunched and his gaze drifted away from David's face.

"I heard you stopped by her place on at least one occasion."

Sam began picking at a non-existent piece of lint on his pants. "Yeah, right. She'd said something to Jasmine about needing some work done. I think she hoped Alex would do it, but he didn't want to. I needed some money so I went over. She just needed some shelves put up, no big deal."

"Did your parents know about this?"

"I'm not sure. Wasn't important anyway. It'd happened months earlier."

Davis didn't know what to make of the strange vibes he was picking up on from Sam. "So you wouldn't have known any of the guys she was seeing?"

Sam shook his head, a little too vigorously. "Nope. Can't help you there."

"Okay. Just seems like it could be something. There's indication that Erin was involved with a few different guys around the time of the murders. Could be she pissed someone off."

Sam nodded, blinking a couple of times. David sat back, taking a sip of his coffee as a cover to get a gauge on what was happening. *Maybe I'm reading something in to this that isn't there?*

"Maybe. Anything's possible I guess."

"I talked with one of the guys and he thinks she might have had something going with a younger guy too. Someone he saw there."

"That so?"

David switched gears. "Any idea why the parole officer pointed a finger at Nathan and Alex?"

His hand twitched. "Guy was an asshole. He never liked either one of them, always hassling them."

"Why?" David pressed.

"He was a real douche. Lots of guys get into professions like that so they can push people around. You must know the type."

His thoughts immediately leapt to Jeremy Black. "Of course. So you think it's nothing more than that, not a retaliation of some kind?"

Both hands were fluttering now, seemingly incapable of keeping still. "Not that I know of."

"What about the deal with the man at Janko's diner. What are your feelings about that?"

The question didn't elicit any telltale signs of stress, or dishonesty. "I think there's a good chance he at least saw something, if he wasn't the person actually responsible."

"I agree. Only problem is no one knows who he is or where he is."

They lapsed into a moment of silence.

"Did you know Jasmine very well?"

Sam looked startled by the question. "Ah, not really, no. Why?"

Another weird response. The guy was on a roll. "I just can't seem to get hold of her. I got the impression she and her mother aren't close."

"Not from what I hear from Alex. After the trial she split, put herself through college, got married and settled down. She's in Brampton now with a couple of kids. I haven't seen her in years."

"Okay, well the only other thing I can think to ask about is the lighter? Any thoughts on how it got to the park?"

Sam gave a near perfect response, all thoughtful nods and

concerned expression, but David caught the tiniest crack in the façade. "I think he dropped it there one day and it got moved by kids or someone who'd picked it up. We used to walk through there all the time."

"You're probably right. Anything else you'd like to share."

"Just that I hope you find the guy. And if you need more money for expenses I'd be glad to pitch in."

"That's very thoughtful of you, but I'm good for now." Per the usual drill he handed over a card.

"Well, you know where I am if you have any more questions."

He walked David to the door. On the elevator ride down David could not shake the feeling that he'd somehow been duped. How and for what reason he could not flesh out. On instinct he sat in his car and waited.

Sam appeared about twenty minutes later, pulling out of the underground parking lot in a snappy red Lexus. His look was intent, focused on getting on his way as quickly as possible. David pulled in behind him, trailing at a discreet distant. Following him onto the 401 proved a challenge, the congested traffic making quick lane changes arduous.

A blue turn-off sign came into view and Sam hit his turn signal to indicate he'd be taking it. As he followed suit, David wasn't the least bit surprised to find himself on the way to Brampton.

Looked like he might be talking to Jasmine after all.

Once off the highway it became harder to perform a discreet tail, though David didn't detect any attempts to be shaken from the task. He imagined Sam to be too caught up in his panic, a state that would hamper his perception skills. David kept cool and continued driving.

Soon Sam pulled into a nice, middle-class neighbourhood, where there appeared to have been only three styles of housing designs to choose from. Variation in siding materials, garage doors, and trim colour were the only things allowing any type of individualization in a bleary stretch of otherwise nondescript homes. Sam drove the length of the main road, passing countless houses, but continued on to a nearby commercial district. He pulled into a lot that fronted several retail outlets and eating establishments. He parked before a large chain restaurant and hurried inside.

A glance at the clock made it clear he wouldn't be getting back to Toronto in time for dinner with Jamie. After a quick review of his options he pulled out his phone.

"Hello," Jamie said.

"Hey, it's David. I'm going to be late. Don't hold dinner for me."

"Okay. What's up?"

"I'm not sure yet."

"Where are you?"

"Brampton."

"I'm not even going to ask. Explain when you get home."

"Will do. See you in a bit."

"You owe me," Jamie said, laughing.

"I'm good for it. Bye."

David watched through the large front window as Sam took a seat in a booth across from an attractive woman with long blonde hair. She immediately launched into an animated speech to which Sam seemed unable to do anything but nod. He had the posture of a scolded child; hunched shoulders and eyes averted away from the source of his admonishment. A waitress appeared, interrupting the tirade. While orders were placed, the woman tapped her stiletto-heeled boots under the table and glared daggers in Sam's direction. As soon as the waitress departed the verbal lashing began again.

David waited until their drinks had been delivered to their table, knowing it would mean risking a "dine and dash" scenario if they attempted to make an abrupt departure. He entered the front door, indicating to the hostess that his party had already arrived. He kept a bland smile on his face as he sauntered to Sam's table, where he was greeted with looks of surprise and contempt, from Sam and the woman respectively.

"Hi there. Mind if I join you?" He didn't wait from an answer, forcing Sam to scuttle over in the booth to make room for him to sit.

"What are you doing here?" Sam asked.

David ignored him. "I assume you're Jasmine Snider?"

The woman looked at him, expression challenging, but David continued to smile. She was achingly beautiful. Thick blonde hair cut and styled like a model's framed her heart-shaped face to maximum effect. Her features were delicate, a classic beauty not unlike a young Grace Kelly. The only blemish was that one of her eyes had a larger than normal pupil, a condition that all but hid the grey-blue iris. The effect distracted him, bringing his attention back to the one side of her face.

"Yes, I am, but its McClelland now, not Snider," she answered. She stared back at David, something in her gaze haunting him.

"Why did you follow me?" Sam asked, breaking the moment.

David looked in his direction. "Because you couldn't have acted any more guilty. Believe me, you have no chance of a career in politics."

"Sam never was a good liar. That's what got us into this whole mess to begin with." Jasmine crossed her arms on the table top.

David settled back, happy to let the two divulge the story in their own way. He couldn't help but feel the animosity between them, as evident as an arctic wind blowing through their booth. He'd been in many uncomfortable situations over the years, and this had all the telltale signs of being a doozy. Sam's gaze locked on the table top, while Jasmine shifted in her seat. He stopped the waitress as she passed the table and asked for a cup of coffee, allowing the two a few minutes to decide how to proceed.

As he was adding sugar to his cup Jasmine launched in. "I suppose I should apologize for not getting back to you. I just really didn't want to deal with this again. I've made my peace with the past, and have made damn sure my present is a million times better than anything I left behind."

"Okay," David said, not quite getting where she was going.

"I think we should clarify, we don't know who did this. We really don't, but we also know that there's no way it was Nathan, Alex, and John."

"And how do you know that?"

"Because we were there that night. In Simcoe Park."

David felt a surge of surprise, and then understanding. "Go on."

Jasmine sighed. "We need to back up a bit. You have to understand the stuff that was going on at the time. I was extremely messed up. I was big-time into drugs back then, I had terrible self-esteem. I mean, who wouldn't coming from my home life?"

David thought about Jasmine's mother, the sad housing complex, and had to agree.

She continued. "We were in that accident where Blake got killed and Trevor got sent to jail. I totally went off the rails after that. I dropped out of school and I was desperate for attention. I didn't really care where I got it."

Sam looked like he'd just been kicked in the family jewels.

"So how do you fit into all this, Sam? And what does this have to do with the murders?"

Sam sighed. "I was fooling around with Jasmine in those days. Had been for a couple of months. None of the other guys knew about it, especially not Alex. He would have kicked my ass if he'd found out."

The two locked gazes. David's frustration was on the rise.

"And?" David asked.

"I wasn't the only one Sam was screwing," Jasmine said. He couldn't tell if her tone was disgust or remorse.

David looked at Sam and made a "get on with" gesture with his hand. Sam took a hard swallow of his coffee and slumped a little lower in his seat.

"I was sleeping with Erin Gagnon too," he said at last.

A-ha!

"So you were the young pup Angus saw at Erin's place?"

"Yes."

"How did this come about?"

"I met her at the hospital," Sam explained. "One time when I went to meet my mom for something Erin and she were chatting. My mom introduced me. I thought she was hot. I waited around until she was done with her shift and I went up and talked to her. I was being cocky, and she fell for it. Invited me over to do some work, but we both knew what she was really asking."

David took a moment to let the information assimilate. When he replayed what Sam had said it triggered some confusion. "Okay, but you were home the night of the murders. Your dad told me he'd had your password to the alarm cut-off."

"I went through his files and found his password. He went out for a bit after dinner and I slipped out then. Didn't come back till late, after he was in bed. As long as he didn't go in my room I was covered. I met up with Jasmine, and then I went to Erin's place."

"You guys went to Erin's together?"

Sam had the good sense to look embarrassed. "No, nothing like that. I left Jasmine at her place. I didn't realize it, but she followed me over to Erin's place. She was suspicious about what I was doing."

"So what happened then?"

"I stayed till about eight, right before it got dark. That's when she'd told the boys to be back and she didn't want them to see me. We got high and had sex."

"I'd waited outside till he came out again," Jasmine said, interrupting. "I confronted him and we ended up going over to my friend Jenna's place. We dropped acid and it got ugly."

"So when did you go to the park?"

"About two in the morning. Jasmine needed some air, she wasn't having a good time. We started fighting again, ended up wrestling around on the ground. I think that's when I dropped the lighter."

"So you dropped the lighter?"

Sam nodded. "We got interrupted by someone coming down the path. We ran up to the cabin, and waited till they'd left again."

By this time Sam's tone had changed dramatically. His hands were trembling, and the simple act of talking seemed to cause him physical pain. Jasmine's face drained of colour as she watched his lower lids brim with tears.

"What happened then?" David prompted.

Jasmine got herself under control before Sam. "We came out. As we were walking back toward the path we saw there was something lying near the creek bed. As we got closer we realized what it was. We freaked and ran back to the park."

"It was the boys' bodies?" David asked, already knowing the answer.

"Yes. We couldn't believe it. I mean we were stoned, and I'd never seen a dead body before. And it was little kids! Jesus, I didn't even know it then that it was Erin's boys, but it really freaked us out."

"We ended up back at the park. We didn't know what to do. I mean we were both high and we didn't want to get mixed up in anything like two dead kids. I acted like a total dick, I'll admit that. I left Jasmine in the park and went home. I stayed there the rest of the weekend. I didn't talk to her again until the next week."

"So you guys saw the murderer then?" David said, incredulous.

Both shook their heads. "Not really," Jasmine answered. "It was dark and we weren't really looking. I couldn't tell you anything that would be helpful."

"They didn't speak?"

"No. It was pretty quick. We didn't even realize what they'd done till we just about tripped over the bodies."

"Yeah, then when the lighter was found and the guys got accused I was terrified. I kept my mouth shut, hoping it would blow over. I mean I knew they didn't do it. I'd called them from Jenna's house like an hour before we left and they were still at Nathan's."

They were both suddenly too quiet. Neither one of them would make eyes contact with David or each other, a decidedly guilty act that prompted a prickly sensation to crawl down his spine. "There's more?"

"After Sam left I was going to walk back to Jenna's house. I started back, but I was really upset and high and I got myself turned around. I ended up near Simcoe and Rosalind, not the best place to be. Anyway this car stopped and a guy asked me if I wanted a ride. I recognized the guy so I said sure. Turns out he had recognized me too."

"Okay, I'll play. Who was it?"

"Jonas Vukovic."

"Alex's parole officer."

"Yeah. Alex didn't have a license, so I sometimes drove him to his appointments. I knew the guy had seen me waiting for him. He started coming on to me, told me he could get Alex's record cleared if I was nice to him. I said yes, thinking I'd take off when he stopped. He drove me to this house. I didn't know where I was. Another man came out, and they forced me inside. They…they raped me. When they were done they dropped me back at my complex and drove off."

Sam was fighting back tears. "I should have walked her home and then none of that would have happened."

David felt something click. "How does this fit into Vukovic accusing Alex and Nathan?"

"He'd told me if I said anything to anyone he'd make Alex's life hell. He'd fake drug tests, report violations, whatever he could. He implied he had the power to get other charges against both of us."

"When she told me I couldn't believe it. It was a big fucking mess. We were scared, but we decided to go to the police anyway. I went with her to the police station. We were waiting to talk with someone when this man came over to us. Jasmine looked like she was going to throw up as soon as she saw him. He brought us to his office and it turns out he was the second man. He threatened us that if we tried to tell anyone else he'd get us arrested."

"I think Vukovic giving up Nathan and Alex's name was to scare us," Jasmine said, "probably thinking it wouldn't stick. When the police went with it, he couldn't exactly recant."

David's stomach shriveled, tightening with his utter disgust. It seemed he just couldn't get away from creeps who liked to prey on the weak these days. He pushed that grim thought aside in order to focus on the situation at hand.

"Couldn't you have said something else, Sam? Like that you'd dropped the lighter another time or something. Why let your friends hang?"

"I was scared. And I did stick up for them. I told the cops I spoke with them a couple of times on the phone, which I did. It just wasn't from home. Once they got arrested I was too afraid that if I said something I'd get arrested too. I didn't want to go to jail."

David didn't press the issue, even though the truth felt as

though it had caught in the back of his throat like a lump of phlegm. He tried to imagine himself in a similar situation. What would he have done?

Jasmine spoke up. "We both decided to be quiet. This was my own brother, so it's not like it was an easy decision. We just didn't see how hanging ourselves out to dry was going to help them. And me going to the cops to accuse Vukovic and some cop of rape was only going to look like a gimmick. Seriously, who would have believed me? Some low-class girl with a druggie mom and a reputation for sleeping around. Wasn't going to happen. Lookit, the guy's still working as a PO, the cop is probably still working too."

David knew she was right, though the validity of her words didn't sit well with him. Everyone was guilty of assumptions and stereotyping, even the legal system.

"So someone dropped those boys' bodies off in the park, and it wasn't the men who are sitting behind bars. Did you see anyone around the park that night?"

"No," Jasmine said.

Something tickled at David's memory. He glanced back through his notes until he found what it was. "Someone made a statement about seeing Nathan and Tammy in the park that night. Maybe it was actually you two."

"Maybe? I sure didn't see anyone."

Sam shook his head.

"What about the cabin? Did you guys actually go in it?"

"No, we just went around back. The whole thing only took about ten minutes."

"And when you came out you didn't see any vehicles or hear anyone driving away." David wasn't sure where he was going with the line of questioning, but he thought he may as well ask everything that came to mind.

"No, like I said it was dark, we were high. I don't even know why we were hiding, we had as much right to be there at that time a night as anyone. Lucky we freaked out. God knows what would have happened to us if the killer had known we were there."

Jasmine nodded. Though she was not as visibly moved as

Sam, the woman's tight posture and wide eyes showed the effect the memories had on her.

"Did you speak with Erin after the boys' bodies were found?" David asked Sam.

"Yeah, I called her. She agreed that we should just keep things between us. It wasn't going to look good for her that she'd been smoking dope and sleeping with a teenager while her kids were going through God knows what."

Again David could see the logic in the decision to withhold information. *I wonder what that says about me?*

"I can see that. No sense wasting time with the cops looking into her when the killer was free."

"That's what she thought."

"Did you talk about the guys' getting arrested with Erin? How did she react?"

"We only talked once, then she didn't want to speak to me anymore," Sam said. "She was messed up. I don't know if she had an opinion of her own on what happened, but she told me she didn't think it was them."

"Do you know if she ever said this to anyone else, like the lawyers or the police?"

"She never said."

"What was the name of the police officer that assaulted you?"

Jasmine paled even further. "Rob LeClair."

The name brought a jolt of recognition, then disgust. Detective Brown had mentioned the same name only the day before. He would always think of himself as a police officer, whether he was actively serving or not. His life always had, and still did, revolve around the pursuit of the truth and protecting the people who needed his help. The thought of taking advantage of people who were vulnerable made him see red. He didn't know what to make of the new information, except that it offered an explanation for the accusation.

David was at a loss. His mind scurried along several trains of thought, each one bringing him to more questions than answers. The restaurant suddenly seemed too bright and warm. Sam and Jasmine looked equal parts guilty and sad, though unlike Nathan and Alex they'd walked away with their freedom. He didn't know if the decade of self-loathing had been a fair trade or not.

After letting them know he'd most likely need to follow up at some point, he finally left the two to commiserate in their shared ordeal. As he walked back to the car a light snow started to fall, though the temperature hadn't stayed cool enough to let much accumulate on the ground. The soft swooshing of the wiper blades instilled an odd sense of calmness, as though cleaning away some of the effect from the dirty secrets he'd uncovered. The yellow chevrons on the sparsely populated highway lulled David into a near hypnotic state on the way home.

Jamie and Jenny were in the living room when David got home a few minutes past nine o'clock. Jamie had a case file open on his lap and a pen twirling in one hand, while Jenny lounged on the couch watching a show about three magical sisters. She was also applying a coat of plum- coloured polish to her nails and sipping on a smoothie. Both looked his way as he entered the room and plopped down on the couch beside Jenny.

"You spending the night?"

"Yep. Thought it was easier since we have that appointment first thing," Jenny answered without taking her eyes off her nail polish.

"Everything go okay earlier?" Jamie asked.

"Yeah, great actually. I uncovered some new information."

"You want to talk about it?"

"Not at all. I'm bushed. I just want to hit the hay."

"That some gay slang for wanting to get laid?" Jenny asked, smirking.

David laughed, but Jamie's cheek tinged pink.

"No, but now that you mention it…" He gave an exaggerated eyebrow waggle and licked his lips.

David and Jenny cracked up. Jamie shot them a look that could have curdled milk and dropped his gaze to the file on his lap. David gave the girl a peck on the cheek and started out of the room.

"I'll be there in a few minutes. I just need to finish this," Jamie said.

"No problem. I'm going to take a bath anyway. 'Night, Jenny." He'd made it to the stairs when he suddenly remembered. He doubled back and peeked his head into the room. "Listen I forgot to ask, but can I use you guys again tomorrow night? I have some photos to show around, and if I have a couple of people we could cover more ground."

"Sure, but I want food first," Jenny answered, gaze already drifting back to the television.

"Yeah, sure. You should ask Sean too. I'm sure he'd help," Jamie suggested.

"Good idea. Thanks."

Breakfast consisted of coffee and a donut from the closest drive thru before they started for the school. David and Jenny had mumbled their way through their greetings as neither was much of a morning person. He was glad to see that Jenny wore one of the new tops he'd bought her and a nice pair of boots. The jeans were a bit tighter than he would have liked, but since she didn't look like she was about to walk Hollywood Boulevard he didn't comment. Even her makeup was more subdued than usual and she wore her hair pulled back in a low ponytail.

The school occupied a one-story, rectangular building that looked as though it could have been a grocery store in another life. The parking lot was a shared area with a similar-sized building to the left and another that backed onto the space from the street running parallel behind the school. The lot was nearly full, but they grabbed one of the still-open spots.

A young woman sat at a reception desk just inside the front door. A rack with brochures explaining the various programs offered sat next to a Scandinavian-style couch where David and Jenny parked themselves to wait for the administrator.

She appeared within minutes, a middle-aged woman in dress pants and a cranberry sweater. Her hair was cut into a jaw-length bob, which she'd tucked behind her ears. She wore small wire-rimmed glasses and smiled brightly at the sight of her potential new student.

David rose to shake her hand. "Hello, I'm David, this is Jenny."

"Hello. I'm Honey Stradwick, but please call me Honey." She ushered them past the reception desk and into a narrow hallway.

Jenny made eye contact and mouthed "Honey." David shrugged. He'd heard worse names.

They went through the whole rigmarole, reading the course itinerary and viewing the classrooms. In the end Jenny seemed pleased, so David signed all the financial papers and wrote a cheque for the first installment. She'd be starting in about three weeks and with the fast-track course load would be done mid-August.

Since they were already together they made their way to the closest shopping mall to pick up the items on the supply list they'd been given. Jenny seemed in good spirits, she didn't complain or give David a hard time about anything. After they'd bought the required items they decided to stop for an early lunch in the mall's food court.

He'd yet to mention the visit from Sharon, something that had been weighing heavily on his mind. He didn't want to upset Jenny, but he didn't feel right about keeping the interaction from her either. They had a very open, trusting relationship and he didn't want to jeopardize it.

"So your mom came by my office yesterday," David said.

Jenny stopped her fork halfway to her mouth. "What did that bitch want with you?"

"She talked with Rhea and got my name. She thought I might be able to convince you to talk with her."

Jenny put the fork down. Her whole body had tensed and her eyes brimmed with tears. "Not a chance. I hope you told her that."

"I did. I know how you feel about her, even if you really haven't told me much about your past. It doesn't take a genius to get how bad it has to be for a fourteen-year-old to leave home." He placed a hand on Jenny's, feeling it tremble. "You can talk to me about anything. You know that, right?"

She nodded, but avoided eye contact. "Yep, I know."

"I'll always have your back. You have any trouble with your mom, let me know. I'll deal with it. The only thing you need to be worrying about is getting better."

"I am better, David. Better than I can ever remember being in my life. I want to keep feeling like this. That's why I don't want her around. She turns everything to shit."

"Understood. Let's not talk about it anymore, okay?"

Jenny nodded, but David could see the pain in her eyes. She played such a good game at being tough and unflappable that David often forgot a vulnerable, young woman was hiding somewhere underneath. Her wall of indifference and the habit of keeping her emotional connection to people at a bare minimum proved difficult to penetrate. He knew that few would ever really know her, or be the recipient of any type of affection from her. There were no words for how honoured he felt to be one of those who had seen the true Jenny, the girl he'd come to love.

They left soon after. He dropped Jenny back at his grandmother's house and he continued on to the office. He fidgeted about making coffee, listening to his phone messages and in complete desperation even filed the pile of paperwork that had been sitting on his desk since before Christmas. David was antsy, angry, and unsure how to proceed. Nothing in his life seemed to be under control. Where only one week before he'd felt more secure than he had in a decade, now Jamie's family life was under duress, Jenny needed guidance and protection to help her put her past behind her once and for all, and he'd yet to make any progress on bringing Jeremy Black to justice. On top of all of the personal distress he was muddling through, the case seemed to be going nowhere.

He tried Erin Gagnon again, getting her voicemail. He didn't see any point in leaving a message. He also tried Alicia again, expecting a similar result. When a female answered the phone he was caught off guard.

"Hello," a woman said.

"Yes, hi. Could I speak with Alicia Marsten please?"

"This is." The voice now sounded hesitant.

"This is David Lloyd calling. I've left a few messages for you this week."

"Yes, right. I meant to call you back. I've been busy."

"Of course. No worries. I have you now. So I'll just jump right in here, so I don't waste any more of your time."

"Well, okay."

He cut her off, leaving no chance to weasel out of the conversation. "So as I said in my messages, I've been hired to look into the Gagnon murders. I'm touching base with all the people involved in the investigation and trial. I understand that you were interviewed and gave a statement about witnessing some occult involvement by Nathan, Alex, and John. Is that correct?"

"Um, yes. I mean it's been a long time and everything. I never said I knew anything about them killing those boys you know…um…just that they were like into weird stuff."

"So did you actually see the boys doing any of this weird stuff?"

"Ya, of course. I mean everyone knew about it."

"Gossip and actually witnessing something are two different things, Alicia."

"I know that. I said I saw them, okay. Listen I have to go now. I need to leave for work. I really don't have anything else to tell you anyway." She hung up.

Everybody's pissing me off.

A call through to Alberta caught Chuck Gagnon before he'd left for work. The man had nothing to add to the investigation but his remorse. He knew he'd been a terrible father, and his sons' deaths haunted him still. David detected no animosity or secrecy on his part, in fact he willingly offered contact information for his work, current girlfriend, even his therapist. Jimmy had already run the man's record and he'd come up clean.

Sean had indeed been coerced into helping distribute fliers and question people about the mysterious Janko's man. David had devised a detailed breakdown of all the areas, shelters, and known hang-outs, and divided them between Jamie, Jenny, Sean, and himself. Even with the extra hands he expected the task to take them into the wee hours of the morning. There were no immediate breakthroughs, but he felt better for the effort. In his gut he knew that someone, somewhere, knew something that would break the case against the accused. Every minute walking the cold streets and every hostile face he looked into was a chance. He needed to chase every possible avenue, no matter how unlikely it might seem. At this point all he had was hope.

CHAPTER 14

Friday morning David had an appointment with the audiologist. It was an annual thing to check that he wasn't encountering any further problems, and that his hearing aid was adequate for his needs. Nothing had changed as far as David was concerned, and he was glad the doctor gave him a positive response to the testing. He really didn't need anything else to worry about.

He hit the gym before going to the office. The burning ache from the workout revived him, and this time he was able to settle into the humidity-induced numbness in the sauna that he so enjoyed. He felt almost human when he emerged to dress for work.

Noon was fast approaching, heralded by the growling in his stomach. For the second time that week he hit a fast food restaurant for lunch. He knew he was attempting to alleviate the discouragement he felt from the lack of progress in the case with food and misdirected anger, his own personal vices.

The first order of business had been to contact Nerine Minniker, the tech Vukovic had been dating. She'd been in her office and had no objections to speaking with him. After a few minutes David realized she knew nothing helpful, but did share that she'd dumped the guy after realizing he was screwing everything "with a heartbeat" behind her back. After that he looked over the cases Jimmy had faxed him, not seeing how any would connect with the Gagnon murders. He did want to thank him for the effort and run something else by him. He tried Jimmy at his office number and got voicemail. The man's cell phone netted the same result. Though he hated to do it he put a call through to his home. He needed some advice and answers.

"Hello," Shawna Benson answered.

"Hi Shawna, it's David Lloyd calling. Jimmy home?"

"No, I'm sorry he's not, dear. He's at an appointment. Should be home in an hour or so. Can I have him call you back?"

"Sure thing. I'm at the office. He has the number."

"All right then. Bye."

It was more like two and a half before he heard back from the man. By then he'd gone in to work, though wonderful woman that she was, Shawna had gotten in touch to pass along the message.

"Hello."

"Hey, Dave. It's Jimmy. Shawna said you called. What can I do for you?"

"Wondering if you can give me some background on a detective? Name's Rob LeClair."

"Doesn't ring any bells, but I can see what shakes loose. Anything else?"

"Yeah, now that you mention it."

David pulled up to the small duplex about an hour after his call with Jimmy. Alicia Marsten's address had been in the system as she'd encountered a few brushes with the law since her high school days, and Jimmy had been most obliging in slipping it David's way. There'd been nothing serious on her record, a few minor drug busts and a shoplifting conviction. It appeared she'd been clean for a few years, but her information was still accessible to those in the know.

A rust-mottled hatchback sat in the driveway. David had driven a similar car back in his high school days, and the vehicle looked as though it came from that era. He parked at the curb and made his way up the slush-covered walk. A rustle at the curtains let him know he was being watched.

The door was answered by a young woman with a generous layer about her mid-section. She wore a loose robe over a pair of men's flannel pajamas and thick socks. "Yes?"

"Alicia Marsten?" He waited for her acknowledgement before proceeding. "I'm David Lloyd. I called yesterday."

The look of cautious interest was quickly replaced with alarm. Her eyebrows shot up and the fingers curled around the edge of the door turned white with the sudden force of their grip. "I told you everything. I really don't have anything more to say…" She started to close the door, but David stuck his boot in between it and the frame.

"Actually I think there's a lot you're not telling me."

Alicia started to cry. She backed up, hand held to her chest. David stepped in and closed the door behind him.

"Look, I'm not going to hurt you, and honestly I don't want to make trouble, but I need to know the truth. Innocent lives are at stake here."

She collapsed into a nearby chair, which groaned in protest to the sudden deposit of weight. "I don't want to get involved. Please. This mess has been following me around for years. I just want some peace."

David knelt down in front of her. He took one of her hands in his much larger one and did his best to keep his tone soft. "Tell me what happened, Alicia."

She pulled her hand away to bring both up to her face. She cried quietly for a few minutes, which David waited out with the last bit of his patience. At last Alicia got herself under control and took a deep breath. "I was told to say those things about Nathan and the other boys. Me and Jake." Her words were little more than a whisper.

"Who told you to do it?" David pressed.

"My parole officer. I don't know what was going on exactly, but he had it in for Nathan and Alex."

"Was your parole officer Jonas Vukovic by any chance?"

Her head snapped up at the mention of the man's name. "Yes. Do you know him?"

"Unfortunately. What did he have on you guys?"

"Jake and I got ourselves into some trouble back then. Drugs. We both got busted and put on probation. Vukovic caught us out one night making a big score. It probably would have sent us to jail. He made us a deal though. We said this stuff about Alex and Nathan, and he'd let it slide. He kept the drugs as collateral, told us he could plant it on us any time. We didn't have any choice, you know. I didn't want to go to jail."

"He never mentioned John."

"Nope, I think he just sorta got dragged into it."

David paused, pushing the new information around in his mind. "You know you helped put three innocent men behind bars?"

"I didn't know that then. I was just a stupid kid."

"Why haven't you come forward since?"

"What difference would it have made? They were found guilty. Then after Jake died it was only my word against his."

Something about the woman was so pathetic and maddening he wanted to throttle her. Instead he stood and paced about the narrow room.

"I don't know what this means just yet, but believe me I'm not letting this go. This isn't the end."

He left Alicia sitting in the chair, red-faced and so full of shame he could taste it.

On his way back to the office David had driven by Erin Gagnon's place, only to find it dark and without a vehicle in the driveway. He even went so far as to take a tour of the property, trying all the doors in the off chance that one had been left unlocked. He felt certain the strange message he'd received had come from her, a feeling cemented by her reaction upon being questioned about it.

Does Vukovic have something to do with that too?

He returned to the cold car and sat, steaming. His frustration had taken on a life of its own, riding along with him on a daily basis. The lack of clarity mocked him. Even what little had turned up seemed to have nothing directly to do with the case at hand, in fact it seemed to be highlighting a series of other crimes. How they were related and the reason for their enactment remained murky.

The shrill bark of his cell phone made him jump. He knocked his head against the top of the car's interior, and fumbled while retrieving it from his pocket.

"Hello," he gasped.

"Can I talk to David Lloyd?" a male voice asked.

"You got him."

"Oh, okay. Cool. Look I saw them pictures you were showing around last night and I recognize the one guy."

"You do?" David couldn't believe what he'd heard.

"Yep, calls himself Josie. He's a real wanderer and I haven't laid eyes on him in years, but I'm pretty sure it's him."

"How do you know him?" David asked, while scrambling to pull copies of the photos from his bag where he'd stuffed them the night before.

"I used to be on the streets myself. Was on the meth and whatever else I could get my hands on. Josie and I holed up together once in a while. He was an okay dude, like not violent or pervy or anything like that, just a bit weird. Like, um, mental problems. Never bothered me though."

David looked at his copies, checking the names he'd jotted on the backs. There was no Josie, but he did have a Josiah Maitland. He had a history of mental health issues, long-standing homelessness, and run-ins with the law, though he hadn't come through the Ontario justice system until after the murders in nineteen ninety. He'd been picked up for different charges, the last being a break and enter in April of nineteen ninety-eight. He'd failed to show for his hearing and hadn't been seen about the area since. Detective Brown had been kind enough to share the background of each of the possible Janko's men he'd sent to David's attention. He also recalled that on the first go around with questioning one of the homeless men he'd spoken with had mentioned the name of Joseph, which was pretty close to Josiah.

"Sorry, what's your name?"

"Burgess."

"Can I come speak with you, Burgess?"

"Sure, I'm off work today." He gave David an address and told him he'd be waiting.

David felt like he'd won the lottery. In his haste to get to the man's apartment he nearly got himself pulled over for a speeding ticket. He saw the cruiser parked on the side of the road just in time and slowed down to only five kilometers over the limit.

Burgess lived in an area of Toronto that David hated to visit after dark. He imagined the building to be full of fleas, cockroaches, and other creepy-crawlie life forms. The building's front doors had obviously had a run-in with someone's foot. The glass was patterned with spiraling, spider-web cracks under the generous coating of grime. David gingerly made his way inside and pressed the button for Burgess's apartment.

The buzzer roared and David grabbed the door to let himself in. Two young men were walking toward the door as he stepped inside. They were engaged in a loud discussion about a woman named Rolanda, so engrossed that one of them knocked into David as they passed.

"Yo, sorry man. Didn't see ya there," he said and kept walking.

"She got titties the size of watermelons," the other man said before the door closed behind them and cut off their conversation.

David shook his head. The elevator was out of order, but thankfully Burgess only lived on the third floor. The door opened onto a narrow hallway with a carpet whose pattern was busy enough to induce seizures, and nicotine-stained wallpaper. A man had his head peeked out of an open door about halfway down the corridor.

"You David?' he asked.

"Yes."

"I'm Burgess. C'mon in." He ducked back inside, leaving the door open.

David moved ahead, feeling uneasy and defensive. It wasn't like he expected someone to burst out and attack him, but you never knew.

The apartment was sparsely furnished, but very neat. Burgess sat on a sagging couch in blue jeans and a faded Maple Leafs sweatshirt. His feet were bare. David closed the door and came to join him. He sat and pulled the bag from his shoulder. "Thanks so much for having me over."

"No worries," Burgess answered.

The man appeared to be close to David's age, about forty. He was thin to the point of looking unhealthy, with milky skin peppered with a few days' growth of beard.

"Right." He pulled the photo of Josiah from his bag. "Is this the man you mean?"

Burgess glanced down at the photo and nodded. "Yep, that's Josie."

David smiled. "You have no idea how happy this makes me."

"You don't say."

"How did you come across this if you're off the streets now?"

Burgess gave a self-conscious smile. "I volunteer at the Helping Hand shelter. I was there last night for the supper. I looked through the photos." The place he mentioned was within a few blocks of Janko's diner, which could be significant.

"Well it's good to be giving back, right?"

"Sure. Helps keep me sober too. Seeing the state some of them guys are in…" He made a face as though he'd tasted something bitter.

"Fair enough. Now were you hanging out with him back in 1991?"

"Could have been. Hard to say for sure, those years are sort of a blur."

"So you couldn't say for sure where he might have been on a given night?"

"I don't think so."

That was disappointing. "You know the areas he liked to stay in?"

Burgess talked a bit about Josie's haunts, all in and around the neighbourhood where Simcoe Park was located.

"Did he go to Janko's?"

"Sure, I went there with him myself a few times. Good food when we could afford it. People who run it are decent."

"Now you said you hadn't seen him in a number of years, but would you have any idea where he might be?"

Burgess shook his head. "Can't say for certain, but he did like to travel the West Coast. He had a daughter there, though I don't think she had nothing to do with him."

"You know where on the West Coast?"

"Vancouver."

"Okay. Did Josie ever work, like did he have a skill or something he might be using to support himself?"

"Not really. He couldn't work most times, like when he wasn't on the meds. If anything it'd be like something manual, under the table. You know cleaning or something like that."

"Right, but if he needed medication then he must have seen a doctor."

"Makes sense."

"Or he could be on assistance?" David said, thinking aloud.

"Yep. As long as he had an address. No address, no cheque."

"You have any idea how to find him if he is out in Vancouver?"

"I'd try what you did here, hit the shelters, food and clothing drop-ins. Stuff like that."

"That will take time."

"Yep, now the bigger problem will be getting him to talk with ya. He don't like people in general, and he's real paranoid about strangers. Thinks they're demons and crap like that. He'll run."

"Would he talk with you?"

"Maybe, if he remembers me. Why, whatcha thinking?"

"Can I get back to you on that?"

"Sure. Anytime."

"One last question. Why didn't you come forward when the police did their investigation after the murders?"

"Must have missed me somehow. Like I said, times from back then are pretty much a blur."

He gave David his home and work number, and let him know his shifts for the next week. David had a crazy, desperate idea in mind, but he needed to get the okay first.

He left Burgess's building and drove around the city. At about five o'clock he stopped and picked up a bottle of wine, as he'd told Jamie he would, then headed home. He waited another half-hour until Jamie got home. David picked up on his partner's foul mood before he even spoke. He watched him walk into the kitchen.

"Hi babe," David said and planted a kiss on Jamie's cheek.

"Hi."

"Everything okay?"

"Just a rotten day at work. You know, and this thing with my parents has been eating at me. Do we really have to go?"

"Have to, nope. But we should. Let's just get it over with then we can come home and get good and drunk."

"I'm holding you to that."

"Beer's already in the fridge."

The drive to Jamie's parents was tenser than any moment he'd ever had with his partner, including the time a few months previous when he'd spoken out about his unhappiness with Jamie keeping their relationship a dirty little secret. In fact, those events were what had triggered the current situation. In coming to terms with his sexuality and his relationship with David, Jamie had been forced to reveal the truth to those closest to him. The revelation had gone by without ruffling any feathers at work, but at home it had really hit the fan.

Samantha's and Caroline's cars were already in the driveway when they arrived. Though he had never been to Jamie's parents' home, the sisters had been to their place a few times and he recognized the vehicles. The house was just as he expected it to be; it was large, attractive, and set on a lot larger than most in Toronto would be able to afford. In addition to the familiar cars a sleek black Mercedes sat in the drive.

Jamie parked. He leaned back against the seat, very quiet in the darkness. David placed a hand on his shoulder, but didn't speak. He understood the gravity of the moment better than most.

"Okay, let's do this," Jamie said at last.

"Remember, you give the word and we're out of here."

Jamie nodded and exited the car. David wasn't surprised that he didn't take his hand as they walked to the front door. Jamie was no doubt feeling angry and self-conscious.

Samantha answered the door and ushered them both inside with a hug and kiss to the cheek.

"You guys look great," she said as David handed over his coat.

Jamie had on the charcoal suit he'd worn to work, minus his tie. David had put on some dark pants and a dress shirt with stripes of crimson, and as usual felt like the ugly step-sister next to his handsome partner.

"You too," David said. Good looks ran in Jamie's family.

"They're in the kitchen," Samantha said. Jamie handed over the bottle of wine they'd brought.

Two small boys came barreling into the room, one tripping over his own feet and sliding across the marble floor. He seemed unfazed, jumping back onto his feet and lunging at his uncle.

"Hi, Uncle Jamie. Can you come play Nintendo with us?"

Both boys gave David a curious look before turning their attention back to their uncle.

"Maybe in a bit, guys. We just got here," Jamie said, laughing.

"Boys, this is David. Remember I told you about him?" Samantha cut in.

One of the boys snickered and looked to his mom. The other looked completely uninterested.

"David this is Josh and Brian. Boys, say hello to David."

"Hi," they said in unison. Josh leaned toward his brother and whispered something in his ear. When Brian did nothing, Josh gave him a nudge with his knee.

"Are you really Jamie's boyfriend?" Brian asked. His cheeks flamed.

David made eye contact with Samantha, who nodded and smiled.

"Yes, I am," David answered.

"Do you like kiss him and stuff?" Josh asked.

Now it was Samantha's turn to blush. "Joshua."

"It's okay, Samantha. It's an honest question."

"So do you?"

"Sometimes," David answered and looked the boy square in the eye.

He thought about it for a moment. "Okay. Do you know how to play Super Mario brothers?"

"I sure do."

"Come play with us." Then a small hand reached toward David and began tugging him across the foyer.

"I'm going to go talk with my parents. You okay for a bit?" Jamie asked.

David said he was fine and let himself be dragged into a giant den where the boys had taken up residence. There was a bar, a full-sized pool table, and an enormous television screen with a frozen image of Mario on it. The boys plopped down on the brown suede coach, and Josh handed David one of the game controllers.

They had been playing for about twenty minutes when Jamie returned. He looked stoic, though not as angry or upset as David might have expected. He leaned on the back of the couch.

"Who's winning?" Jamie asked.

"David's kicking butt!" Brian said with undisguised reverence.

"Just 'cause I'm old doesn't mean I can't play video games."

"Can you come with me?"

David caught Jamie's gaze. "Sure. Josh, take over for me."

He followed Jamie from the room and down a long hallway. The house was enormous, even larger than David had gauged from the outside. At last they arrived at a kitchen bigger than the entire first floor of their house. Susan sat at a large table by a row of windows looking out onto a greenroom-type space. She swirled a glass of wine with one hand. As they entered she looked up.

Samantha and Caroline, and Caroline's one-year-old daughter, were also at the table. The baby was being fed her dinner, most of which she seemed to have smeared on her face and the top of her high chair. All three women smiled as they entered.

"Hi, David. Nice to see you again," Caroline said.

"You too, Caroline. And this must be Morgan?" David said, coming to the high chair.

Morgan reached out for him with one squash-coated hand, giggling like a hyena. David let her grab his finger, which made her laugh even harder.

From his peripheral vision David had caught another person

standing by the gigantic island. He managed to pull his finger away and after wiping the grime from his skin with a napkin helpfully supplied by Caroline, he looked to Jamie for guidance.

Jamie stood at his side, tension drawing his shoulders high and tight about his neck. In what David guessed to be an automatic response, Jamie reached back and grabbed David's arm.

"David this is my father, Richard Brennan. Dad this is David. My boyfriend."

David took a few steps forward, reaching out his hand. "Hello, Richard. It's a pleasure to meet you."

Richard hesitated, then grasped David's hand. "Likewise."

Richard was a good-looking man, not unlike his son. They both had dark hair and vibrant green eyes; even the shape of their noses and chin were similar, but the elder Brennan stood a few inches taller than his son and was more substantial in build. Not that he was in any way overweight, the man simply had a large frame. *He would have made a great linebacker,* thought David, though he bit back the comment at the last second in case it wasn't taken as a compliment.

"Why don't we go into the dining room? We can all sit down and have a glass of wine," Susan suggested.

"Good idea," David said.

She flashed him a look of encouragement as her husband walked from the room, then hooked her arm through his to lead him in the correct direction. A small sitting area before a large bay window separated the kitchen from one of the grandest dining rooms David had ever laid eyes on. The room was at least twenty-five feet long, with warm walnut paneling and ivory silk curtains. A low-hung crystal chandelier hung over a table that could seat eighteen. One end had been set for their party to encourage an atmosphere of intimacy that David suspected would not be easy coming.

"Have a seat everyone," Susan called out. She'd brought the bottle of wine from Jamie and David, and set about pouring everyone a glass.

Caroline had remained behind to clean up the baby, but the other five took a seat about the table. Jamie sat to David's right, in between him and his father at the head of the table. The women sat opposite. He touched Jamie's leg under the table.

"So tell me a bit about your family, David," Richard said, his gaze so focused on him that David felt as though he were boring a hole in his forehead.

"What can I tell you? I'll be thirty-nine next month, I was born and raised in Toronto. I have great parents, my mom's a secretary at a doctor's clinic, my dad's an accountant. My younger brother Sean manages a medical testing lab and he just got married a few weeks ago. I like football and hockey, I read when I get the chance and I'm pretty handy around the house."

"You were married before, is that right?" The directness cut deep.

The question surprised him but David didn't let it show. "Yes, that's true. Didn't work out for obvious reasons, but Dana and I are still friends."

Richard nodded thoughtfully. "I understand you've taken in a young girl, a former prostitute if I'm not mistaken."

"I've helped a young woman named Jenny get off the streets, yes. I met her during an investigation a few months back. She's living with my grandmother at the moment, and I recently helped her get enrolled for school. I'm hoping she'll come work for me in the future. I've become very fond of her. We both have." David indicated Jamie with a wave of his hand.

"This happen often? These types of people coming into your work?"

"I'm not sure I know what you're getting at?"

"Me either," Jamie said.

The hostility in the room gave David a sensation like choking, but he continued to smile despite his discomfort.

"Well, you're a private detective, aren't you?" Richard asked.

"Yes, that's right. About five years now."

"And before that you were a police officer?" The tone was smooth, but David nonetheless felt the effects of an interrogation.

"Yes. I was on the force for ten years."

"That's how we met. David was a witness in one of my cases," Jamie said.

David picked up on a tightening of Richard's jaw as the

man's eyes moved in the direction of his son. For a split second he thought the man might strike out, and then the impression vanished.

"That's what your mother told me. Now Susan also said you had some trouble. That you got hurt and had to retire," he said and took a casual swallow of his wine.

David wasn't sure he'd classify the attack on him as "some trouble," more like a major life-changing catastrophe, but he wasn't going to pick a fight. "Yes. I got jumped one night while I was out and lost the hearing in one ear and hurt my knee pretty bad. I'm healed up now, but it was enough to take field work out of the equation. So now I work for myself and it's going well."

"But unpredictable, right? I mean you can't guarantee when or if you'll be working."

"Dad, please," Samantha said, shooting the man a look of pure annoyance.

"I have a right to ask, don't I? If you and Jamie are living together your life will no doubt have an effect on his." He looked right at David then, daring him to disagree.

"Of course, Richard. Just like any couple, what affects one affects the other. Though I am happy to say I've never had any long periods without work. I'm reliable with money, I have savings and own my own home." Susan was staring at him, but David waved away her silent offer to intervene. "I'm certainly able to pay my own way."

"What are you getting at here, Dad?" Jamie asked. His tone dropped the temperature in the room several degrees.

"I'm simply trying to get to know David, Jamie. I want to know what kind of person my son has gotten involved with. Any good parent would do the same."

"I'm not a gold-digger Mr. Brennan, if that's the implication. Though I don't think its Jamie's financial well-being you're actually concerned about. Nor is it what type of questionable persons I might be involved with through my work. What's really eating you is the fact your son is sleeping with a man, right?"

An angry silence filled the room. Jamie shifted in his chair, but reached down to brush David's hand, which still touched his leg. Samantha glared daggers at her father, and Susan looked as though she might cry. Only David and Richard kept their composure with icy smiles and rigid posture, their gazes locked across the table.

"I think it would be a good idea for David and me to have some time to chat alone," Richard said.

"I don't think so. Besides, anything you have to say to David you can say in front of all of us," Jamie answered.

"It's fine, Jamie. Richard and I are both gentlemen. There's no need to worry." David turned his look to Jamie.

Jamie glanced at his mother and sister, neither of whom looked convinced that leaving was a smart move, then to his father and back to David. After a sign of acquiescence he stood, and with a hand cupped about the back of David's head leaned down to kiss him. David knew the action was more to irritate Richard than to offer David comfort, but he didn't mind.

"I'm right outside the door," Jamie whispered before walking away. Susan and Samantha followed him from the room.

Richard waited until the door closed behind them. "Let's cut the shit, shall we?"

"Agreed. I've never been fond of playing games."

"Now I don't know you from Adam, and I'm not saying you're not a decent guy, but this whole thing has really thrown me for a loop. I was shocked when Susan told me. I'm not comfortable at all with this and I certainly can't say I approve. Never in a million years would this have been a life I would have picked for my son." Richard's face had become quite flushed and fine beads of sweat dotted his hairline.

David chose his words carefully. "This is not your choice Richard. Or Jamie's either, if we want to be blunt. He is who he is, and gay or straight he's still your son."

Richard made a face as though he were holding back tears, not something a man as proud and strong as he would give in to without a fight. "I love my son, no matter what. That's not the issue. I just don't know if I can ever be okay with this…with him being with a man, with you. Every time I think about this I see red."

"He's happy though. And I can tell you that I am one hundred percent in love with Jamie, he's the most wonderful person I've ever known. He's my best friend and I would never do anything to hurt or disrespect him."

"That's good to hear, but I can't tell you that it makes me feel any better about the situation. Jesus!" The chair shrieked across the floor as he suddenly pushed back from the table. "Jamie should be married and raising kids like his sisters."

"Maybe he will one day," David said.

Richard's eyes burned with anger. He took three long strides to come and stand before David's chair, a finger pointed at his face. "That's not the way things are supposed to be."

"Richard, that's the way things are. Jamie and I have had many discussions about this, and if you don't find a way to at least tolerate him being gay you're going to lose him. It took everything in Jamie to come to terms with this himself, and he'll never go back to hiding or feeling ashamed of who he is. He has no reason to be ashamed."

Richard's hand dropped to his side. He took a long, shaky breath and his impressive stature seemed to crumple in on itself.

David stood. "Listen Richard, if you want to hate me or resent me then do it, but just do it silently. Keep that crap to yourself. I know you love Jamie and you want to be a part of his life."

"You really love him?"

"I do. We've been together a good chunk of time now and I can't even imagine my life without him."

Richard seemed to realize they were standing very close to one another and he took a hasty step back. He smoothed his hands along the front of his shirt though there wasn't a wrinkle in sight. David knew Richard was conflicted and far outside of his comfort zone. Though he really didn't want to, he was going to cut the man some slack.

"Why don't we get everyone back in here and we can have a nice dinner together. The best thing to help right now is time. You need to adjust to the new status quo, just like we did. If you want to talk with me again another time you know how to find me."

"Fine. Let's do it." He turned on his heel and walked to the door.

As the door opened, the small group clustered just outside came into view. Caroline had joined her mother and siblings, and all four looked up with anxious curiosity plastered across their faces. Richard passed them without a word. Jamie rushed to David's side.

"I'm fine," David said.

"You're still in one piece. That's a good sign." Jamie gave him a quick visual once over.

"Did you settle things then?" Susan asked. Both sisters stared at him, eager for the reply.

"For now. I think the best thing is to back off and let things come through in their own time. I mean, he didn't throw my ass out on the sidewalk, so I'm good with that," David answered. He *was* good with that, in fact it was more than he could have hoped for.

"Where's my dad going?" Jamie asked.

"I'm not sure."

"Samantha why don't you get the boys, I'll round up your dad and we can get dinner started," Susan said.

The two women strolled off, leaving David, Jamie, and Caroline to regroup in the dining room. In the distance Susan and Richard were talking, the sound too low and muffled to make much sense. They sat at the table, David and Jamie returning to their previous seats as though from habit. But David didn't see coming to family dinners at the Brennans' happening as a regular occurrence any time soon.

Caroline poured herself a glass of wine and downed half the contents in one neat swallow. "So this is fun."

"I'm a barrel of laughs, that's why your brother puts up with me. Didn't he tell you?" David's words dripped with sarcasm.

Both Jamie and Caroline laughed, spurring David to join them. He had to give in to the futility of the situation. The resolution was out of his hands, he could only play as nicely as possible and hope for the best. Even that was a stretch. He often found it hard to bite his tongue and wasn't the most adept at handling delicate situations.

"I thought it was because you have a nice ass," she quipped back when her laughter subsided.

"Caroline!" Jamie cringed with embarrassment.

"I do have a nice ass, but I can't say what attracted your brother to me. In theory we are total opposites, but it seems to work."

"Oh, I don't think you're that different," Caroline said. "You're both very driven, hard-working and painfully honest. Plus you strike me as someone with a good sense of decency and loyalty."

David never knew how to take a compliment. "Well, thanks."

"She's right. You might be a little rough around the edges, but you're a good guy underneath." Caroline smiled.

"I liked her compliment better."

Brian and Josh came running into the room, their presence announced moments before by gales of laughter. To David's chagrin they fought over who would get to sit next to him. He must have made a good impression with his video game skills. Brian won out, and Josh was relegated to sitting next to his mother, who had returned with Susan and Richard in tow. Richard had poured himself a scotch three fingers deep. David could have used a stiff drink himself.

The group made their way through the meal without any unpleasant incidents. After helping clear the table and tidy the kitchen, Jamie and David ducked out. They drove home in silence, both ruminating over the events of the night.

On impulse David decided to cruise by Jonas Vukovic's house, which he realized was quite close to Jamie's parents' home, though on the fringes of the affluent neighbourhood. They made a tour of the block, noting a car in the driveway and lights on in several rooms on the lower level. The second time around they parked a few houses down the street and watched. It was just after nine o'clock and for the most part the street was quiet. They waited until ten before their patience paid off.

Jonas Vukovic exited his house and got into his car. He drove across town to an area dominated with two-story town houses and parked out front of one in particular. He could be seen making a call from his vehicle and about five minutes later another man came out of one of the units. It was too dark to make a positive identification, though David was quite certain he didn't know the man.

They drove off together, with David and Jamie trailing at a discreet distance. Soon familiarity began to tingle at the base of David's skull, and as he pulled onto a street he'd visited several times in the proceeding days. David's stomach gave a sharp twist as the car pulled into the driveway of Erin Gagnon's house. Vukovic gave a quick look over his shoulder before entering the premises when the door opened.

"What the hell is that about? And who's that other man?" Jamie asked, words dripping with disgust.

"I don't know, but it's not cool. That's for sure."

The house was dark and the men did not come back out for more than an hour, so they decided to cut their losses. Once inside their own home Jamie went straight to the cupboard, bypassing the beer David had purchased. He pulled down a bottle of rye and poured them both a glass. A couple of rounds later, both were feeling calmer.

"What a night," Jamie said, and David did not miss the sarcasm.

"Full of interesting revelations."

"What are you going to do about this Vukovic thing?"

"Not sure yet. I need to think on it a bit."

"Seriously though, thanks for everything," Jamie said.

"Of course, though I don't think I did anything too spectacular."

"You stood your ground, for yourself and us. That means more to me than anything else."

David swaggered up to his partner, pressing himself against Jamie's body. "How are you going to thank me properly?"

Jamie smiled. "I have a few ideas."

CHAPTER 15

"David you have to report this," Jamie said. He slammed his coffee cup down with such force that some of the contents splashed over onto the tabletop. On seeing the mess he'd made, Jamie immediately went to the sink to get a cloth and mop it up, an action David found amusing but knew better than to comment on during their current discussion. They'd been enjoying a pleasant Saturday morning breakfast when David had decided to bring up the information he'd gotten from Alicia Marsten.

"I know and I will. I just want to get more details, maybe some proof. God knows if the guy was pulling this kind of shit back then that he's probably still at it now."

Jamie sat down again and took a careful sip. The sunlight streamed in the window, casting a line of light across the table and haloing Jamie's damp hair. "Of course. People like that rarely stop of their own volition. They need to be caught."

"Exactly. There must be a way to get names of current people on his roster, maybe I can talk to some of them. I might be lucky enough to get someone to talk."

Jamie's eyes lit up and he gave David a cheeky grin. "Maybe we can beat him at his own game."

"What do you mean?"

"Well, it sounds like he trolls areas where he knows his clients hang out, or maybe he's just hitting known areas for drugs, crime, prostitution. That's probably how he crossed paths with Jasmine. I don't think he was necessarily looking for her, just someone in the area that he might be able to threaten or intimidate. It was just her bad luck to be there at the wrong time."

"You're probably right."

"Why don't we do the same? Maybe we can hit up some of the people we know on the streets to keep an eye out for him. You know, we could catch him red-handed."

"Not bad. I think my immoral, underhanded ways are rubbing off on you. Wouldn't your dad be disappointed?"

"Fuck him. This is good stuff. We're helping take scumbags off the street."

"Again with the we." Not that David was complaining, he liked working with Jamie. They made a good team.

"Yeah well, to be honest I get more satisfaction from the small bits I help you with than even the biggest cases at the Ministry. I've been looking at things a lot differently lately. It makes me sick that a professional like Vukovic would be doing this."

"People are often not what they seem. I run into this time and time again. Doesn't matter what kind of job you have or how much money, a creep is a creep."

"Agreed," Jamie said in a wistful tone.

David wanted to let that matter rest until he'd worked out exactly how he planned to proceed. If he was lucky he'd get one shot at the bastard, and he wanted to make it count. Like Jasmine had said, an accusation against the man would not be received with open arms. Many would think it to be a desperate attempt to shift blame away from the accused, one of whom was her brother. David needed to look at the situation with Vukovic like a separate case, even though the man's actions had clearly influenced the outcome of the Gagnon trial. If he could find the proof for the real killer then perhaps he could offer enough to the police to warrant a proper investigation of Vukovic's past transgressions.

"Listen, something else came up yesterday that's pretty interesting."

"What's that?" Jamie asked.

"I might have identified the Janko's man."

"Seriously? How'd you pull that off?"

"A man called me yesterday. He'd seen the photos we'd passed around and he thought he recognized one of the guys.

The name he knew him by is pretty close to the legal name, and the issues he knew this guy to have sound a lot like the Janko's man's behaviour."

"Does he know where he is?"

"That's the kicker. He suspects the man's in Vancouver. Says he used to go back and forth, might have a kid out there. Even if that's where he is it'll be difficult to track him down. Unless he's in hospital or jail, or receiving assistance, he'll be a ghost. You know how these guys are, they can stay off the radar for years."

"Yeah, and Vancouver is a big city. I wouldn't wish that on anyone. Might be tricky with cross-provincial police too. You know how territorial these things can get."

"Yeah, a lot of macho bullshit. All puffed like a cockfight."

"Yeah, plus you'd need the okay to cover the costs, right? Sandra might not want to put out for a trip that could go nowhere. You'd be looking at a few thousand dollars for your travel and hotel, your time."

"Yep, I've been thinking about that."

"And even if you do track this guy down, who says he even saw anything. Maybe he is just some nut that got into some other trouble the same night. I know it seems unlikely, but things like that do happen."

A ringing started and both men reached for their cell phones. A strange number lit up on David's call display. He frowned and snapped it open. "Hello?"

"Hi. Could I speak to David Lloyd?" An older male's voice.

"You got him."

"Great. This is Lester Racelli calling. Got your name from Art Brown."

It took David a few seconds to put the name in context. "Oh, right. You were Art's partner on the Gagnon case."

"Yessir. He knows how much this case has bothered me so he called me pretty much as you left his office. I've been stewing on this since then, and I just couldn't stand it any longer. So I gotta ask, have you turned anything up?"

David hesitated in saying anything to the man. What he'd discovered was flimsy at best, and as Jamie had just pointed out might not actually have anything to do with the case. "Well I'm following a few leads, nothing solid yet. I don't want to get into anything just yet in case things don't pan out. I'm sure you can understand."

"Right, right. I getcha. Can't even tell you how much this case got to me. It's one of the reasons I went for early retirement. Just could never shake the feeling I'd been part of something real bad. I don't believe those boys are guilty."

"I'm with you on that score. Seems like they got railroaded."

Jamie was staring at him expectantly. He jotted a note on a piece of paper and slid it across the table.

"Something was definitely rotten. Could never figure out what was going on with a few of the players, like the mother for one and that smug-ass probation officer for another. Yet the lawyers just ate it up, pushed the damn thing through with nothing to back it up."

"I don't disagree Mr. Racelli. Look, I promise to keep you in the loop if anything concrete turns up. Can I reach you at this number you're calling from?"

"Yep, this is my home number. You need anything call me. Nothing I'd like more than to get to the truth on this before I take a dirt nap. Don't need this shit trailing me to the afterlife."

Dave fought back a bout of inappropriate laughter. The old guy had spunk, he had to give him that. "Sure thing, Mr. Racelli. I'll be in touch."

"Good to hear, and call me Lester."

"All right Lester. I'll talk with you again soon."

David put the phone down. The conversation played for a second run in his mind. The case had a number of people up in arms, yet no one seemed to have a clue about exactly what had happened.

"You have a lot of people on edge with this," Jamie said after a few minutes of thoughtful silence.

"Yep. I'm guessing the one I piss off the most just might be our killer."

Jenny had come over to the house for dinner and to get ready for Stella's event at The Scarlett Letter. She'd bought herself a new dress, a low-cut, shimmery number that made both David and Jamie break into cat calls when she came downstairs to show them. Jenny was a very attractive girl, more so now without the heavily applied makeup and questionable clothing of her former profession. Her natural, sandy-coloured hair better suited her fair complexion than the bleached style she used to wear. With a bit more meat on her bones she didn't seem as gaunt, and softening her harsh appearance had let her natural beauty through.

David realized he and Jamie were looking at Jenny like parents with a child going off to prom. She looked pleased at their reaction, and slightly self-conscious, but still gave them a little twirl and sassy toss of her hair.

There'd been consensus among the three to push aside any personal and work issues, and devote themselves fully to a good time. As such they all partook of several drinks before heading to the club in a taxi around ten p.m. The flash of the ten-foot neon sign could be seen for several blocks, and the three exited the vehicle to a sidewalk lined with expectant patrons. David moved toward the two large bouncers guarding the velvet rope, one who David remembered from his last visit to the club, a night that had ended with several shots being taken at him. The man was enormous, a dark-skinned black man that looked as though he could bench press a small car. David gave his name, and the familiar man shot David a look that mirrored his own.

"Hey, now. I remember you. Now we ain't going to have any trouble tonight, are we?" He grinned, revealing several gold-capped teeth. He remembered the shoot-out David had been involved in at his last visit to the club.

"Nope. We're here purely for social reasons."

Jamie and Jenny had stepped in behind him. The man gave them a quick glance and re-checked the list he had in his hand.

"Stella put down your name David, and guests. Go on through." He opened the red velvet rope to allow the three to pass, garnering a small eruption of complaints from those in line. "Settle down. You want in, you wait. You piss me off and you'll be standing here all night."

Inside a young woman with spiky blonde hair and one arm

fully tattooed from shoulder to wrist checked their coats. She flirted with Jamie, going so far as to stroke his hand when she passed across the tickets. Leaning in she said something close to Jamie's ear that garnered a smile from him. He jerked his thumb back in David's direction and she looked up, lips pursed.

"Get a good offer?" David teased.

"Interesting," was all he had to say.

Inside, a line of topless women were dancing a techno-styled rendition of the can-can to the rapt attention of paying customers packed in like sardines. The three made their way to the closest bar, one of two on the main floor, and ordered drinks. David let his gaze wander over the crowd, catching sight of a few people he knew, before he spotted Stella standing near the door that accessed the dancers' dressing area. She wore tight leather pants and red halter top, with her long hair loose down her back.

David pointed in her direction and Jenny immediately went to speak with her. At the sight of the girl Stella threw her arms about her and pulled her into a crushing embrace. They were both laughing and looking one another over. After a few moments Jenny pointed back to where he and Jamie sat at the bar. David raised a hand, waving.

The lights dimmed, allowing the large ensemble to clear the stage. Filler music, heavy on the bass, began to thump. David could feel the vibrations crawl up his leg from the floor, a not unpleasant sensation. He'd remembered to turn the sound on his hearing aid down before they'd left, saving himself a painful reaction to the impressive decibel level.

The curtains snapped open. A woman was draped across a chair, long hair swaying and almost touching the stage. The lights caressed her body, trailing along every inch of her long, toned legs. She broke out into a re-imagining of the classic *Flashdance* scene, right down to the spray of water at the end of the number. It took David most of the dance before her realized he was watching Roberta. Her natural auburn hair had been covered with a long, pale-blonde wig and the elaborate makeup all but disguised her.

She turned as the water dripped to the stage, flashing

the crowd her smile before the darkness stole her away. The thunderous applause drowned out the music for a few moments, the passion of her followers a heavy, smothering presence.

Someone touched his arm and he found himself looking down on a beaming Stella and Jenny. Stella pulled David into a hug and rose to her tiptoes to place a kiss on his cheek. She followed suit with Jamie before stepping back to look them over.

"I'm so glad you guys could make it. Roberta told me you said you'd come, but I had my doubts," Stella said.

"I insisted," Jenny cut in.

"And look at this one. She sure cleaned up nice, huh?" Stella remarked, giving Jenny another quick hug. "I need a drink." Stella pointed to the beers David and Jamie were holding. "You guys good?"

"Yeah, for now. Thanks."

She ordered for her and left instructions for the bartenders to give David and company whatever they wanted on the house. The music had changed again, and the stage remained dark. Stella crooked her finger, indicating they should follow her. She led them to the second level, where several private tables were watched by men with physiques straight out of Greek mythology. Her table sat on a slightly raised platform, giving it a view of the whole club. She chatted with the man assigned to her area then walked up the three steps to take a seat.

They sat and chatted for a few minutes, aware of the interested, jealous gazes flickering in their direction. David felt out of place, but somehow also content. It was nice to be out with Jamie and Jenny, worries locked away for the night. Seeing Stella strong and happy, free of the demons of only a few short months ago, proved to be a tonic for the weariness he'd been plagued with.

Two women approached the table. Roberta had lost the wig and changed into a form-fitting unitard. She had her arm about the waist of another woman who was attracting stares from all that she passed. David marveled at the outfit she wore, which consisted of tiny thong briefs over black fishnets and a bra-like top that could barely contain her ample breasts. Her short dark hair was thick and pushed back from her face, highlighting her big blue eyes and scarlet- coloured lips. David had caught a glimpse of the Asian-themed scene covering her entire back as they approached. A row of silver rings ran along both ears. The pulsating lights flashed streams of colour over her milky skin, plenty of which was uncovered. If David had been into women he'd have had a massive boner.

The man by their table let the two women pass, giving them both a hungry look as he did so.

"Hi guys," Roberta said. Her companion gave her a poke in the ribs with her elbow.

"Oh, Jesus, sorry. David, Jamie, Jenny this is Jennafer, my girlfriend."

"That's Jennafer with an a," she said, giving them a thousand-watt smile.

David reached out to shake her hand, and found himself being pulled across the table by the front of his shirt instead. The girl was taller than Roberta and she had impressive four-inch heels on, allowing her to be almost eye-level with David. She leaned in, pressing her lips against David's and lingered. When she pulled back she reached for Jamie, then Jenny, giving them each a kiss in turn.

Stella laughed. "Jennafer's a bit friendly."

"Well nice to meet you. I gather you're a dancer?" David asked, indicating her outfit.

"Yes. You missed me actually. I'm done for the night, so it's time to get a drink."

The women sidled into the booth so that Jennafer was pressed next to Jamie. He gave David a perplexed look and grabbed his leg under the table. Stella got the attention of one of the waitresses, a tiny waif of a girl, and after a brief discussion placed an order for the table. The waitress returned a few minutes later with a man in tight pants and a bow-tie, both carrying trays with racks of shots, bottles of beer, and mixed drinks. The shots were passed about and consumed in quick succession, three per person, to be followed with beer and a rye and Coke. Within an hour David had consumed more alcohol than he normally would in months. He was a casual drinker, a beer or two to wind down after a tough day or a glass of wine with dinner.

Jamie's face was flushed. He grinned at David, eyes sparkling. His hand began to creep up David's thigh. "You look hot tonight."

David laughed. "You're drunk."

"Getting there, but that's not the point. This is fun. We need to get out more."

"Sure, I can agree with that, but to the strip club?" David asked. In his peripheral vision he could see that Roberta and Jennafer had begun to kiss and touch one another in ways that would no doubt get temperatures rising.

"Well no, I don't mean here specifically. I just want us to enjoy ourselves..." Jamie started kissing David, and his hand moved a little further north.

Confliction seized him. He wanted to give in to Jamie's touch, give himself over to the uninhibited, carefree part of himself that rarely came up for air. He knew the desire was spurred by the sexually liberated atmosphere and the alcohol he'd consumed, but did that matter? Jamie had been expressing a confidence and happiness with himself that David had never seen. His partner was opening himself in ways never allowed before, and it was heartening and inspiring to see. He needed to ride along on the voyage with him.

I think way too much. Funny how he was always thinking Jamie needed to loosen up, and now the shoe was on the other foot.

Several different dancers and staff stopped to chat or join them at the table for a drink. David lost count to how much he'd consumed, and as the evening wore on he found he didn't care. Myriad numbers graced the stage, from the purely artistic to the downright raunchy. Both David and Jamie enjoyed the military-themed number performed by a small group of chiseled men, a performance that ended with the collective dressed only in barely-there red briefs, the cut and fabric of which left little to the imagination. At one point David was even convinced to get out on the dance floor with their motley crew, though he didn't last more than a couple of songs. Jamie stayed with Jenny, while he returned to the table with Roberta and her very affectionate girlfriend.

After a good amount of time spent trying to ignore the women with their tongues down each other's throats, and with the consumption of several more drinks, David felt Nature's call. He let the two know where he was headed, then gladly escaped to the washroom. Standing brought on a wave of dizziness and he found he wasn't seeing too clearly. It took a lot of concentration to get to the washroom.

Once inside he splashed some cold water on his face and took several deep breaths. While standing at the urinal another man took the spot beside him and launched into a spiel about how much he'd been enjoying the show. The stranger seemed completely indifferent to the fact they were both standing there with their dicks in their hands, and if he hadn't been going on about the size of several dancer's breasts David would have thought he was being checked out.

As he wandered back into the main area of the club he realized he was good and truly wasted. He hadn't been this drunk since the night he'd been jumped, a parallel he didn't appreciate. When the room gave a lopsided whirl he mentally cut himself off. He stopped about midway to the table, leaning against the railing that overlooked the lower floor of the club. After a bit of searching he picked out Jamie and the others still dancing.

Without realizing he'd decided to follow through on the idea that had popped into his brain, David found himself on the first floor of the building, heading toward the front door. Fresh air would be a welcome relief to the intense heat of the enclosed space and the rush of negative, alcohol-induced sensations. A group of women sat at a table to his right, nothing more than a blur of faces and overly loud laughter, but something his brain was not quite able to process brought him to a standstill. He looked back, gaze locking on a woman staring back at him. Her lips were slightly parted, her posture tense.

Erin Gagnon.

As soon as she saw the recognition on David's face she bolted. She made a nimble bypass of a large group next to her table, who in that same instant started walking in David's direction. He scrambled out of their way, and in the confusion lost sight of Erin. He rushed to the front door, hoping she hadn't doubled back.

The cold air hit him like a brick wall. He blinked several times, eyes stinging from the drastic change in temperature. The cold crawled over his body, and he had to swallow to keep a hold on the bile burning in the back of his throat.

The crowd shifted and David caught sight of Erin making her way up the block without a coat over her short skirt and top. Her dark hair fanned out as she cast a nervous glance behind her. Her gaze travelled over those milling about the front of the club, but she didn't seem to see David. She turned back and kept moving, appearing as though she were going for a grouping of taxis parked on the next block.

David picked up his pace, having to push aside a few in his way, much to the other parties' irritation. One man even grabbed at him, forcing David to body check the guy to break free. Erin had just about reached the taxis when David caught up with her. He grabbed her shoulder, which she tried to jerk free of without even looking back.

"Cut it out," he said.

She stopped resisting and looked back at him with venom in her eyes. "Leave me the fuck alone."

"I don't think so. Not after the phone call and you running like this. We're going to talk."

Several people passed, one man looking back as though thinking about intervening. David let his hand drop, but Erin shooed them away with abrupt wave of her arm.

"Then get in the car. I'm freezing and I'm going home."

David had no choice but to follow or physically haul her back out of the taxi. He thought the former would be the most prudent choice of action, and the one least likely to have the police called on him. The driver most likely assumed they were a couple who'd gotten into a fight during their night out. Erin barked the address at him and the man didn't say boo, though he frequently cast glances back at them in his rear view mirror.

They sat in contemptuous, defensive silence for several blocks. David reached for his phone, ignoring Erin's obvious irritation. "Hey Jamie, it's David."

"Where the hell are you? I came back to the table and Roberta said you'd gone to the washroom and never came back." There was a slight slur to Jamie's words that on another night David might have found charming.

"I ran into Erin Gagnon and I'm in a cab back to her place as we speak."

"What?"

David cringed. He could almost see the steam coming from Jamie's ears. "Yeah, um sorry. I saw my chance and I took it."

Erin shot him a look that caused his blood pressure to spike.

"Whatever, tell me about it tomorrow. I'm not sure when I'm getting home. Jenny and I are having a pretty good time here."

"Noted. And you deserve it. I'll see you later."

"Yep. Bye."

He and Erin passed the remaining fifteen minutes of the ride in silence. When the car stopped Erin jumped out without paying. David forked over some money and followed her to her front door.

Erin's home was a duplex set on a corner lot, the structure set far back from the street. She'd left an outside light on, the weakness of the bulb casting her in a yellowish hue as she stood retrieving her key from her purse. She unlocked the door and entered, leaving it open behind her. David followed her inside.

She deposited her purse on a long shallow table to the left of the door. Her heels were kicked off and left helter-skelter on the faded linoleum. David wiped his shoes on the mat and continued straight down the hallway where he'd seen Erin going. The passage opened onto a family room, where he found Erin sprawled on a couch. Her eyes were closed and she was pinching the bridge of her nose as if to ward off an oncoming headache. David was pretty certain he'd have a doozy of one himself later that morning.

Erin had turned on a small table lamp, which cast a murky circle of light about the inner space of the room. A shadowy glare to the far end of the room David took to be a set of sliding doors leading to the backyard. He fumbled his way to a chair across the table from where Erin lounged and dropped himself in it. His stomach knotted in protest to the sudden movement.

After a few minutes his eyes began to adjust and he was able to make out more details of the room. A tall cabinet stood beside the couch, full of books and other knickknacks. A series of framed photographs lined the top of the structure. Erin still wasn't speaking, so with an inward groan David pushed himself to standing and, with careful steps, made his way over to the photos.

As he'd suspected they were all of Jake and Robert. The smiles and innocent expressions were a jarring contrast to the .crime scene photos sitting on his desk. It was almost more than his alcohol-soaked brain could bear, as though the boys were staring back at him, accusing. He felt like a colossal douchebag standing in the home of their mother and wondered if he shouldn't turn around and march his butt out.

"You going to ask me something or not?"

Erin's voice snapped David back. "Yeah, of course."

She pulled herself up on one elbow, staring at him. The contempt leaked from her pores. "Then ask."

"Do you know who killed your boys?"

"No."

"Do you suspect someone?"

"I don't know."

David had started to feel unsteady on his feet so he returned to the chair. "Why haven't you done anything? I mean why not go to the police and tell them what you think?"

"I have no proof," she answered. She patted the space about her, looking for something. With a sigh she went back to the hallway. When she'd returned she had her purse in hand, and once seated again pulled a pack of cigarettes and a lighter from its depths. She lit one up and took a deep drag.

"Fuck proof. You're the mother, the police would listen to you."

"Hardly. The police messed everything up. I don't even think they cared who killed my boys. I could tell what they all thought of me."

"Is that why you went to Vukovic? You think he could help you out?"

The question obviously startled her; she almost dropped the

cigarette into her lap. It took great effort to guide her shaking hand to the ashtray to flick of the ash. "I don't know what you mean."

"I saw him and some other guy come over here Friday night."

"You fucking spying on me? Jesus, what gives you the right."

"I'm trying to find the truth. That gives me every right."

"He don't have nothing to do with anything. I knew him long before my boys were killed."

"Yeah, how?"

Anger replaced her shock, and she sneered at him. "I met him at a bar. People do that you know. We still see each other every now and again. What consenting adults do with each other is no one else's business. I knew people wouldn't understand when all this was going on, so I never said anything."

"Fine, if he has nothing to do with this, who are you covering for?"

"No one."

"Bullshit. Tell me what's going on Erin." The room was spinning, his temperature rising with every passing minute. He didn't know how much longer he could stand the heat mixed with the offensive cigarette smoke, neither of which helped with the large amount of alcohol sloshing about in his stomach.

"The only thing opening my mouth would do is get me killed."

The seriousness of her statement gave David a sudden chill. "What's that supposed to mean?"

She smoked for a few moments and David waited her out. "I was doing a lot of stupid shit back then. Chuck had bailed on me a few years before, never helping out with the boys, always skipping out on the support. I started doing pretty much anything that would give my life some pleasure. Drugs, sex, you know."

"I can understand that. You got a bum deal like lots of mothers do. "

"Yeah, but the boys should have been what made me happy, don't you get that? They were wonderful and I didn't appreciate my time with them at all. I was so fucking angry and resentful all the time. You know I actually considered giving them up? Back to their dad, their grandparents, whatever could be worked out. What the fuck was I thinking?"

"You're losing me here."

Her face snapped up, eyes as sad as any David had ever seen staring out at him. The makeup around her eyes had smeared and the thin straps on her top had slipped off her shoulders, making her seem even more tragic. "I don't want to talk about this. I made my peace and now I'm happy to just get through each day as they come. I know I did wrong and I have no right to expect life to give me any more chances."

"Everyone deserves a chance Erin. So you smoked some pot, slept with a couple of guys. That hardly makes you a pariah."

"Nothing you can say will make me feel any better about this."

"You don't think freeing two innocent men would make you feel better? C'mon, that's bullshit. Tell me who you think did this."

David's heart thumped and his skin felt clammy. He licked his lips, desperate for a glass of water, but he didn't dare break the momentum. Erin lit up another cigarette and began to tap her bare heel against the carpet.

"I told you I don't know who did this! The courts think those boys did, so who am I to say different. Please go away!"

"I'm not going anywhere Erin. You can talk to me and let me dig up the proof or I can turn this over to the police. I can guarantee I'll be much nicer to work with."

"So now you're threatening me. Nice. Like I haven't had enough of this shit in my life."

David was drunk, angry and away from his warm bed. He wanted nothing more than to reach across and give the woman a good shake. He made himself count to five, which allowed his blood pressure to slip down into normal range.

"I'm not threatening you. I'm trying to figure out what happened to your kids. Why won't you help me?"

"I can't help you. It's done, they're gone." A long section of ash crumbled from the end of her cigarette, floating to the floor like soot-coloured snow.

A thought came to him. "I know about Sam."

Erin's empty hand clenched into a fist. "What about him?"

"I know you were sleeping with him. I spoke with him and he told me everything. I know he was here the night the boys were killed."

Erin stubbed out the cigarette with short, hard thrusts. She settled back in the couch, arms wrapped around her torso, but she didn't respond. He took her silence as confirmation.

"Look I understand you didn't want to open yourself up to anything else, you know, for sleeping with an underage boy, but this information could have made a huge difference in the investigation. Sam and Jasmine were in the park that night. They were there when the killer dumped the bo...boys."

"They didn't see anything. It wouldn't have made any difference."

"But Sam dropped the lighter, not Nathan. That at least puts some doubt on their guilt. C'mon you have to know this!"

"I can't help you."

"What the hell do you know, Erin?"

"I don't know anything!" Erin burst into angry tears. She kicked at the table, knocking aside a pile of magazines and dumping the contents of the ashtray to the floor. Her hands trembled and she would not meet David's eye.

He bit the inside of his cheek to try and force himself to calm down, but the pain was just another irritation. David did what he could to keep his tone in check. "Tell me, Erin. I will help you, I promise."

The reaction took a long time coming. David sat still and silent, letting Erin cry until she seemed to have exhausted herself. From under the couch Erin withdrew a crumpled accordion folder, and after pressing it to her chest as though clinging to her firstborn, placed it on the table. She opened it, and after flipping through several pages pulled out a group of photos. She removed the paperclip holding them together and shuffled through a few until she found what she was looking for. She stared at the photo for several minutes before handing it across to David.

He took the eight by ten, not surprised to find one of the

photos from the crime scene package. He had a copy of the very same photo in his own file. The subject matter Erin had singled out did surprise him, though he wasn't certain why. The item had triggered speculation on his part as well, though there had really been no indication that it had been any more telling than any of the other pieces recovered from the area around the bodies. He tapped the well-worn photo against his hand, thinking.

"What about the belt buckle Erin?" he asked.

"I think I recognize it. At least I did then."

"Okay, so who do you think it belongs to?"

She all but choked on the words when she answered. "Mark Ester."

"Sandra's ex-husband? How can you be sure?"

"'Cause I seen him wearing it."

David didn't know what he'd expected her to say, but the implication couldn't quite compute. Sure, Mark had seemed like a class-A jerk when he'd spoken with him, and the accusations of infidelity hadn't scored him any points, but David found it hard to wrap his head around the man killing two innocent children. Then again, it was difficult to imagine anyone being capable of such depravity.

"Okay, I'll bite. Why were you with him?"

Erin sighed. "I told you I was doing some stupid things back then."

"So Mark was one of the things you were doing?" When she gave him a sharp look he added, "Sorry. You know what I mean."

"Yeah, we were on and off for over a year. By that time he'd been separated from Sandra for about six months, though it had started before he left. I don't know, he was good-looking and he came after me. I guess I was flattered, at first. The sex was good anyway. Then after the marriage ended Mark changed. He got weirdly controlling and possessive, like showing up unannounced, hounding me at work. It got old really fast. Especially when he started putting the pressure on to send the boys to their dad's. I guess that was one of the big issues in his relationship with Sandra, he just wasn't into kids. He didn't want any of his own, and after the years with Nathan he didn't want to look after anyone else's again."

"There's a big difference between not liking kids and killing them."

"We'd had a huge fight a couple weeks before this happened. He caught me with Angus and the two of them got into it. I told him to get lost, made it real clear it was over. I remember the look in his eye, like he couldn't believe I'd want to end it with him. His eyes were dead, like looking at pure evil. It gives me the chills now ten years later just thinking about this. He called me a whore, and told me no man would ever want to be with me, especially not with a couple of kids."

"Did you talk with him again before the murders?"

"No, but he called me a few days after. He told me... I got what I deserved. He fucking laughed at me, the sick bastard. I hung up and I've never spoke to him again."

David could see she was telling the truth. Every bit of her body language spoke to her experience, and how the conversation was forcing her to relive the pain and shame. "I still don't get why he'd do this. I mean why not knock you around or come trash your house or something. From what little I know about the man it seems more his style to go out and screw everything with a heartbeat to make himself feel better, not something like this."

"He's a fucked-up man, David. His whole sense of himself is based on how adored he feels. He can't understand why anyone would reject him."

"You really think he killed your boys?"

She shook her head, crying again. "I don't know for sure, but if I had to guess that's who I'd look at."

He looked at the photo again. "And this is his?"

"It looks just like one he was wearing near the end of our relationship. I couldn't swear on it, but I'm fairly certain."

"You're not giving me a lot here Erin. No real proof, no admissions of guilt, no witnesses, nothing I can take to the police. I mean yeah we can say you think this is Mark's belt buckle, but after all this time we'd be hard pressed to get the case reopened with just that."

"That's why I've kept my mouth shut. If he killed my boys, can you imagine what he'd do to me for going to the cops. And I have a sister, and parents, two nephews. I don't want anyone else close to me getting hurt." She paled at the thought.

David didn't know what to say. As a police officer and as a private detective he'd been known to go with a hunch, but he just couldn't seem to get a handle on Erin's revelation. Maybe once the alcohol had cleared his system he'd feel differently.

"I'm going to work on this. I may need to ask you some more questions, so if you're going to be away please let me know."

"Don't let Mark know I said anything. Please."

"I'll be as discreet as I can."

He left her on the couch, softly crying. Shadows clung to her small form, like some ghoulish manifestation of her inner torment. It was only after he'd made it down the front steps that he remembered he didn't have a way to get home. He pulled his cell phone out and called a taxi.

It was nearly two a.m. when he made it home. Jamie had yet to arrive and the empty house unnerved him. After scrubbing his teeth he crawled into bed and fell into a heavy sleep.

CHAPTER 16

David peeled his eyes open the next morning with caution. He expected the light in the room, what little there was, to be a painful assault. Jamie had come in sometime after three, rousing David from sleep with the bump of the front door, drunken laughter and a difficult voyage up the stairs. It had been a significant struggle for him to get his shoes off, and after the accomplishment he had fallen onto the bed, asleep within minutes.

Jamie was still sleeping. He was fully dressed except for his shoes, and hadn't even managed to get under the covers. David folded his side of the duvet over his partner and shuffled to the bathroom. After relieving himself he took a good long stare in the mirror. Despite the visible bags, he didn't look too bad. At least he hadn't come home with any new bumps and bruises. Or bullet holes.

He peeked in the guest room before heading downstairs. Jenny was passed out in a similar fashion to Jamie, her shoes and purse lying where she must have dropped them by the bed. He pulled the blanket from the foot of the bed across her and closed the door behind him. Downstairs he went straight for the coffee, standing by with cup in hand until enough had brewed to fill it. The brew touched his tongue like liquid heaven.

It was early yet, not quite nine o'clock. He felt unsteady, dehydrated and achy, much as he should have for what he'd consumed the night before. He expected Jamie and Jenny to be a little green around the gills whenever they made an appearance. Truth was Jamie had been so tightly wound for much of his life that he needed to let loose. Didn't mean David wouldn't tease him though.

He thought about eating some cereal, but the idea of milk made his stomach clench. Instead he grabbed a couple pieces of leftover pizza, refilled his coffee and sat at the table, which often doubled as his home office. He knew he could use the room Jamie had converted into an actual office, complete with computer, but he liked him to have a sense of his own space. They were sharing the home after all.

After his stomach had settled and his head began to clear, the revelations from Erin flooded back. He replayed the conversation over in his mind, trying to draw out the nuances and the body language she'd displayed. No doubt about it, she'd believed what she said. The woman had been truly fearful and full of remorse. David grabbed a pad and jotted down everything he could remember. He also added his notes from his talk with Burgess, and kept coming back to the same conclusion: he needed to take a trip.

He tried Sandra's house, getting her answering machine. He didn't feel what he had to say was something to leave in a message, so he hung up. He needed something to keep him busy so he thought he'd start the laundry and grab some groceries. Sweats seemed suitable for the local Loblaws, and a half-hour later he was parking in the nearly empty lot. The only people shopping at such an hour were senior citizens and mothers with children under two. He stocked up, taking his time to read labels and compare prices, something he didn't usually have the patience for. Satisfied he'd covered all the bases, David paid and returned home.

As he came in the side door he heard the radio playing, so he knew at least one of the party animals was up. He came around the corner with bags in hand to find Jamie sitting at the table, hands clasped around a mug of coffee. A bottle of Tylenol sat before him. He turned bleary eyes in David's direction and tried to smile, but the effort caused a shudder. David knew the feeling well. He'd had a couple years of hard partying while working his way through college.

He let Jamie sit in his misery while he brought in the rest of the groceries. When he started to put things away he ordered Jamie to take a long, hot shower and promised when he was done he'd have brunch waiting for him. He cooked up a huge pan of bacon, made some French toast and threw on a fresh pot of coffee. Jamie arrived as he was filling mugs, and he marched right to the table. He was barely seated when he started to shovel food into his mouth.

"Feeling better?" David asked after their plates were cleared.

"Yep. Tylenol's starting to work and the food and coffee took the edge of. Wow, I don't know how people do that on a regular basis."

"You build up a tolerance."

"No thanks. Once in a while is more than enough for me." He took another sip of coffee.

"You were having fun, nothing wrong with that."

Jamie said, "Sure, having fun is fine, but I have to be careful with my reputation. You know how it is if the wrong thing gets back to work."

"I don't have to worry about that stuff now."

Jamie gave a thin smile. "Right. Anyway I'm not a big partier."

"I don't know after last night. I wish I'd had a video camera to get you dancing with Jenny and the others. It was awesome."

"Stop it."

"It's fun. You looked hot."

"Seriously, cut it out."

David let it go. He poured himself yet another cup of coffee and decided to pick Jamie's brain while he had his full attention.

"So are you coherent enough to go over some stuff about the case with me?"

"Sure." He yawned. "What have you got?"

"Well, my talk with Erin turned up some interesting stuff."

"Like…"

"She was having an affair with Mark Ester for one."

"Nathan's dad?"

David nodded. "And Jonas Vukovic, who I guess she's still involved with."

"Seriously. Who hasn't this woman slept with?"

David ignored the catty remark, even though he'd had a similar reaction. "Mark was the step-dad. Yeah, I guess the guy slept around, has quite the ego from what Erin says. And she thinks it might be his belt buckle that the police found in the park."

Jamie made a noise somewhere between coughing and choking. "You're kidding! Why the hell didn't she say something before?"

"She's scared. She thinks he might try and hurt her or her family. I guess he threatened her and called after the kids were killed to tell her she got what she deserved."

"This is crazy. The guy was never even considered, I mean he was only spoken with because he was a parent. There was no reason to think anything else. Why would he act like that?"

"Erin seems to think it's because she ended things with him. And what if she's wrong? Maybe he was just being an asshole and really has nothing to do with this. There's no proof and no one else has ever suspected him."

"Wow." Jamie leaned back in his chair, pulling at his lower lip as he did when lost in thought.

"Could still have something to do with Vukovic. His ratting them out seems personal to me. Then again, he could just be some sicko who likes to screw with people's lives. "

"Could be."

"So this brings me back to the conversation I had with Burgess." When Jamie made a face as though he didn't understand what David meant, he clarified, "The guy who called in about the fliers."

"He identified one of the guys Detective Brown gave you, right?"

"Right."

"But David, just because one of these guys got recognized doesn't make him the Janko's man. That's quite a stretch."

"The way Burgess tells it the guy, Josiah, liked to hang out in the right area and knew about Janko's. This is a good a lead as I've had, Jamie."

"Didn't you say he thinks the guy is in Vancouver?"

"Yep, that's the catch. I need to sell the trip to Sandra."

"You need more proof."

"Like what?"

"I don't know. Maybe the Janko's staff? People saw this guy, right?"

"Sure. I can try that. Good idea. You wanna come with?"

"No way. I'm going back to bed for a while." He pushed his chair back from the table with a sigh. Coming around to David's side Jamie gave him a kiss and started to shuffle away.

"Want some company?"

He left Jamie to nap and headed over to the office where he had his files. He put in a call to Mike the manager, not surprised when he didn't answer. The man did work nights, so he was most likely still asleep. He left a message. In the interest of being thorough David looked up the other staff members from the names and numbers Manny Janko had given him, who had been on when the Janko's man had come in. He got a hold of Martha Van Koughnett, the cook, but didn't connect with the waitress. Martha agreed to meet with him after he explained what he wanted.

A call back to Janko's connected him with Manny, who confirmed that Mike would be in later that evening. David asked that he let him know he'd be stopping by. Martha had already agreed to meet him, so he changed the location, thereby killing two birds with one stone. He passed the remaining hours of the afternoon with his grandmother. Rhea always had an unlimited amount of errands and a penchant for company while doing them, and enjoyed being chauffeured by her grandson. He loved her dearly, and found it hard to say no to her.

When it got close to suppertime he dropped his grandmother off and headed over to Janko's Diner. Manny was at the front, speaking with a hostess who thankfully wasn't Lila. He gave David a nod and pointed toward the counter. Mike was nowhere to be seen, but a middle-aged woman sat there, drinking a cup of coffee. From the back she reminded David of his high school librarian, who'd had the same halo of fuzzy hair, and shoulders to rival those of a professional football player.

He tapped her on the shoulder. She turned and looked at him blankly.

"Are you Martha?" he asked.

"Yes. Oh, you must be David." She offered her hand, which he shook. When she smiled she revealed a large gap in her front teeth and dimples deep enough to fall into.

"Right. Is Mike in the back?"

"Yup, he just went back." She stood up and made eye contact with the cook who could be seen through the cut-out in the wall behind the counter. "Send Mike out."

The man nodded and disappeared from view. After a few moments the door opened and Mike appeared. He gestured toward an empty booth and David and Martha followed him over to it.

"Thanks for meeting with me."

"No worries. I hope I can help," Mike said.

David made eye contact with the man, and like their previous encounter he felt strongly that he wasn't playing with a full deck. Martha sipped her coffee.

"Right. Okay I have a photo I'd like you guys to look at. I think it might be the man who came in here the night of the murders."

He pulled the photo from the envelope he'd brought and laid it on the table top. Both pairs of eyes scanned the face before them, Mike with his eyebrows scrunched low and Martha still sipping at her coffee.

Mike made a series of faces, almost like involuntary tics and then gave David his attention. "It sure looks like the guy. Hard to say for sure 'cause he had a hat on and him acting all crazy, but I think so."

"Me too." Martha said. She closed her eyes for a minute as though trying to recall the incident. Mike watched her intently and, seeming to think he should follow suit, squeezed his own eyes shut. The only thing that would have made the image more perfect would have been if a large dunce cap had materialized on his head.

"Yes," Martha said. Mike opened his eyes again when she started talking. "I think this is the man. Pretty sure he came in other times too, late at night. Sometimes by himself, sometimes with a friend. He usually just bought coffee, but if he had some money he'd get fries or a piece of pie. Never talked much, at least not from what I could see from the kitchen." She pointed to the cut-out.

It took the utmost restraint for David to not jump from his seat and do a little happy dance. "Thanks. You've been very helpful. I have to advise you if this goes any further the police may want to question you."

"Sure. You know where to find me," Martha said.

He left them in the booth together, feeling as though he'd finally made some headway. The next obstacle would be locating the man, who may not even be alive any longer. Jamie was right, it was going to be a tough sell to Sandra.

Sitting on the plane with Burgess at his side, David couldn't quite believe what had transpired in the previous eight hours. Sandra had been far from difficult to convince. All he'd had to say is he might have identified the Janko's man and she was writing off a cheque to cover his travel expenses. She didn't even bat an eye when he'd asked to bring Burgess along. Of course he hadn't been completely honest with her. His suspicions about her ex-husband had been kept under wraps, and though he'd never directly said as such, he knew she believed that the Janko's man was a suspect rather than a potential witness.

He'd been lucky enough to connect with Jimmy before he'd left as well, using the man's resources to his advantage. Jimmy had put him in touch with a detective in Vancouver who would be able to help guide his search. Having a police professional bridge the gap would be extremely helpful, and David hoped the man's local knowledge would cut his time down significantly.

That was how he found himself on a three-a.m. flight to Vancouver, armed with little more than a photo and an intense desire to succeed. They landed a few hours later, in the early morning hours when the sun had just begun its ascent. The horizon was bathed in shades of purple, which David watched dissolve into a soft gray-blue sky as they waited for the car rental booth to open.

After checking in to their hotel he and Burgess grabbed breakfast at a nearby restaurant and then jumped back in the car to get to their meeting with their police contact, Detective Marin Breckinridge. Burgess proved a worthy navigator, a must in a sprawling metropolis like the port city of Vancouver.

After scouring the multi-level lot David spotted an empty space near one of the staircases leading to the main level of the actual police department building. The temperature was much milder than the one they'd left in Ontario, with no snow or ice to be seen. The proximity to the Pacific Ocean had a moderating effect that David could appreciate.

At the front desk they announced who they were and the person they were to meet. The staff member regarded them with suspicion and told them to take a seat while she tried to track the detective down. Even at the early morning hour the space bustled with activity. David found the nature and tone of the passing conversations easy to connect with, like a phantom limb of his former work life. Burgess by contrast seemed mildly anxious and unsettled.

When Detective Breckinridge appeared he greeted them warmly, offering his massive paw to shake with both men. He was a giant of a man, easily six and half feet and thick with muscle. David would have bet money he had to have his shoes specially made. Yet almost in defiance of his burly, hyper-masculine stature his face was smooth and round, like a man in his early twenties. He had thin, pale hair and looked like he wouldn't have been able to grow a mustache to save his life.

As they meandered back to his office he chatted with the men about their trip. David noticed he was quick to smile and projected a warm, easygoing charm, which attracted many waves, nods and hellos from fellow employees. His presence was a breath of fresh air in a profession that often led to a disconnect with humanity at large.

The end of their voyage brought them to a large space on the third floor that had been divided into smaller sections filled with clusters of desks. Around the perimeter were several private offices, one of which Detective Breckinridge led them to. He took his seat behind the desk, leaving David and Burgess to the ones before it, a couple of mismatched chairs that looked as though they'd been brought in from some other area. David noticed a file with a picture of Josiah Maitland on top.

Detective Breckinridge moved the photo aside and cracked open the file. "So you think this Josiah Maitland is somewhere in Vancouver?"

"Yes, that's right," David answered.

"And what is your reasoning?" he asked, still smiling.

"Well Burgess here is an acquaintance of Josiah's and he told him that he had a daughter here. Though he's transient, he seems to have favourite locations, Vancouver and Toronto being the top choices."

"Yep, that's what he told me anyway," Burgess said.

Detective Breckinridge nodded enthusiastically as David spoke. "You're right on the money there my friend. Not only does Josiah Maitland have a daughter here, he himself was born in our fair city. He's been in the system on and off since his teens. Nothing terrible, it's more sad than criminal in my opinion. The guy's been diagnosed as manic-depressive with paranoid tendencies. When he's on his meds he goes off the radar and when he's not on them he has his run-ins, you know, people calling in for odd behaviour, sleeping in public parks, panhandling, that type of stuff. Not known to be violent."

"So you know where we can find him?" David asked.

"I didn't say that. He was picked up last year for public intoxication. The daughter came and bailed him out, so we had her contact info on record. I took the liberty of calling her, and she says she hasn't seen her dad since shortly after that incident, but she suspects he's still in the city somewhere. Something about there being monsters in your neck of the woods."

"Yes, I've heard that before. Something I need to clarify."

"And this has to do with these murders of yours?"

"That's what I need to find out. I suspect that Josiah witnessed something that really traumatized him, and since he already had mental health issues it was just too much to process."

"You think he saw the murders?"

"No, I think he may have seen the kids' bodies being dumped in the park. The spot's a favourite for homeless folks and kids messing around."

"I see. Well, Yolanda had no problem with me giving you her number, and I've drawn up a list of some places that should help you out, areas where Josiah's been picked up before, shelters and meal providers, that kind of thing." He handed over a couple of sheets of paper, including a more recent mug shot.

"I don't suppose you've run him with social assistance?"

"I did, and he is not drawing a cheque anywhere at this time."

David smiled. "Wow, you've gone above and beyond here, Detective Breckinridge. I appreciate the effort."

"No problem, I'm happy to help, and please call me Marin." He pulled a card from the tray on his desk, and scribbled some numbers on the back. "That's my extension here and my cell number on the back. Give me a call if you have any trouble."

"Thanks. I owe you one. Anytime you have something in Toronto I'm you're guy."

"Good to know. And good luck."

When they reached the lobby David put a call through to Yolanda Lake, Josiah's daughter. To his surprise she answered after a few rings. "Hello."

"Hello there. Is this Yolanda?"

"Yes, can I ask who's calling?"

"Yes, my name is David Lloyd. A Detective Breckinridge spoke with you recently."

"Yes, that's right. Last night."

"Is it possible to come by and speak with you about your father?"

"Right now?"

"Times against me I'm afraid. I only have a couple of days in Vancouver."

She sighed. "All right then. Come on over." She recited an address that David jotted down.

In the car the men located the street on the map and set off. Like Toronto, Vancouver was vast and sprawling, the home of many neighbourhoods. Yolanda's home was actually located in Victoria, a separate city on nearby Vancouver Island. With the drive and ferry over it was more than an hour before they reached their destination. At last they pulled into the driveway of a gorgeous two-story home that many Canadians would love to own but could not afford. In the drive sat a new Grand Caravan.

David parked and the two men went to the front door. He had barely touched the bell when the door opened. An attractive, light-skinned black woman stood in the doorway with a finger pressed to her lips. The men stepped inside.

She led the men down a hallway of highly polished dark wood, passing a family room where a group of pre-school aged children sat watching a video. A baby gate had been locked across the open entryway to keep the little ones in check. They continued down the hallway until it opened up into a gorgeous gourmet kitchen complete with double ovens, a wine fridge and a granite island large enough to host parties on.

Yolanda was dressed in a pair of jeans and a long-sleeved knit top. Her hair was loose, with a soft curl that fell midway down her back. She had a tray with coffee and fixings waiting on the table.

"Please sit down. I've got the kids set up with a movie so they should be okay for a little bit. I run a home daycare, which you probably figured out." She poured three cups as the men took a seat.

"I'm David Lloyd, this is my associate Burgess Knowles. I appreciate you taking time to talk with me."

They shook hands. "I don't mind, that's not the issue. I'm sure you can appreciate that this has nothing to do with wanting to help and everything to do with my relationship with my father. Or lack thereof might be more accurate."

"I'm very sorry to stir up bad feelings. My only concern here is finding the murderer of two little boys."

"Yes, Detective Breckinridge gave me a brief explanation of what's going on. I can't for the life of me understand how a human being could be capable of such violence."

David hadn't formed any preconceived notions of what Yolanda would be like, but he felt surprised nonetheless with her eloquence and articulation. With a father like Josiah he supposed he thought she'd be somehow more lower class, rougher.

"I've worked in law enforcement and as a private detective for many years and I've seen a lot of horrible things, and believe me it never gets easier," David said.

"My husband says the same thing. He's in the military over at the Canadian Forces Base Esquimalt." She pushed across the tray with the cream and sugar.

David gladly loaded up his cup. "Oh, a military man. Have you moved around a lot?"

"A few times. Mostly within Canada, but once overseas. We've been back in B.C. for the past seven years."

"I see. Well I guess there's no polite way to get into this so I'm just going to start asking questions."

"Ask away."

"Do you know where your father is? Or where he might be?"

"I don't know where he is, but I feel pretty certain he's still in Vancouver."

"Why is that?"

"They last time I saw him he'd been picked up for being intoxicated. He'd actually passed out on someone's front lawn. I got him into a place where he could dry out and get back on his medication. He stayed there for about two weeks and I talked with him a few times. He told me that there was something evil living in Toronto and that he'd seen it. Last time he'd been back he saw it again, whatever that means. So he's been here ever since."

Burgess nodded in David's direction, agreeing with Yolanda's description.

"Is this unusual not to have spoken to him for so long?" David asked.

Yolanda let out a soft giggle. "Not at all with my father. He's not what you'd call stable."

"So your relationship is not that close?"

"Not at all. I didn't even know the man till I was sixteen. My mom was a drug addict, they met on the streets and she got pregnant. He split and she raised me on her own for a few years.

I got taken away from her when I was four, went into foster care then on my own when I was sixteen. I decided to go looking for him then. It took a couple of years but I finally found him at one of the area shelters. He's been in and out of my life since then, mostly out."

"I'm sorry to hear about this Yolanda. I can't imagine how tough it must have been for you as a kid."

"It was terrible, believe me. All the kids used to make fun of me, and I was always being shuffled around. I made it work for me though. I studied really hard, and got into university. I got my Bachelor of Ed. I had a baby two years ago, so I took a break from teaching to be home with her."

"Wow, I'm impressed."

"Well sometimes life gives you a kick in the ass, but you can't let it keep you down."

"True enough. Can you give us any insight into your dad's issues?"

Her lips give an almost unperceivable quiver. "He's got a lot. He's bi-polar, with paranoid thinking. Also addictions issues and suspected ADHD. Plus now that he's getting up in age he's had some heart problems and I suspect maybe diabetes. As you can imagine he doesn't eat well and doesn't see a doctor regularly. He's not a well man by any stretch of the imagination. I have escaped his demons, thank God. I can't imagine living the way he does."

"Me either. It's very sad."

"Now you don't think my father is involved in this, correct? You think he may have been a witness?" Yolanda asked.

"That's right. I really think he saw the bodies being dropped off. I think he was sleeping in the park that night, and it was a classic case of wrong place, wrong time."

She took a long sip of her coffee, eyes lowered. "I'm so glad to hear you say that. After everything I don't think I could bear finding out my father is a child killer."

David pulled out the list Marin had given them. "Can you look this over and tell me if there are any other places we should check. Maybe some names of friends, even dealers, anything that might help us find your dad?"

Yolanda looked over the neatly typed list over. "I can add a few." She grabbed a pen and jotted down a couple of places, including the clinic where he'd gotten help. "The counselor's name was Sally Painter. If you give her my name she should speak with you. I know places can be stubborn about confidentiality."

"Thanks for this, Yolanda. I'll make sure to let you know if we track him down."

She walked the men to the door and bid them good luck in their search. David supposed the best thing for Yolanda would be if Josiah had disappeared for good. Though she'd made no overt statement about her relationship, he imagined the man gave her more grief than warm fuzzies. Like Jenny, blood relations didn't always bring happiness to one's life.

Inside the car Burgess finally spoke up. "This is a wild goose chase isn't it?"

"Could be," David agreed as he looked the list and then the map over. "Let's be positive about this though. It could be the difference between life in prison or freedom for two men."

"I'm game. Let's do this."

CHAPTER 17

By the end of their second day in Vancouver David and Burgess were both exhausted, starving, and frustrated to no end. They took a detour into a local greasy spoon to refuel.

David read the menu, practically salivating at the list of homey comfort foods. He settled on Salisbury steak with potatoes, heavy on the gravy. Burgess took a more traditional route with a bacon cheeseburger and fries. They both took a beer with their meals, and not a word of conversation passed between them until their plates were cleared and they'd sent the waitress off to get them both a piece of cherry pie and ice cream.

Pulling out the list, David crossed off various places they'd already reviewed as he ate his pie. He was so overrun with sugar and fat he had to fight back a moan.

"So, getting to the nitty-gritty here," Burgess said. He was pushing his fork around the plate, careful to get every crumb.

"Yep. We've done most of the shelters and soup kitchens, the Sally Anns, and the addictions clinic. We'll have to finish up with the shelters tomorrow. Maybe we can hit a few parks tonight."

"Sure. It's only nine," he said after peeking at his watch. "Lots of time yet."

"Damn this pie is good. I'm getting another piece to go."

The majority of the shelters they hit could not give a definitive answer on whether Josiah had ever stayed there or not, and the two who thought they did recognize him also said he hadn't been there in some time. The clinic had not had any contact with Josiah since he'd left against medical advice some ten months before. They were able to verify that he'd taken his prescription with him, but trying to track down where and when he might have had it filled would have been an exercise in futility.

David settled up with the waitress, leaving her a nice tip, and the men returned to the rental car. By one thirty they were both done. They hadn't found Josiah or spoken with anyone who knew or would admit they knew the man. The car was parked at the curb of a street close to a park that had been identified as a spot popular with transients. There was quick access to nearby restaurants, public restrooms and places to score drugs. In their final encounter a man with a patch over one eye had pulled a knife on them, which David took as a sign to call it a night.

As they hit the sidewalk, headed back to the car, a cluster of people on the next block caught their attention. All about them were businesses closed for the night or catering to questionable clientele, either way no one seemed to have taken notice of activity in plain view. A man was passed out on the sidewalk while several others rifled through his coat and the contents of his bag that had spilled on the ground next to him. One person was even removing the man's boots.

"Hey!" David called out. He started to run at the group.

"Wait David. Be careful," Burgess said. When David kept going he added, "Fuck, wait up."

Seeing two men rushing towards them sent the group scattering. The man on the ground didn't budge. When David knelt down next to him the fumes coming from the man made David gag. Two of the scavengers had stopped across the street and were staring at David and Burgess, waiting to see what would happen next. David stood up and crossed the street in their direction. He was about halfway across when recognition hit him like a sledge hammer.

"Jesus, it's him. Burgess, it's Josiah."

One of the men made eye contact with David, fear and surprise frozen on his face. The man had lost weight and there was significantly more grey in his hair and beard, but there was no doubt in David's mind it was Josiah. They stared at one another for a heartbeat, then Josiah took off. For an old guy he could motor.

David threw the keys back at Burgess. "Go get the car."

He took off after Josiah, thankful the streets were sparsely populated at that hour. Even so he bumped into a few not-so-happy people, one who grabbed his arm and connected a punch to the back of his head. He broke free and kept going despite the nauseating throb in his brain and his desire to retaliate. Up ahead Josiah took a hard right.

Coming to the area he'd seen Josiah enter, David realized it wasn't an actual street, but a cut-through between two large warehouses. Doors lined the sides of both structures, along with sets of metal stairs to the upper levels. He tried the first few doors, finding them locked, and assumed the rest were as well. David slowed his pace. The dark between the intermittent lights was so intense he could barely see farther than the length of his arm. He listened, hearing nothing but his own breathing and a few snatches of drifting conversation from the nearby street. He crept further, on alert to anything that might suddenly come at him.

A crash up ahead made him burst into a run once again. Something brushed his side and then he found himself toppling over a large solid object that he struck with his shins. Cursing he picked himself up and kept going. Ahead a small, steady beam of light beckoned. He headed toward it, figuring Josiah to have done the same. If he had ducked into an unlocked door or had hidden in the shadows somewhere only to double back after David had passed, then he was screwed.

At the source of the light, a large orb dangling from a wire that ran diagonally between two buildings, David paused to get his bearings. The street he'd come from was lost in the darkness. Ahead seemed to be another street, and two smaller alleyways transected the one that he stood in. He could have gone three different ways.

"Fuck!" he said and took off running. He choose to keep going straight through to the far side of the block, or what he believed to be the street running parallel to the one he'd come from. As he skidded out onto the sidewalk the rental car raced past. David started running after it, hoping he didn't lose them as the car screeched around the corner.

He could taste his heartbeat as he ran. His shoes pounded along the uneven concrete. The few people in the area stared as he ran past, but did nothing to interfere. He rounded the corner too quickly, catching his hip on the corner of a building and almost toppling himself. He flailed his arms to keep his balance and kept running. The car was stopped about a block ahead with the driver's side door open. He skidded to a slower pace as he reached the vehicle, the sound coming from somewhere just beyond the front bumper making the hair of his neck stand at attention.

Josiah lay on the road, his face pressed to the concrete and the lower half of his body twisted at the waist. The closer David got the more his injuries became apparent. The man was bleeding from several cuts to his face and one arm was bent at a completely unnatural angle. Burgess stood still with his one hand clamped over his mouth. His eyes were wide pools of light in the darkness.

Burgess seemed to suddenly be aware of David's presence. His hand dropped and with a voice that had to fight its way out of his throat he said, "I hit him. I didn't mean to, he just cut in front of me."

David pulled out his phone and called 911. He had to get Burgess to run to the corner to get the name of the street they were on, a long, anxious thirty seconds while Josiah lay motionless and bleeding. Five minutes later an ambulance and a cruiser arrived. Josiah was taken to the hospital while David and Burgess stayed behind to answer questions from the police. David passed along Marin Breckinridge's name as a contact, hoping that would help take some of the heat off them. Though it was clearly an accident it didn't mean that some kind of criminal charge wouldn't be applied.

Once satisfied the responding officer let the men go. He'd been kind enough to let them know where the ambulance had gone so David and Burgess drove straight to the hospital. Josiah was still being attended to when they arrived. They sat in the waiting room until a doctor came to speak with them.

A middle-aged woman with short grey hair emerged from the back sometime later. She spoke briefly with the charge nurse before coming to where they sat on the uncomfortable plastic chairs.

"David Lloyd?" she asked, he gaze passing back and forth between the men.

David stood. "That's me. How's Josiah doing?"

"He's stable. We've sedated him and he'll sleep for several hours now. I understand you're not family?"

"No, we're not. I passed along the name and phone number of his daughter, but I'm not sure if she'll want to get involved. They have a rocky relationship."

"I see. Well I can't really speak to you about his condition without his consent."

"Of course. I should tell you that Josiah has long-standing mental health issues and is most likely not taking his medication. We can't be sure what condition he's in as far as that goes. We didn't get the chance to speak with him."

"Thank you for letting me know. I'll try and track his history down. Any idea where he lives?"

David couldn't help but chuckle. "Sorry, I have no idea. Most likely he's on the streets."

"Well that's not going to make things easy. If he's been in the hospital system in the province I might get some information, but if he's been seen by various agencies it'll be difficult to get the whole picture." She'd tucked her hands into the pockets of her long lab coat, and she looked exhausted.

"Can we speak with him tomorrow?"

"What is all this about?"

"Josiah might be a witness to a murder that happened in Toronto some time ago."

"I suppose, as long as he doesn't get upset."

"We'll do our best. It's just very important we speak with him."

"Come around nine tomorrow. I'll leave a note with the nurse on the floor he gets taken to." She walked back to the nursing station to drop off her paperwork before disappearing into the back to attend to other patients.

By the time they reached the hotel it was nearly three o'clock in the morning. David parted ways with Burgess to head to his own room. As he started undressing for bed, he pulled his cell phone from his coat pocket, remembering he'd turned it off in the hospital. He sat on the edge of the bed, holding the phone in his hand as though it were going to divine the answer to all his problems. With a weary sigh he lay back and hit Jamie's number. It was three hours later in Ontario and he knew Jamie would be getting ready for work.

"Hello," Jamie answered after a couple of rings.

"Hey, handsome. You naked?"

"Wouldn't you like to know. So how's it going?"

"We found him."

"Fantastic. What did he have to say?" Jamie sounded surprised.

"Don't know. I haven't had the chance to talk to him yet."

"I don't understand."

"Burgess hit him with the car and he's in the hospital. We're going to see him in a few hours."

"Burgess hit him with the car?"

It sounded even worse hearing it parroted back to him. "Yep. Total accident. Listen, I'm beat. I need to get some shut-eye. I'll catch you up later okay? I just wanted to hear your voice."

"Yeah, okay. I'm in the office all day. Call me there."

"Will do. Bye."

He slept like the dead, neither waking nor moving position until the alarm gave a shrill bark at seven. After a call to Burgess's room to make sure the man was awake, David jumped in the shower and dressed in fresh clothing. A hurried breakfast and a long drive later he and Burgess arrived at the hospital. As they got off the elevator on the floor where Josiah was being kept they found Detective Breckinridge seated on a chair outside his room.

"Hey fellas," he said as he came to greet David and Burgess.

"You get a call about our adventures last night?" David asked, shaking the man's hand.

"Sure did. Still can't believe you pulled it off."

"It was plain old dumb luck. We were just heading back

to the hotel when we crossed paths and well, you know what happened after that."

"Yeah. I got the Coles notes from the responding officer. The doc's in with him right now. We had a brief chat and she told me he's going to be okay. Broke his arm and a couple of ribs, some bumps and bruises and a concussion. She wants to keep him here for a few days."

David could see the relief flooding through Burgess, causing the man to lose his ever-present bland expression and actually smile. He rubbed his hand through his unruly head of hair.

"So can we talk with him?"

"When they're done."

They only waited a few minutes before a man and a woman exited the room. The doctor conferred with them briefly and advised that the nurse would remain for their interview as Josiah had been quite agitated for the past few hours, despite being medicated. She explained that he was coherent enough to follow a simple line of questioning, but was subject to rambling and interjections of remarks unrelated to the conversation at hand. She warned that it would be several weeks of proper medication before he would be lucid enough for a thorough interrogation.

"We promise to keep it brief. These men just have a couple of questions and then we'll be out of the way," Marin said.

The nurse, a heavyset man in his thirties, followed them into the room without a word. He stood by the door with his arms crossed, as though having to accompany them was beneath him.

Josiah lay on the bed, eyes wide with suspicion as they approached. One arm has been placed in a cast and the other lay at his side with an IV running from the inner bend. He'd been cleaned, though his tangle of hair and beard remained, and he was dressed in double gowns, one acting as a robe. He looked frail, and his vulnerability pulled at David's heartstrings.

Marin took the lead. He came to Josiah's side and said, "Hello Josiah. My name is Marin Breckinridge and I'd like to ask you a couple of questions. Is that all right?"

Josiah looked past Marin to the other men, gaze steady and questioning. When he made eye contact with Burgess recognition flashed across his face. "Name's Josie."

"Right...Josie." Marin waved the other two closer. "This is David and Burgess. I think you know Burgess from Toronto."

Josiah gave a quick nod.

"How ya doing Josie?" Burgess asked.

"Been better," he answered.

"You okay to talk with these men. They're not here to hurt ya, I promise."

Josiah nodded again.

"Do you remember a night about ten years ago when you were in Simcoe Park. It was summer and you were probably there to sleep at the old caretaker's cabin." David spoke in a calm, friendly manner, mindful not to come across as condescending. Suspicion clouded Josiah's dark eyes as he spoke, and the man licked his lips repeatedly. "I think you saw something that scared you. You ran to Janko's Diner."

The scent of fear radiated from Josiah, triggering a visible reaction from the men who'd come to speak with him. He grabbed at the sheets with his undamaged hand and began to twist from side to side. An odd muttering-humming noise escaped his lips and he would no longer make eye contact with any of them.

"Did you see something Josie?" David asked.

The momentum of Josiah's rocking picked up, accompanied with violent head shaking. The nurse gave them a hard look.

"Josie, please. These men need your help. You're the only one who saw." Burgess came around the far side of the bed to perch on the edge. He reached out and touched Josiah's hand, eliciting a soft mewling sound from the older man. Silent tears slipped down Josiah's thin cheeks.

"A monster," he whispered. The sound crawled over David's skin.

"What monster?" Burgess asked, keeping his hand on his friend's.

Josiah suddenly shot forward. He grabbed at Burgess's arm, his eyes wild. The nurse came to the bedside to intervene.

"He's getting upset," the nurse said. "I think we need to end this."

"Please just let me show him a picture," David pleaded. "Then we'll leave, I promise."

Josiah was openly sobbing and David had begun to feel the man's terror as his own. He wanted nothing more than to flee from the room, from the case and never look back.

"I don't like this," the nurse said, but he moved aside.

David pulled the photo of Mark Ester from his bag and held it before Josiah. At first he would not look, forcing his head back against the pillow with his face turned from David's direction. Burgess leaned in and whispered in the man's ear. His response was an urgent head shake. He said something else that only Josiah could hear, and after a few tense minutes he opened his eyes and let his gaze fall on the photo.

Josiah cried out, swatting the photo from David's hand. He tried to leap from the bed, but Burgess and the equipment he was attached to prevented a hasty retreat. Instead he and Burgess tumbled to the floor, taking the IV stand with them. The nurse rushed to their aid, much faster than David thought a man of his size would be able to.

Burgess had taken the brunt of the fall as he'd instinctively cradled Josiah on the way down. He'd hit his head with significant force on the tile floor and he lay with Josiah resting on his chest. The nurse pulled Josiah back on to the bed, checking his injuries and IV site before dropping down to care for Burgess, who'd remained still on the floor as though dazed from the fall. His eyes fluttered between open and closed and breathing seemed to cause him pain. When the nurse turned his head a small pool of blood was discovered underneath.

The nurse hit the call buzzer and thirty seconds later a second medical professional came into the room. Marin grabbed David by the elbow and gestured to the door. They stepped outside to wait until things settled down.

"You sure know how to cause a commotion," Marin remarked, though not in an unkind way.

"It's one of my specialties," David answered. "I guess I got my answer though."

"I'd say so, though you know it's not official until there's an actual confession. A man flipping out at the sight of a photo is hardly proof positive. We need an actual statement. Even then it might be a hard sell to your investigators. I mean the man is not the most reliable of witnesses."

"I know, but I can't exactly sit on this. Two innocent men have spent the last ten years in jail, and a killer is walking free. This could be enough to get the police to look into other things, like testing some evidence against Mark Ester. I need to get back to Toronto right away. Are you able to follow up with Josiah when he's better and get a formal statement?"

Marin had taken a seat and leaned forward with his elbows on the top of his thighs. "Sure I can. I need to make a report on this whole thing anyway. I need to warn you though, it could be weeks before you get what you need. Remember the doctor said he's in no shape to be interrogated."

"I can't wait that long," he answered.

The door opened and Burgess exited. He moved with care as he came to where David stood.

"You okay?" David asked.

"Yeah fine. Just knocked the wind out of me."

"What about your head?"

"It's fine. No stitches needed."

"We need to get home," David said.

"Be careful with this, David," Marin warned him. "You go off half-cocked and you could mess things up for your guys instead of helping them."

"I'll be careful." He held his hand out, which brought Marin back to his feet. They shook and then he and Burgess took their leave.

Once back at the hotel they put a call through to the airline and secured tickets for a mid-afternoon flight. David tried to get hold of Jamie, but the call immediately went through to voicemail. He assumed Jamie was on the line, so left a message about his expected arrival time in Toronto. They checked out and got themselves a bite to eat before heading back to the airport to return the car and check in for the flight.

As they waited in the airport David put a call through to Sandra to bring her up to speed on the recent developments. For the first time David felt as though he'd made some real progress in the case, that there might actually be a possibility of proving the men's innocence.

"Hello."

"Hi. Is this Sandra?" David asked.

"Yes, it's me."

"Great. David here. Listen I have some news that will make you very happy."

"Go on," she urged.

"I tracked down the Janko's man and he definitely saw something that night. He's in the hospital right now, but the police here in Vancouver will be taking a formal statement from him when he's well and that will get the ball rolling as far as Nathan's case is concerned."

There was such a long pause David thought she might have hung up. "You're kidding?"

"Not at all. I'm pretty shocked about this myself. Finding the guy seemed like a shot in the dark, and he might not have even seen anything even if we did. He couldn't have just been some nut."

"I can't believe this. I was discussing this with Mark just yesterday and it seemed pretty farfetched when I was telling him about this. Even though I've been holding out hope on this for so long, I had to agree that the chances of this amounting to anything were slim to none."

"You spoke with Mark?" David asked, his tone sharper than he meant to use.

"Yeah, I guess after you interviewed him he got to thinking about the past, and wanted to call and check in on me. I hadn't talked to him in years, and I was pretty surprised after the way things had ended. I guess he felt bad."

That's an understatement. "Listen I don't mean to alarm you or anything, but can you keep this phone call to yourself until I get back there and we have a chance to talk. We don't want to risk the chance of spooking the real killer. You wouldn't want them to get away after all this time."

"Sure, of course. I understand. When are you back?"

"Our flight leaves in about an hour," he said, glancing at his watch. "We should be back in Toronto about five. I'll call you when I'm there, okay?"

"Looking forward to it. See you soon."

No sooner had he ended the conversation than Jamie called. They had a brief discussion about the events at the hospital and the implications for the case. Jamie agreed to leave work a bit early and pick them up at the airport. Anticipation was an itch that David could not scratch and it gnawed at him the entire flight home. The truth had seemed to fall into his lap, but using it to the men's advantage would be the true test. Marin had been right in that Josiah would hardly prove a reliable witness in the eyes of the law, and combined with the lack of hard evidence, motive, the length of time since the crime and lack of other support for Mark's guilt, his testimony may not have the effect Sandra and others were hoping for. If Jasmine could be convinced to make a statement against Vukovic the combination of new evidence might get the case reopened.

The plane touched down less than ten minutes later than scheduled. Jamie waited near the exit gate in his dark suit and tightly knotted tie. He shot Burgess a curious look as they approached.

David came to him, unsure of how to greet him, but Jamie took the decision from him. He leaned in for a quick peck to David's cheek, then offered his hand in Burgess's direction. David pushed aside the tease that sprang to mind.

"I'm Jamie, and you must be Burgess," he said as they shook hands.

"That's right. Good to meet you."

"You too. I hear you guys had a successful trip."

At Jamie's lead the men started walking to the parking area. They chatted about Josiah and their encounter with him, and his medical condition. After dropping Burgess at his building and thanking him for his time, Jamie and David headed over to Sandra's house for a discussion that would change many lives.

Smoke curled from the chimney, pale grey against the deep indigo of the night sky. Sandra came to the door, ushering them into the front foyer filled with the enticing aroma of garlic and fresh baked bread. Though she smiled, her manner seemed tense.

"You got here just in time. I'm just serving up some pasta."

"We don't mean to impose…" David said.

She waved off his protests. "Please, I always cook like I'm feeding an army. Tammy and the girls are here, so it's fine. C'mon to the kitchen."

Jamie gave David a shrug. They followed the woman into the other room, as she was apparently not going to take no for an answer. Tammy looked up as they entered, a brief look of animosity flashing across her face before she turned her attention back to getting the girls settled at the table.

"Ah Sandra, Tammy, this is Jamie. I hope it's all right if he's here for this discussion."

"Of course. I have complete faith in you." Sandra placed plates piled high with pasta and tomato sauce in their hands. "Sit. There's bread and salad on the table."

Tammy passed another look their way as they took their seats, and from the set of her jaw and narrowing of her eyes David didn't think she felt the same way as Sandra, but was smart enough not to voice her opinions in that moment. With the children present David didn't think it was a good time to bring up the case, so he waited until plates had been cleared and the girls scampered off to play. The dinner had been wonderful, and hit the spot after numerous meals on the road.

"Thank you for dinner. It was wonderful," David said.

"Yes, thank you," Jamie added.

"All right, now the kids are gone. Let's talk about what's going on here. The last few hours have just about killed me." She continued to run her fingers along a napkin she'd folded and stretched into a strip of material about the size and length of a pencil. She didn't seem to be aware of her nervous act.

"There's no easy way to tell you this. The man from Janko's Diner is Josiah Maitland and he's identified Mark as the man he witnessed in Simcoe Park."

"You're fucking joking," Tammy said as she exhaled a tight gust of breath.

"There has to be some mistake." Sandra shook her head from side to side, eyes glazed as though trying to force David's words to make sense. The napkin slipped from her fingers.

"I'm quite sure, Sandra. He had a violent reaction to the photo of Mark I showed him. Now he is in quite a state and it'll take some time to get him stabilized so that a formal statement can be taken, but I feel very strongly that this is it."

"Why the hell would Mark do something like this?" Tammy asked.

"Not sure exactly, but here's the next bombshell that helps tie this together—he was having an affair with Erin Gagnon."

Colour drained from Sandra's face. "I still don't get it. I knew he was running around on me, but Erin Gagnon?"

"Mark was cheating on you? You never told me that." Tammy's words were sharp and accusatory and she'd grabbed Sandra's arm.

"I didn't know it would have anything to do with this! How could I have known?"

"You should have told me too," David said. "Probably the police back during the original investigation. It may have changed the way things went." He knew his words would hurt Sandra, but it didn't make them any less untrue.

"After everything else I was supposed to air my dirty laundry. Jesus, yes, Mark was a dog. He cheated on me a few times those last couple years. It was terrible to go through, but never in a million years did I suspect Erin Gagnon. And I had no idea it could have helped the case. I mean if I did, of course I would have said something." Sandra's voice had become shrill and loud enough to instill a palpable anxiety in everyone in the room. She stood from the table, pulling away from Tammy's grip on her arm. She walked to the sink where she grabbed the edge with enough force to turn her knuckles white and leaned over.

Tammy sat back like she'd been struck, remaining quiet for several moments before making eye contact with David. "Okay, should-haves aside, I'm with Sandra here. What is Mark's motive for doing this?"

"That I'm not sure about. Erin did say that she'd ended things with him a short time before the murders and that he was being very verbally abusive to her. She also said he'd told her that if she wanted to be with him she needed to find someone to take her kids. He apparently didn't want to be a father."

Sandra shook visibly as David spoke, the truth of the words hitting hard.

"So she dumps him and he kills her kids? What, to spite her? That seems harsh, doesn't it?"

"Maybe something else happened to trigger his rage?" Jamie suggested. "And anyway in cases like this a person's motives rarely make sense to those on the outside."

Sandra made a sound like she were about to vomit into the sink. With slow, deliberate movements she turned to the group at the table. David had seen many people in the grip of violence and the most devastating news over the years, and the expression on Sandra's face mirrored those in the worst of life's circumstances. Like the possibility of someone she'd once loved being capable of such atrocity had begun to kill her from the inside out, she stared outward with blank eyes, limbs heavy. Her voice lacked conviction when she finally gathered enough strength to speak. "How will you prove this?"

"I'm hoping a confrontation might shock him into a confession or provoke some action that will reveal his guilt. Other than that we can only turn over what we know to the police and hope it's enough to re-open the case." His words didn't sound any more comforting to his own ears than he imagined they did for Sandra and Tammy.

"If he's guilty he must pay. Not only for my son, and for Alex, but for those two innocent boys whose lives were stolen from them. Even for Erin. No one could ever deserve to have this done to them. No one." Sandra all but collapsed back into her chair.

Tammy left the room, returning with a small glass filled with an amber liquid. She placed the cup in Sandra's hands and ordered her to drink. The ingestion of alcohol brought spots of pink to her cheeks.

"I agree Sandra, I do. We need to be smart about this though. I don't want this bastard to walk."

"When are you planning to confront him?" Tammy asked.

"There's no time like the present," David answered.

"I'm going with you," Sandra said.

"I don't know if that's a good idea."

"It's not up for debate. I want to be there. And I know Mark, I'll be able to tell by his reaction. I think my presence will make it harder for him to lie too, at least it should."

David started to protest, but Jamie cut him off. "Let her come."

By the time they were parking in front of Mark Ester's house night had fallen completely, draping over the landscape in velvety shades of grey. An outside light illuminated the empty porch and the front lawn, and the fact that the truck David had seen during his last visit was gone. Instead a small sedan was parked in the driveway.

David knocked at the front door. His mind raced with the multiple scenarios of how the conversation to be had would transpire, and none seemed as though it would end in anything less than a shouting match. Movement sounded from inside and then the door opened inward, revealing not Mark, but Carmine.

Recognition lit in her eyes as her gaze settled on David. "Yes?"

"Hi, Carmine. Is Mark home? I need to speak with him."

"He's not here right now," she said. As she stood in the crack she'd opened in the doorway, effectually blocking a view of the interior of the house, she gave a quick glance behind her.

David placed his hand on the door, giving it a firm shove that Carmine was no match to block. The door swung all the way open as she stumbled from the sudden loss of her grip on it. She gave a sharp bark of surprise as David stepped inside.

The front closet door stood open, with several hangers lying on the floor as though items had been removed in haste. A chair had been knocked over and a small vase lay in pieces on the floor. Several pictures lining the hallway were askew, and the contents of a purse had been scattered across the floor. A closer look at Carmine showed a bright red area on her lower jaw from a hit she must have taken in the not-so-distant past. Something sudden and violent had occurred.

"Don't fuck around with me Carmine. Where is he?" David demanded.

Carmine burst into tears. "I don't know where he is. Please, I really don't..." Her word trailed off into a series of unintelligible sobs and snuffles.

Jamie and Sandra had come inside, both standing hesitantly by the doorway. A cold gust of wind crawled inside, prompting Jamie to close the door behind them.

"What happened here, Carmine? Obviously there was a fight of some kind."

Carmine sank down onto the steps, her crying having subsided. In addition to the now evident welt on the right side of her jaw, the rest of her face had become blotchy and a line of snot dotted her upper lip. She used her sleeve to wipe the dampness from her cheeks. "I came home from work and Mark was flying around the house. I asked him what was going on and he just said he needed some time away. When I asked why and where he was going he flipped out and started shoving me around."

"He's on the run," Jamie said.

"He's a smart guy, has money and he knows how to survive in the outdoors. He could be anywhere." David was getting more pissed by the second.

"Sounds like he could stay off the radar for some time," Jamie added.

Sandra, who'd remained quiet the entire episode, came forward. "I have a pretty good idea where you can find him."

CHAPTER 18

After a hurried preparation for the unknowns of the winter wilds of northern Ontario, David, Jamie, and Sandra hit the road. They took Highway 400 north out of town, driving more than three hours till they passed the town of Parry Sound, a medium sized town nestled along the shores of Georgian Bay, before taking a turn to the east. Had they continued farther than their intended destination they would ultimately have ended up at the edge of beautiful Algonquin Provincial Park. Instead they left the relative safety of the public road they'd been travelling to continue down a series of progressively more rugged and remote trails, leading to the heart of prime hunting and fishing territory.

The deeper they found themselves into the forested area where Mark's cabin hideaway was located, the happier David found himself with the choice of his recent vehicle purchase. The weight of the vehicle lent better traction, making the progression easier and less stressful to him as the driver. Another half-hour passed and the trail became impossible to venture any further on. Though winter had shown signs of clearing in the greater Toronto area, in the north the snow and ice had yet the recede. Without proper tires, and possibly chains, the passage of mechanized vehicles was halted.

"How much farther?" David asked.

Sandra looked about, getting her bearings on their exact location. "We're close. Another maybe half kilometer to the next cross junction, then maybe two kilometers to the cabin after that."

Sandra gave an explanation of the exact path that David stored to memory.

"Okay, listen. You two stay here. Jamie I want you to keep trying Jimmy. If you can't get him in the next half-hour call Marco, let them know what's going on. If I'm not back within the next two hours, get back on the road and call 911."

"I'm not letting you go out there by yourself," Jamie responded. He frowned as he leaned into the space between the front seats.

"You two will come with me as far as the road to the cabin, then come back to the car. Don't give me shit about this, Jamie. It's dark, it's cold and we don't need to run the risk of all of us getting stuck out here."

"I don't like this. Not at all."

"I don't either," Sandra agreed. She let her gaze travel over the snowy landscape.

"If he's here we need to get him to confess Sandra. You know this could just be a stop before disappearing."

"Yes." She sighed.

David turned to Jamie. "I'll be fine. I have a vest on and I have my gun and a flashlight. I'm dressed for the conditions and I'm a pretty smart guy. Let me handle this."

Jamie's eyes closed for a few moments as he pressed his lips together. "Okay, right. Get this guy."

They picked their way down the path, following the narrow swath of light from David's flashlight. Though a good amount of snow had accumulated, two wide indentations indicated a vehicle had passed through sometime in the near past. The path came to an end at a T-shaped junction, where the road carried on in both directions along a parcel of land densely packed with old tree growth. A vehicle had taken the left turn.

"Okay, keep walking down this path. You'll pass a couple of properties before you hit Glendale Pass, which is the private road to Mark's cabin. It's about another kilometer more. You'll come to a cleared space with two smaller outbuildings and a large cabin close to the lake shore. Mark will be in the main cabin and his truck should be parked nearby."

"Thanks Sandra. You two stick together okay? No funny business. If you see or hear anything that doesn't seem kosher, get back to a main road and call the police."

Sandra turned on the small lantern she had with her in preparation for the walk back. David reached into his coat pocket and pulled out his second gun, a compact six-shot Ruger Vaquero he'd picked up during one of his earliest cases as a private investigator. He handed it to Jamie.

"Take this. It's not the best gun, but it can do some damage if need be. Just don't be a hero, okay."

Jamie hesitated before taking the gun from David's grip. "Right back at you."

David turned to leave and Jamie caught his arm. He leaned in and planted his lips against David's, kissing him with a quiet desperation that left him feeling raw and unnerved. Jamie stepped in alongside Sandra with worry pulling at his handsome face.

"Be careful David. I don't want any more blood spilled on this," Sandra said as they started to walk away.

Jamie's show of intimacy had rattled David, and it took an intense focus to push the sensation aside. When he looked back into darkness, the forms of his partner and his client had vanished and he could not dismiss the feeling of abandonment. The cold gnawed at his exposed skin as the gentle pass of wind stirred the snow that had begun to fall and whistled through the bare trees. He kept his hands pushed deep into his coat pockets, his right hand gripped about his gun. In his other a small recorder bounced about.

David liked to think of himself as a pretty tough guy, but by the time the cabin property came into view he'd become completely rattled by the cold and a suffocating darkness. The beam from his heavy-duty flashlight did little to guide his way, and he found himself stumbling, and being the victim to sharp assaults by naked tree limbs. Once, he fell so hard he endured a jarring pain as his jaws snapped together and he found himself with a mouthful of blood. The notion of time passing had been lost.

The final hundred yards of the lane onto the property continued on a downward slope as it curled around a small clump of quivering trees. David paused, using the trees as a natural shield while he scanned the property. A thin cloud of smoke drifted up from the stone chimney of the cabin, a subtle difference in colour against the velvet blackness of the sky. Higher above this a shower of stars twinkled, indifferent to the ominous activities of the people below.

After making a careful observation of the layout and location of the various buildings David switched off the flashlight and dropped it into his pocket. He maintained a grip on the gun as he slowly made his way to the left. After a number of cautious steps he made it to the first outbuilding, where he stopped and listened. He could hear nothing but the wind and a soft moan from the settling of one or more of the buildings. At the second building he paused at the wood pile. His eyes had adjusted to the lack of light and he could make out the shape of the cabin, and the steps and porch leading to the front door. Mark's truck was parked right beside the staircase, meaning that David would have to go around it to gain access.

He made it to the truck, pressing himself against the cold metal hulk. His breath hit the air with a ragged exhalation that touched his ears as though produced by some alien being. His heart hammered against his ribcage. A hazy light radiated from a window on the structure's first floor, but there were no other signs of anyone in residence. Slowly David made his way up the steps. His fear had become so palpable he could taste bile in the back of his throat and he had to keep blinking in order to keep his vision in focus. A painful ringing filled his ears, itching at his hearing aid.

Once on the porch he dared a peek in the window and spotted Mark crouched before the fireplace. He noted a shotgun leaning against the arm of a chair to the man's right, about five feet away, and a second one on a table farther to the back of the room. He took a deep breath and burst through the door.

Mark whirled about in surprise, almost toppling to the floor. David rushed inside and ran straight at the man. Mark leaned for the gun, but David reached it a few seconds earlier and kicked it from the man's grasp. He had his own weapon extended before him, aimed at the man's head.

"Don't!" David instructed. The intense heat from the fire

after the long stretch in the cold made David feel faint, but he held his ground.

"You're trespassing," Mark retaliated with a flippant tone. He stayed crouched near the hearth, but his eyes kept sliding to the weapon beyond his reach.

"That's the least of your worries right now Mark, and we both know it." David pressed the button on the recorder.

The men stared at one another as the firelight danced across Mark's face. Looking at him it seemed inconceivable to David that he could be capable of such a heinous crime. There was nothing outwardly sinister about the man, in fact he was a nice-looking, fit, middle-aged man that could have been at home in any number of everyday settings.

"You think you know anything, please. That stupid bitch Sandra should have just let things be. It's not like that hooligan son of hers was going to amount to anything anyway."

"You let three innocent boys go to jail for something you did. Jesus Fuck man, you butchered two little boys. How could you do such a thing?"

Like a flick of a switch the monster behind the façade of normalcy emerged. His eyes narrowed and the grin turned into a menacing sneer. He rose to his feet with hands balled into fists.

"That stupid cunt was fucking every guy in town. You know she had the nerve to try and break it off with me? Like she would ever get a better offer, slut lowlife janitor that she was. Makes me sick to think I was ever with her."

David's arm was starting to feel the strain of his stationary hold and the weight of the gun. A small tremble began at his wrist and ran up to his shoulder. "So you killed her kids because she wanted to end things? That's nuts."

"You don't fucking get it do you?" he said, his voice strained with anger. "I went over there that night to give her another chance. I saw the boys riding their bikes so I picked them up and we went back to the house. I told them to stay in the car 'cause I was going to surprise Erin and take them all up to the cabin, you know, do some fishing and swimming, cut loose. And you know what I found? You know what that fucking whore was up to?" Mark's voice had acquired a tone that made the hairs on the back of David's neck stand at attention. The man was completely lost to the rage and madness the memory inspired. "That fucking slut was in bed with some kid. There she was with her lips wrapped around his cock, and they were both so into it they didn't even notice me standing in the doorway. I turned around and walked out of the house, got back in my truck and drove away."

Sam. "That's still no reason to kill her children. There are a thousand less violent ways you could have gotten back at her."

Mark turned slightly away from David and the gun being held on him, angling toward the fireplace, where he reached out to warm his hands. Something about the casual and relaxed gesture spoke to the man's break with rational human thinking. David knew he was in the presence of a psychopath.

"I wasn't going to kill them, at least that wasn't my first thought. I just wanted to scare the bitch. I brought them up here to the cabin, I thought I'd keep them here overnight and make her freak. At first it was fine, the boys came with me thinking their mom had said it was okay. We ate and played some games. Then Robert started getting whiny, asking for his mom and shit. Boy he was getting on my nerves, and you know that was the whole problem in the first place. I didn't want to be looking after kids, they're too needy and demanding. After a couple hours I couldn't take it anymore and I smacked the little bugger. And that's when everything got out of control."

Sweat lined the inside of David's gloves, bringing with it a terrible itching sensation. "Tell me."

Mark flicked his attention in David's direction. "Jake, the older one, decided he was going to protect his brother. He came at me and we crashed into that table right there," he said, pointing at the long pine table holding the second gun. His eyes hesitated for a split second on the weapon, then moved back to David. "It hurt too, the little fucker. I shoved him back and he fell into the hearth and cracked his head pretty good. That kept him down, but then Robert flipped. He bolted out the door and into the woods. I had to chase him for a good hour before I finally got him. He'd fallen down into a ravine back off the property, think he broke his leg. He'd screamed like a demon when I carried him back here.

"When we got back Jake was still in the same position, breathing real shallow. I knew he was going to croak, and then my options were gone. I had no choice. I killed them, made it look some crazy fucker got a hold of them. I wrapped them up in one of my old camping tarps and drove back to town where I dumped them in the park. I figured no one would ever suspect me."

The complete lack of remorse and compassion from Mark was so unnerving David could barely think straight. He thought he might be sick. "Except you made a mistake. You dropped your belt buckle."

Mark actually grinned then. "Yep. I think the tarp caught on it when I was unwrapping them. Didn't notice till I got home, and then it was starting to get light and I didn't dare come back."

"You also didn't notice you had a witness."

"The fucker from Janko's, right? Of all the dumb luck."

David felt a maniacal bout of laughter bubbling up his throat, inspired by the deranged ridiculousness of the situation. Here he was calmly discussing the brutal murder of two children as though it were nothing more casual than the weather. His own skin felt tight and restrictive, his blood molten lava coursing through his veins.

"Yes, the man at Janko's."

"So now what?" Mark asked.

"Now we get in your truck and drive to the nearest police station where you're going to turn yourself in."

David gestured toward the space behind him with the gun. His arm gave a sigh of relief at him having changed position, then promptly turned to jelly. Mark took a step forward as though he meant to comply when an abrupt change of expression came over him. His smile became a wide O of surprise.

"I have a better idea. Why don't I just end this right here, right now," a female said. A shot rang out, hitting a figurine on the fireplace mantle and blasting it into a shower of ceramic pieces.

Mark dived out of the line of fire, managing to roll underneath the table. David also dropped, scuttling around the side of a well-worn La-Z-Boy recliner. He made eye contact with Mark, who mouthed "Carmine," and made frantic hand gestures in the direction of the front door. David chanced a look around the side of the chair and sure enough Carmine was walking toward them with a rifle clenched in her hands.

"Carmine, wait please! You don't want to do this. He's not worth it."

The wind had whipped her hair into a state resembling Medusa's mane of snakes, and snow had caught on her lashes, melting a line of water over her red cheeks. "Stay out of this David. I don't want to hurt you. This is between Mark and me."

David jumped to his feet gun held out before him. Carmine stopped, frowning at the standoff. She didn't lower the gun.

"C'mon Carmine. We can talk about this."

"No." She took a shot that hit the floor a few inches short of where David stood. *Shit, she means it.*

She kept coming, pushing past David. He made a move to stop her when she suddenly let out a stream of expletives. She turned back to David, eyes blazing. "Where is he?"

David looked to where Mark had been under the table. He was gone.

And so was the gun.

"I don't know, but he's armed now."

David leaned down to pick up the rifle he'd knocked out of the way when he'd first entered. It had slid halfway under the chair. He pulled the strap over his shoulder and ran after Carmine as she made her way to the dark, back end of the cabin. He stumbled into several items along the way before he felt the blast of cold from a door left open. He followed the draft to its source; another entrance. The door stood open, groaning with the movement of the wind. David approached the opening with caution, bending down before he peeked out lest someone decide to take a shot at where his head should have been.

The door opened onto a narrower back porch, stocked with split firewood. The moonlight washed the space and the open ground beyond in silver. He stepped out, taking a quick look in both directions. He didn't see anyone in close proximity. His heart hammered, and his own breathing seemed to be trying to suffocate him. He'd just cleared the steps when gun shots rang out.

He followed the sound around the back end of the cabin, spotting Mark's still-parked truck. Another shot split the night, sounding as though it came from the direction of the nearby lake, which in the dark was a vague, shadowy area several hundred yards in the distance. He jogged alongside the vehicle wishing he could turn on his flashlight to help guide his advancement, while knowing it could also lead to him being exposed, and subsequently shot. He'd been there once, and didn't relish another experience.

As if on cue a shot whizzed past, ricocheting off the hood of the truck. David skidded to a stop and retreated back the length of the car.

"Stay back!" Carmine shrieked from off in the distance.

With a mouth as dry as sand David doubled back and veered to the left to use the closest outbuilding as cover. Since he could barely see five feet in front of his hand, and he certainly could not make out either Mark or Carmine, he felt safe that he wasn't any clearer to either of them. He inched his way along the building to the back. After a quick scan of the immediate area he shot across the open land, running to the tree line that followed the lake's edge before opening onto an area cleared as a small private beach and dock. Just before reaching the beach he hit a patch of ice and went down hard, landing on his already injured knee.

The pain was bright and immediate, and he had to bite down on his lip to keep from crying out. With much effort he got himself back to standing, but moving with any speed was out of the question. Too much weight and the knee buckled. Cursing his luck he hobbled along to the vacant beach.

Shouts from farther along in the darkness caught his ear, along with a quick exchange of gunfire. If he was lucky they'd both damage themselves enough to make escape impossible. David pulled his cell phone from his pocket, not surprised when he couldn't get service. He had no choice but to keep going. Mark certainly knew the area, and even though he wasn't dressed for the weather he could no doubt get himself to some kind of cover or escape route. Carmine might also be familiar enough with the area to use it to her advantage, but David could not say the same. If he lost them he had no recourse.

He passed the dock and empty boat launch. The water was free of ice and lapped against the frozen land and wooden structures. The wind was a banshee's cry across the open water, turning to a dry sigh as it hit the forest. Though the moon was high and bright and a smattering of stars dotted the black sky, it proved difficult to maneuver over the ice-crusted drifts of snow. His aching knee only hindered his progress more.

Carmine came into view so suddenly that David drew in a sharp intake of breath. Certain she'd heard him he lowered to the ground and clamped his free hand over his mouth. He crawled along, daring a peek at her moving form every few seconds. He reached a clump of shaggy, ice-coated brush, which he pushed aside for a clearer view, surprised to find them slick and warm. He brought his glove close to his face, squinting to see what he already knew he'd found.

Blood.

So, someone had been hurt.

"You're not going to get out of this Mark," Carmine screamed into the wind. "May as well give up now."

"Fuck you, Carmine!" Mark shouted back.

Like Carmine, David tracked the sound to her left. From the brief description Sandra had given him he recalled that the only thing in this area was forest, crisscrossed with trails and the occasional hunting shelter. Once Mark got into the woods he'd have the advantage.

He stood, creeping forward with cautious, deliberate movements. A soft crackle came from behind, an unexpected sound, yet before David could pivot enough to view the source a hand clamped on his arm.

"Don't," Jamie whispered against his ear.

David was equal parts relieved and furious at his appearance. "What are you doing here?"

"We saw Carmine coming down the road, so we turned around. She's got good snow tires so she got a bit farther than we did, but she abandoned her car about halfway down the road into the cabin, so I wasn't too far behind."

He made a gesture that they should lower down. "Where's Sandra?"

"She's gone to get the police. The cell service out here sucks."

David gave a soft chuckle. "Yes, it does."

"I heard gunfire. What's going on?"

"Carmine's got a rifle and she's pissed. She's chasing him down. I would have had him too if she hadn't busted in. But someone's hurt, I found some blood back there."

"What do you want to do?"

"You still have the gun I gave you?"

Jamie nodded, sapphire eyes bright with anxiety.

"Okay, look I hurt my knee and I'm going slow. I can use your help here, but I don't want you putting yourself out there. Be careful."

They quickly sorted out who would go where. Jamie retreated back into the shadows, taking a wide berth around Carmine, who'd become stationary about fifteen meters from where the men were watching. David stood up and took a shot, deliberately aiming far to her left side. She whirled about in surprise, managing to pop off a return shot before realizing she needed to reload.

David took advantage and started to close in. With half the pace between them travelled Carmine suddenly pitched forward and the rifle few from her grip. She rolled onto her back, taking an experienced swing at Jamie, and he crumpled to the ground with her. They tussled while David struggled to get close enough to help.

The woman fought like a wildcat, arms and legs flailing, backed with her rage-induced strength. Jamie seemed to get her under control at last when she got a hand free and raked her nails across his cheek. Without even thinking he struck her back, knocking the woman unconscious.

"Shit. Are you okay?" David asked when he reached them.

Jamie grabbed a handful of snow and rubbed it over the wounds. "Don't worry about me. Get the gun and let's go." He reached inside her coat pocket and pulled out the pack of ammunition she'd been attempting to get hold of.

David grabbed the gun and handed it to Jamie. He still had his own handgun and Mark's rifle over his shoulder. Together they approached what they could now see was the mouth to a trail wide enough to accommodate a snowmobile or other all-terrain vehicle.

"I'm going to go in through the woods, you take the trail. It'll be easier with your knee," Jamie said. He walked forward a couple of feet and then dropped to his knee.

David peered over his shoulder, what he'd spotted coming in to view. More blood.

"He's hurt," David said.

"Yeah, doesn't mean it'll slow him down. He has everything to lose here."

"Yep, be careful."

"You too." Jamie sprinted off, soon to be lost in the impenetrable darkness of the dense forest. David followed the trail, but kept close to the edge to afford himself what little protection he could. The odd time he thought he heard something ahead, only to find it was his own accelerated pulse mimicking the sound of urgent movement. His knee throbbed and he'd burst into a chilled sweat in response to the unrelenting pain.

Up ahead, but much closer than he would have suspected, a gunshot blasted. A second shot soon followed, this one with a different sound, indicating two weapons. A man cried out, followed by a series of primal grunts and the snapping, crumpled sounds of a tumble of something heavy through the brush. A third shot reverberated through the night.

David pushed himself as hard as he could, all but dragging his bad leg along behind him. He could make out the shape of a figure couched by the edge of the path, and ragged, pained breathing filled the night.

"Jamie!" he cried out, stumbling and having to drag himself the rest of the way.

The figure turned, and when David could see Jamie alive and breathing before him he expelled the breath he hadn't realized he was holding. Jamie scrambled over to him and helped him to his feet, letting David rest his weight on him like a crutch.

"Are you okay?" David asked.

"I'm fine. I hit Mark though, I think. He's not moving."

David fumbled with the flashlight in his pocket, finally managing to pull it free, and swept the beam over the area before them. At first all he could see was trampled brush and overlapping footprints. A trail of blood appeared, scarlet and telling against the blanket of snow, leading to Mark's still body. David did his best to hold the beam steady as Jamie checked his vitals.

"He's alive."

It took more than two hours before the police and emergency services made it to the cabin. By then Jamie had managed to drag Mark back from the wood using his coat as a makeshift gurney, and David had forced a groggy Carmine along with them at gun point. After she made a few attempts to flee, they finally tied her to a chair.

Mark had taken two hits. One from Carmine had hit him in the thigh, causing a serious amount of blood loss. The second from Jamie's gun had hit him in the chest, but had not exited. Mark weaved in and out of consciousness, while Carmine wailed and spewed insults. The approaching sirens had been music to David's ears.

WRAP UP

Many things came to light in the weeks following the standoff at Mark Ester's cabin. Though Mark refused to make a confession to the police, Carmine, in exchange for a much reduced charge of her own, gave a formal statement about the conversation she'd overheard between David and Mark. Instead of facing an attempted murder charge, the police processed her with aggravated assault, which would translate to minimal jail time because of her cooperation. *Ah, the criminal justice system.* David understood the choice between the lesser of two evils, but the thought of a woman like Carmine on the streets was enough to make David think twice about the city he called home. In reality it was the best scenario they could hope for since his recorder had tumbled from his pocket during the struggle with Carmine, and when the police had recovered it the next day the cold and wet had rendered it useless.

With Josiah Maitland stabilized and coherent, the authorities had also secured his firsthand eye witness account of the boys' bodies being dumped in Simcoe Park. Testing of the cigarette butts and other items as Tammy had suggested early on produced positive results. The saliva matched Josiah, proving he'd been there, and the prints on the shoe and belt were tentatively matched to Mark Ester, who until that time had never been tested. He'd never been arrested, been in the military, or held a job that had required his prints to be on file. Once the ground was no longer frozen the police would search for the boys' bicycles they believed had been disposed of on or around Mark Ester's property. It was more than enough to re-open the case and make an application for a new trial. All things going as they should, Alex and Nathan would be free men in a matter of weeks.

Sam and Jasmine had come forward to give their version of events of that fateful night, actions that added to the pressure to re-open the case, and led to a new and separate investigation against Jonas Vukovic and his partner in crime, Detective Rob LeClair. With their statements on record, Alicia Marsten had been inspired to also come forward, and with the two separate complaints the police had put David and Jamie's idea of surveillance into action. They'd succeeded in catching Vukovic picking up one of his clients, and going to a nearby hotel to engage in extracurricular activities. In short order Vukovic had been excused from his duties without pay, pending a full investigation. David had no doubt formal criminal charges would be forthcoming.

The most surprising and disheartening news had come when David had been taken to the hospital to tend to his knee injury. While waiting in emergency Marco Arabetta had come to see David, and he'd brought more than well wishes. He let David and Jamie know that Jimmy had been brought into hospital the day before, hence his being MIA when they'd tried to get him on the phone. Jimmy had been quietly fighting a battle with cancer, but the latest round would be keeping him out for the foreseeable future. David had suspected something was up, but even so, hearing the truth about a dear friend had been painful.

The damage to David's knee was not as bad as he'd expected, though he would require a few days of bed rest and then several weeks of physiotherapy and a gentle transition back to weight training. Jamie hovered over him like an old mother hen, much to David's chagrin. Secretly he loved every minute of it. Jenny pitched in by coming to tidy the house and run errands, while Grandma Rhea cooked enough food for a small country to help get them through.

Erin Gagnon had remained silent, even after the news had hit the papers. David had reached out to her with a couple of phone calls, none of which were ever returned. He concluded she'd chosen to deal with the news as she'd had the first time

Liz Strange

around; quietly and alone. Maybe she'd find some peace at last and finally break free of the darkness that had held onto her for so long.

One afternoon as David sat on the couch reading, after an intense therapy session and a long visit with Jimmy, who was responding well to his new treatment regime, there came a knock at the door. He'd lost the crutches already, proud and determined to heal in a timely manner. Walking to the door there was only the slightest imperfection in his gait, and he felt strong and clear of mind.

He opened the door to find Sandra Klassen waiting. "Hello Sandra, this is a surprise."

"I hope I'm not bothering you," she said with a beaming smile.

"Not at all. Please come in."

They settled at the kitchen table with mugs of coffee. Her happiness was palpable and contagious, and David found himself grinning in response.

From her large, well-used handbag Sandra pulled out a brown manila envelope, which she pushed across the tabletop in David's direction. He picked it up and pulled the contents free. In his hands he found a trip itinerary, with hotel and flight reservations to a five-star resort in Greece in his and Jamie's names. For a moment he literally couldn't speak.

"I already cleared the time with Jamie, and he helped me pick the resort."

"I don't understand. You've already paid my bill."

Sandra laid her hand on David's, meeting his gaze with tearful eyes. "This was more than just a case, or the process of settling a bill. You've saved my son's life, and Alex's, and given both these men their freedom. There is nothing in the world that could show my gratitude for that. This is just a token."

"Sandra please, I'm happy that you're happy, but this isn't necessary."

"It is, David. You're a wonderful investigator, and more than that a real, honest, dedicated man. You should be proud of the way you conduct yourself and the man you are. You deserve a break and some time to kick back, have some fun. Spend some alone time with that fella of yours. He's a keeper by the way."

David laughed. "Agreed. Probably better than I deserve."

"Well now, don't sell yourself short. Anyway I'll get out of your hair. You have a trip to plan for."

David walked Sandra to the door, where she had a slip in her composure. The tears she'd been holding back escaped and she gripped David in a desperate, smothering embrace. He let her cry for a few minutes while awkwardly patting her back and making what he hoped were reassuring noises. After a flurry of additional thank-yous that caused embarrassment and poignancy on both sides, Sandra bid goodbye. David watched her walk to the car and drive away, overcome with a feeling of deep satisfaction.

And that was how David found himself on the beach, soaking in the sunshine with a frosty beer in hand and Jamie at his side. He'd long dreamed of a chance to travel with him, leaving the stress and complications of real life far behind. In an unspoken promise there'd been no mention of work, family strife, or unavenged wrongs. Just two blissful weeks of sleeping, sex, and sightseeing, aided by the occasional shot of ouzo.

"So I think I've made a decision," Jamie said on their second to last day of their vacation.

David took a sip of his beer. "That so?"

Jamie looked at him with his calm steady gaze. "I have. When we get back to Toronto I'm putting in my notice at the Ministry and I'm going to go to work for myself."

"You're kidding."

Jamie laughed, and it was a wonderful sound to David's ears. "I'm totally serious. In fact I thought I might come to work with you."

David nearly choked on his beer when the understanding of Jamie's statement sunk in. "Holy shit, really?"

"Yes. I've been thinking about this for the last couple of months, especially after the stuff at the cabin. I'm not happy where I am. I mean I know I do a good job and all that, but I want to help people more. I thought I could help you out on your cases and maybe do some private legal work, even run like a clinic for low-income earners to help with family courts rs, small claims and civil suits. I don't know exactly, I haven't worked out all the details. Jenny could assist us both, you know it could be a good thing for everyone."

"Sounds good to me. I can always use the backup."

"And someone to keep your ass out of jail."

"That too. Are you good with giving up a secure future, pension, all that crap?"

"Now you sound like my dad."

"That's a low blow."

"You're right. No, I'm good, I'm sure. And you now what? I'm really excited about this. In fact I can't remember a time in my life when I've ever been happier."

David agreed. Life was changing, and definitely in a good way.

Bring it, he thought as he took another swig of beer and let his gaze drift over the endless expanse of blue skies and sea.

ABOUT THE AUTHOR

Liz Strange is the published author of ten novels and several short stories. She has also written multiple scripts for both film and television.

Curious about other Crossroad Press books?
Stop by our site:
http://store.crossroadpress.com
We offer quality writing
in digital, audio, and print formats.

www.ingramcontent.com/pod-product-compliance
Lightning Source LLC
Chambersburg PA
CBHW030242200626
46816CB00002BA/479